MURDER AT MEREWOOD HOSPITAL

MICHELLE SALTER

B

Boldwood

First published in Great Britain in 2024 by Boldwood Books Ltd.

Copyright © Michelle Salter, 2024

Cover Design by Nick Castle

Cover Photography: Shutterstock

A CIP catalogue record for this book is available from the British Library.

Paperback ISBN 978-1-83751-078-8

Large Print ISBN 978-1-83751-079-5

Hardback ISBN 978-1-83751-077-1

Ebook ISBN 978-1-83751-080-1

Kindle ISBN 978-1-83751-081-8

Audio CD ISBN 978-1-83751-072-6

MP3 CD ISBN 978-1-83751-073-3

Digital audio download ISBN 978-1-83751-076-4

Boldwood Books Ltd
23 Bowerdean Street
London SW6 3TN
www.boldwoodbooks.com

1

JUNE 1919, MEREWOOD FARM, HAMPSHIRE

When she heard the door to the ward open, Helen didn't bother to look up. She always knew exactly where Dr Bingham was in the hospital without needing to see him. Was it intuition, or had she caught the sound of his soft tread and the slight rustle of his starched white coat? Perhaps she'd detected the faint aroma of his sandalwood cologne.

In the three years Helen had been a nurse at Merewood Farm Hospital, she'd taken no more notice of Samuel Bingham than any other doctor. Now they were the only medical staff left at the hospital, she was conscious of his presence from the moment she came downstairs in the morning to when she carried a candle to bed with her at night.

'Helen.'

She recognised the deep voice of Morgan Jennings. She'd repeatedly told him not to use her Christian name and wished she'd never been goaded into telling him what it was.

She'd left her office door open so she could keep an eye on the patients and hear if they called. As there was no urgency in

Morgan's voice, she didn't rise from her desk. He was bored and in need of company rather than medical attention.

A year earlier, dozens of wounded soldiers had cried to her from their beds. Doctors, nurses and orderlies scurried between the six wards, numbered in order of severity. Ward one for the most traumatic cases through to ward six for those with minor injuries, whose stay at the auxiliary hospital would be brief.

Helen hated to admit it, even to herself, but she'd relished the intensity of those frantic days. Everyone had worked together to save as many lives as they could. Now the war was over, and only one ward remained.

'Sister Hopgood,' the voice called again.

She smiled at the wheedling tone.

Glancing at the wall clock, she was surprised to see it was after nine. It was still light outside, and she hadn't realised it was so late. She must have spent over two hours making inventories of the medical equipment and supplies, beds, and linen that needed to be collected by the Red Cross. They'd given instructions for all items no longer in use to be transferred to their temporary infirmary at the rear of the Royal Victoria, a large military hospital in Netley, near Southampton.

Helen got up, stretched her back and went next door to what had once been ward six. These days, it was just called the ward.

Morgan peeked at her through downcast lashes as if chastened, though a smile hovered on his lips. She walked sedately over to him and touched his forehead.

'What is it? Are you feeling poorly?'

He reached up and moved her fingers down to his lips. 'I thought you could do with a break from those bloody lists.'

She pulled her hand away but couldn't be bothered to reproach him. Morgan flirted because it was the only way he knew how to speak to a woman.

'The inventories are taking longer than I expected,' Helen admitted wearily.

'The longer it takes, the longer we have together.' His eyes blatantly rested on the curve of her breasts. He leant forward to pull her towards him, and she nimbly stepped out of his reach.

'Is that your reason for interrupting me?' she said reprovingly but without vigour.

'I need a little more time. We all do.' He leant back in his chair and motioned to the other occupants of the ward.

'Mr Wintringham isn't going to close the hospital until you all have somewhere to go.' It was what Joseph Wintringham had said. In truth, they both knew the men couldn't stay there much longer.

Only five patients remained in the hospital. If it could still be called that. Morgan was their unelected leader. From military stock – his father had been a major – an army life was all he'd ever known. Sadly, the army had no further use for him.

The remaining patients all had one thing in common, apart from the fact they'd been left to languish in the last ward of Merewood Hospital. They were currently too damaged to return to the lives they'd once had.

Their problems were as diverse as the men themselves. Some had physical ailments, some mental disorders. Or perhaps they all had both. In the case of David Cowper, it was difficult to tell.

David was seated by the open patio doors and seemed to be staring unseeingly at Merewood Manor. For all Helen knew, he could see the house as clearly as she did.

Ward six had once been a drawing room and had a set of glass doors that opened out onto a flagstone patio. Beyond the patio, the lawn dropped down towards Merewood Lake.

On the other side of the lake, up the hill, Merewood Manor nestled on the outskirts of Gibbet Wood. The Wintringhams' country home had the appearance of a giant doll's house. It looked more like an ornate folly built on a grand scale than a place people lived in.

Charles Wintringham had favoured a gothic French style of architecture, and the upper floors had sharply pointed dormer window arches that jutted from a severely sloping roof. The windows were further highlighted by grey stone surrounds that contrasted with the red brick façade of the rest of the building.

Merewood Farm was a later addition to the estate, built by Charles's son, Joseph. It no more resembled a farm than it did a hospital. In keeping with the mansion that looked down on it like a poor relative, Merewood Farm boasted an ornate red brick exterior and arched windows.

Helen didn't know much about farming. She was a city girl. Her only experience of working the land had been when she was twelve, and her father had taken them on holiday to Kent. Only it hadn't been a holiday. Her father had expected her and her mother to pick hops. They'd lasted a week before taking the train back to London. She'd never seen her father again after that. She presumed he'd gone home to Ireland.

Helen had occasionally stayed in farmhouses when she'd been posted to the field hospitals of northern France. Even with her limited knowledge of agriculture, she'd seen enough to realise that Merewood was a toy farm. A rich man's hobby rather than a working man's way of life.

'Sister Hopgood. Would you read to me?' Albert Gates was smoking while he sifted through the letters he regularly received from his fiancée, Emma.

Helen used to tell them off for smoking on the ward. Recently, she'd relaxed this rule. Morgan, Albert and Nathan smoked cigarettes while Oliver sucked on a pipe. David never smoked but didn't seem to mind the others lighting up.

'I'll be over in a moment,' she replied.

Albert would ask her to read a passage from one of the letters and then question her as to what she thought his fiancée meant by it. Helen was sure he must know every word by heart. She certainly did.

All was quiet, and the patients had changed out of their hospital blues into their pyjamas. She decided to make a start on turning down their beds in the hope of an early night. Nathan Smith was still reading a book, and Oliver Edwards was sketching. With any luck, they'd retire soon.

Helen returned to Morgan's bedside, and as she bent to fold the covers, he reached out to pull her towards him. She gently removed his hand from her arm.

He smirked. 'I get it. You don't want the good doctor to think you're getting too friendly with the patients. That would be highly improper.' He gave a crude smile. 'Of course, you and the good doctor are nothing but professional.'

She ignored him, glancing over to where Dr Bingham was measuring out a sleeping draught for Albert.

Morgan leant closer and said in a mocking low whisper, 'I hope he doesn't creep upstairs to your bedroom at night.'

'If anyone were to creep upstairs in the night, they'd find my door locked,' she whispered back, feeling unkind as she said this. Morgan wasn't capable of navigating a flight of stairs unaided, let alone creeping up them.

She couldn't help wondering if it had crossed Dr Bingham's mind to venture up the oak staircase and seek her out.

'Don't you ever get lonely up there all alone? Or frightened? Surely Merewood must have a ghost lurking around somewhere.'

'The farm was only built twenty years ago,' she retorted. 'Isn't that too soon for a ghost? Even the manor house is only sixty years old.'

Morgan considered this. 'Surely it's about how someone dies

rather than the age of the place they haunt? Perhaps the ghost of a beautiful young nurse in a blue uniform and saintly white cap roams Gibbet Wood and comes to Merewood Farm in search of her killer?'

Helen felt a chill. She was glad Morgan was still whispering. The patients would never settle if they started to discuss the murder of Isabel Taplin.

2

Samuel Bingham's eyes sought out Sister Hopgood as they always did when she entered the ward.

Morgan Jennings was pawing at her again. He was becoming a bloody nuisance. Samuel watched with satisfaction as Sister Hopgood firmly removed the man's hand from her arm.

Hospital was no longer the place for Morgan. Nothing more could be done for him medically, although a good exercise regime would help. The important thing was for him to come to terms with the fact that he'd always walk with a pair of sticks. After they'd removed the shrapnel embedded in his thighs, he'd been left with considerable muscle damage. Morgan should count himself lucky he'd survived and make the best of the situation.

Samuel chastised himself. Perhaps the same could be said for Albert Gates and Nathan Smith. They both got a little stronger each day, though their mental afflictions caused them to present with physical symptoms. David Cowper and Oliver Edwards were another matter. They did need ongoing medical help; he just wasn't sure what sort.

He turned his attention to Albert. 'Any pain this evening, Albert?'

'No, Dr Bingham. Just itchy.'

'That's a good sign, it means the skin's healing. But you must try not to scratch, you don't want to make your scars worse. I'll ask Sister to apply some cream.'

'How long before they fade?'

Samuel sighed. Albert asked the same question every day, hoping, it seemed, for a different answer to the one he always received. 'It's difficult to say. You'll heal faster if you stop scratching. They'll gradually diminish over time, but you will be left with some permanent scarring.'

The young man nodded, and Samuel glanced at the bundle of letters clutched in his hands. Poor, scarred Albert and his blasted fiancée. Sister Hopgood must know those damned letters by heart.

Albert was still here because he was afraid to leave. Sooner or later, he'd have to face the world again. And more pertinently for Albert, his fiancée. The poor chap wasn't even that badly scarred. Samuel had seen worse. Far worse. It was just unfortunate the shell fire had scattered over his face rather than somewhere less obvious.

As he moved on to Nathan Smith, he called, 'Sister, could you put some cream on Albert's sores?'

'Of course, doctor.'

She gave him a brief glance, which he interpreted as gratitude for rescuing her from the crude attentions of Morgan.

Samuel noticed Albert pass Sister Hopgood one of his letters. The silly boy had become too attached to her. It wasn't her fault. She'd shown him such kindness. But it was time to cut the apron strings.

Standing by Nathan's bed, Samuel realised he had a habit of seeing each patient in order of concern. Albert Gates and Nathan

Smith were the ones who worried him the least. Perhaps because they were so young, both only twenty-two. Time wouldn't erase, but it would heal. Although they were left with scars, mental and physical, they had the potential to live full lives.

Nathan received him with his usual stammered greeting. The young man was in constant motion. It was something he had no control over. His eyes twitched, his legs jerked, his arms shook, and his lips trembled as he spoke.

Samuel could find no physical cause for his symptoms. Instinct told him that tranquillity and time to recover in peaceful surroundings were all that was needed. He hoped this was the case. Nathan had nice manners and a boyish charm that would take him a long way if only he could overcome his present difficulties.

They chatted for a while before he moved on to Morgan.

'How are we this evening, Morgan?'

'Same as every other evening, doctor.'

The insolent tone irritated Samuel, as did the smoke rings emanating from Morgan's mouth. Reluctantly, he'd agreed with Sister Hopgood's suggestion to allow the patients to smoke. She was a good nurse, knowing when to exert her authority and when to relent a little. Normally, he'd never allow smoking on the wards, but these were far from normal circumstances, and smoking seemed to calm the men's nerves.

'I expect you can't wait to get out of this place,' he said jovially.

Although Morgan had his problems, he too could leave the hospital and go on to lead a full life, albeit different from the one he'd imagined.

'And miss the tender care of Sister Hopgood?' Morgan's lips curled into a slight smirk, which never failed to enrage Samuel. 'And your own healing powers, of course, doctor.'

With an effort, he produced a rigid smile. 'I'm afraid I've done all I can for you, medically speaking. From now on, it's down to you to increase your strength. Keep doing the exercises you've been shown, and you'll make steady progress.'

Morgan bowed his head in a show of acquiescence.

Samuel suspected he was exaggerating his symptoms – putting on that limp for the sake of female attention. Wintringham's silly stepdaughter, Georgina Vane, fawned all over him.

Usually slow to move on to Oliver Edwards and David Cowper, today, Samuel couldn't wait to leave Morgan's bedside. He always left this pair till last – mainly because they troubled him the most.

With caution, he approached Oliver Edwards, who was bent over his drawing. Samuel examined the pencil sketch of Joseph Wintringham's thoroughbred horse, Flame. It was a remarkable picture. The man had talent – he'd managed to capture the motion of the horse in full flight.

Looking up at him, Oliver slammed the stump of his left arm on the wooden table, sending his drawing box flying.

'How can the bloody thing hurt when it isn't even there?'

'Steady, man.' Samuel caught the box before it fell to the floor. It was a lovely piece – antique mahogany with a decorative shell inlay of satinwood. He'd often admired it and tried not to be irked by the casual way Oliver handled it. Samuel knew it stemmed from the patient's frustration at his disability. 'I'm afraid it's your brain playing tricks on you. It's a common occurrence. Give it time, and it will sort itself out.'

He felt like a fraud saying this. He'd treated patients who'd experienced phantom pain years after the loss of a limb.

'How much time?' Oliver demanded.

'It's difficult to say.'

'Will I be like this for the rest of my life?'

The despair in the man's voice was painful to hear.

'It will ease over time. What a splendid drawing,' he said in an attempt to change the subject, then immediately regretted it. He sounded like a nursery schoolteacher talking to a child playing with coloured chalks. At forty, he was only six years older than his patient, though the younger man's face showed the ravages of all he'd been through. Lines crossed Oliver's forehead and his sandy hair was greying at the temples.

'Can't you give me something for the pain?' Oliver asked. 'Pills, I mean. Not that damn cream.'

'It's a little tricky with nerve pain. Drugs don't always hit the mark.' Particularly if the mark isn't there to hit, Samuel added silently. In Oliver's case, the feelings he experienced were below his left elbow amputation. 'I've been researching phantom limb pain, and the mainstay of rehabilitation is in the realms of psychiatry.'

Oliver snorted and went back to his drawing. Samuel knew he'd been dismissed.

The amputation wound had healed well. What Oliver was left with was nerve pain and violent mood swings. Samuel wondered if these could be the result of a head injury. Or was it the frustration of partially losing a limb? His symptoms could even be a type of psychosis brought on by the horrors of what he'd been through. During his time in the cavalry, Oliver had witnessed the mass slaughter of men and the brutal destruction of so many of his beloved horses.

Oliver was an old friend of Richard Locke, the estate manager of Merewood Manor. Locke said Oliver had once been blessed with a sweet nature and good temper. This left Samuel in a quandary over how to treat him. Should he refer him to a brain specialist or a psychiatrist?

He left Oliver and moved on to David Cowper, who was sitting alone, staring out of the open doors. At thirty-seven, David was his oldest patient. It was the youngster, Nathan, David seemed to get on with best. They would often sit together, rarely speaking but seeming to find comfort in silent companionship. While Nathan was in constant motion, David was usually still, gazing blankly into the distance.

Was David blind? His was a case that had caused all the doctors at Merewood Hospital to scratch their heads. Most of the time, David lived in his own private world, occasionally talking, though most of the time content to be silent.

David had been exposed to mustard gas, which had led to temporary loss of vision. But eye experts could no longer find an organic reason for his ongoing blindness. That didn't mean there wasn't one. However, it could be that David's mind had just decided to shut out the horrors of the world.

Like Oliver, David wasn't an easy patient to treat. Was he blind? Or did he simply choose not to see?

The light was beginning to fade, and Samuel caught a whiff of sulphur as Sister Hopgood turned on a lamp. The gas pipes at Merewood Farm seemed to have their own peculiar odour. It was ever present but intensified when the lamps were lit.

Samuel chatted with David for some time, all the while watching Sister Hopgood do her rounds. When she stretched up to light the wall lamps, he noticed her trim waist, the cord of her crisp white pinafore tied neatly around her blue linen uniform.

Before, in the chaos, he hadn't taken much notice of her. She'd always been efficient. A cut above some of the other nurses he'd encountered. But he hadn't looked at her. Not really.

Since the rest of the hospital staff had left and it was just the two of them, he was constantly aware of her presence.

He hadn't felt desire like it since Isabel Taplin. He could still picture the girl's laughing blue eyes and enticing smile. God, she'd been beautiful. That bloody Frederick Wintringham had certainly thought so, always sniffing around her.

At night, Samuel would fantasise that it was just him and Nurse

Taplin left at the hospital. Unable to resist, she'd creep downstairs in the dead of night while the patients were sleeping and come to him. He was ashamed of how this fantasy would end, and he kept trying to banish images of her from his mind.

Isabel Taplin was a tragedy he didn't like to dwell on.

3

Richard Locke spotted Sister Hopgood on the patio outside the ward and was wondering how he could contrive to speak to her away from the patients. He was only half listening to Frederick Wintringham, who'd caught up with him by the gates of Merewood Manor.

'My grandfather put a curse on this place.' Frederick's horse, Blaze, was getting restless, but his rider was too caught up in his tale to notice. His gun dog, Dexter, had already run ahead. 'No, not a curse. A protective spell.'

Richard tried not to roll his eyes. He also had to resist the urge to reach out and pull Blaze's reins in. His own horse stood placidly enough.

'Misfortune will befall any Wintringham who tries to sell Merewood. It must stay in our family,' Frederick continued. 'My father doesn't seem to be paying heed to this warning.'

'Your father isn't selling the manor. Just the farm.' He could also have pointed out that Merewood Farm hadn't been built until a year after old Charles Wintringham's death.

The Wintringham banking dynasty had made vast profits from

the slave trade in the British West Indies, enabling Charles Wintringham to build Merewood Manor in 1859. His son, Joseph, had added the farm in 1896 after inheriting the manor following his father's death. The only purpose of the farm was to provide produce for the Merewood estate – and it had even failed at that.

'Can't you talk to him? I don't understand why it's all so bloody expensive to run,' Frederick moaned. 'Now the war's over, we can get the farm back on its feet. We just have to economise. It doesn't help that my bloody stepmother feels the need to be lady bountiful and give aid to the undeserving poor.'

Dorothy Wintringham was the most decent person in that family, Richard thought. Joseph wasn't a bad man, but his son, Frederick, took for granted the privilege he'd been born into.

'Labourers need to be paid, horses need to be shod, livestock fed and tended,' Richard explained. 'Merewood Farm cost more to run than it produced.' If Frederick had ever bothered to examine the accounts, this would be blindingly obvious. All he had to do was look at the expenditure column to see that every year it had cost more and more to keep the place going.

Frederick scowled. 'Maybe all that's required is a new manager. Perhaps you need to try harder.'

Perhaps you need to shut your stupid mouth, he was tempted to reply. Instead, he shrugged. He was losing his job anyway. What did he care for the insults of this spoilt brat? The farm had been losing money long before Richard had become estate manager.

Unsurprisingly, when the Red Cross had come calling in 1916, Joseph Wintringham had been more than happy to accept the government grant to turn the farmhouse into a temporary hospital. By then, he'd realised how much his hobby was costing and his passion for agriculture had waned.

It certainly wasn't the magnanimous gesture Joseph boasted of. It had saved him from having to give up a wing of Merewood

Manor. Far more convenient for the family to accommodate the hospital at arm's length on the farm instead of in their home.

Now Baden Knight was sniffing around, keen to acquire Merewood Farm to extend his own neighbouring estate. Richard was certain Joseph would accept his offer. Though, to his credit, he'd said no sale would take place until the last patient was rehomed. This was probably due to his wife's influence.

'I have plans I'm going to talk to my father about. First, we need to get rid of that lot.' Frederick gestured to where the patients were seated in deckchairs on the patio.

'That lot? You mean those men who bravely fought for their country?'

Richard saw his comment had hit the mark by the flush that rose up Frederick's face. To be fair, the young man had spent time in the trenches. He'd lasted a year before being honourably discharged in 1917 after suffering an injury to his left hand. It was rumoured that it hadn't been caused by enemy fire. Rather, he'd used his own service revolver to shoot at his finger. Richard glanced at Frederick's left hand, which was clutching the reins. He'd lost the tip of his ring finger. Hardly in the same league as the wounds Oliver had sustained.

'The war's ended. It's 1919. Time to move on.' Frederick stared at the patio where Georgina Vane was seated next to Morgan Jennings. 'My bloody stepsister doesn't help. Fawning over that Jennings chap. Everyone knows he's a chancer.'

Richard didn't reply. For once, he agreed with Frederick, though he wasn't about to admit it. Oliver had told him the only reason Morgan was still at the hospital was because he'd gambled away all his money and had nowhere else to go.

Richard also knew Morgan wasn't as disabled as he pretended to be. He'd seen him walking in the grounds after everyone had gone to bed. During the day, Morgan walked slowly with two sticks.

When Richard had seen him sneak out of the ward at night, he'd only had one stick, and his gait had been stronger and faster.

He suspected Morgan was secretly meeting Georgina, ignorant of the fact that she was unlikely to provide the financial solution he sought. Joseph Wintringham wouldn't be prepared to cough up any sort of dowry unless he approved of the match. At thirty, Georgina was six years older than her stepbrother but equally as oblivious to the realities of life.

He watched Sister Hopgood tending to David Cowper. She was no fool, that one. Did she know Morgan was faking? It wouldn't surprise him if she did. She wouldn't be taken in as easily as Georgina. Perhaps, like him, she chose to keep silent. After all, what concern was it of theirs? Morgan had suffered. Was still suffering. Who could blame him if he was putting it on a bit?

Richard was more worried about Oliver. Something dark had happened to his old school friend. He wasn't the man he used to be. He and Oliver were planning to go into business together as soon as they could find livery stables with suitable accommodation. But he was concerned. Oliver had developed a temper, and he'd heard he could sometimes scream in his sleep. He wanted to seek Sister Hopgood's advice, but he had to get her on her own, away from the patients and that pompous prig of a doctor.

'It wouldn't surprise me if he had something to do with it.' Frederick was still staring malevolently at Morgan Jennings.

Richard didn't have to ask what he meant.

While Frederick scowled at Morgan and Georgina, Richard's eyes flitted toward Gibbet Wood. He could still picture her lying there. The grey skin and unseeing eyes of a face that had once been so warm and alive. He remembered the cold smell of death mingling with the warm scent of the pine needles she rested upon.

If anyone had put a curse on Merewood, it wasn't old Charles Wintringham. It was Isabel Taplin.

4

'Where will you go when this place closes, Helen?' Morgan was seated by the side of his bed, flipping his cigarette case over in his hand.

'Sister Hopgood,' she corrected automatically. 'And that's not your concern.'

'I want to know more about you. Let's sneak out for a moonlit walk by the lake.'

Helen turned her back on him and began to adjust the sheets on his bed. As she did, she spotted a note under his pillow.

It's a full moon. Meet me by the lake. Usual time. G.

She recognised the childish looping handwriting of Georgina Vane. Helen had long suspected Morgan was sneaking out at night. However, she hadn't thought Georgina would be so stupid as to meet him. The woman must be desperate, though for what, she wasn't sure. Did she really want Morgan, or was he just a way to avoid becoming the spinster of Merewood Manor?

Helen told herself off for being unkind. Morgan was a war hero.

And a good-looking one at that. He'd shown her snapshots of himself taken in 1914, newly promoted to captain, broad-shouldered and square-jawed, wearing a uniform just waiting to have medals pinned upon it. Even in the grainy image, he'd radiated arrogance and expectation with his shock of blond hair and defiant grin.

Five years later, Morgan walked with his shoulders hunched over two wooden crutches to support his damaged legs. He'd crawled into no man's land to rescue a wounded pal. She glanced at him and smiled. He still had a strong jawline and dancing eyes, though these days his features were less chiselled and more haggard.

It was evident Georgina's note had given him the idea to ask her for a moonlit walk, and he'd known what her answer would be. Helen was sorely tempted to agree to his proposal just to see the look of panic on his face.

Instead, she replied, 'I'm needed here.'

'Bingham can take care of things. It's not as if that lot are going anywhere.'

This was true. The patients were occupied with their usual pursuits. Nathan was reading, Albert gazed at Emma's letters and Oliver worked on his sketch of Flame. David was holding a small clock in his hands. It was a beautiful little thing left to him by his father. A gold travel clock that folded into a leather case lined with velvet. David liked to wind it up and listen to it ticking at night. He was in his usual spot, by the open patio doors, staring out towards the manor. The fresh evening air provided some relief from the haze of cigarette smoke and the pungent odour of Oliver's pipe.

Noises were coming from Merewood Manor. The Wintringhams must be entertaining. Helen thought she heard the faint sound of laughter drift across the lake. The family and their guests were probably in the drawing room. It was a warm night, and the doors to the terrace would be open.

Helen decided to turn the beds down early and put the patients' medication out in preparation for Dr Bingham's final round of the day. That way, she could go straight upstairs afterwards.

The patients didn't usually require attention at night unless one of them had a bad dream. Fortunately, the five men got on relatively well. Oliver could be moody at times but rarely took his anger out on his fellow patients.

Dr Bingham's bedroom had always been in the downstairs quarters so he could be called upon in an emergency. This left her with the whole upper floor to herself. Never before had she had the luxury of her own bathroom. It was bliss not to have to wait your turn to run a bath. She wasn't sure where her next post would be, wherever it was, she doubted it would offer the private accommodation she currently enjoyed at Merewood Farm.

As she worked her way around the five beds in the ward, she noticed Morgan watching her.

'Are you and the good doctor planning an intimate dinner for two this evening?'

The patients had eaten earlier, and she and Dr Bingham were going to have a late supper together.

'We'll be having our meal in the kitchen as usual,' she replied in a tone that suggested it was another chore to be completed before the end of the day. In fact, she was doing the beds early so she could enjoy a soak in the bath and change into something other than her uniform. She didn't have many dresses. By now, Dr Bingham had seen her entire wardrobe, but changing for dinner made her feel like there was more to her life than just being Sister Hopgood.

Helen had arrived at Merewood Farm with a team of nurses in the August of 1916. Dr Bingham had been the most senior doctor, and she remembered the way he'd made a show of greeting each one of them individually. His ponderous manner had irritated the nurses who'd been impatient to get to their quarters.

In the following years, she'd paid little attention to Samuel Bingham. Then the war had ended. One by one, the patients had been discharged; most back to their homes, some to permanent medical establishments, and a few had died. The other doctors and nurses had packed their bags and left to start new lives.

Even the orderlies and kitchen staff had gone. Meals were brought over from the manor by the Wintringhams' kitchen maid, Kate, who was also tasked with cleaning the farmhouse.

Each evening, Helen and Dr Bingham had their meals together in the kitchen, making polite, civilised conversation as they ate the food prepared for them. She would go so far as to say they'd formed a friendship. It was difficult to tell in such an unreal setting.

She was certainly more aware of his physical presence than she'd been before. He had a large frame that seemed to take up more than its fair share of space. He wasn't as handsome as Morgan had been – still was in his way. But Dr Bingham had a goodness about him, with intelligent grey eyes and an earnestness that made him attractive. Was it her imagination, or had he begun to look at her differently, too?

Helen was irritated to find Morgan's eyes still fixed upon her. His expression suggested he knew what she was thinking, and this caused a surge of irritation. Did he imagine her sole purpose in life was to nurse men like him?

'Meet me by the lake at midnight,' Morgan whispered.

'Don't be silly.' She cast him a reproving look before moving on to light the wall lamp. To her annoyance, she found the mantle had broken. She'd talk to Kate about replacing it in the morning. It was still light, and if the patients wanted to stay up, they could use the candles by their beds.

'It's Midsummer's Eve,' Morgan called after her. 'The night before the summer solstice.'

'Is it?' Helen found it hard to believe that they were so far into

June. She recalled the elation of Armistice Day and the heady feeling that she'd be leaving Merewood Farm within a month, two at the most. Seven months later, she was still here.

'No. Midsummer's Eve is tomorrow,' Oliver snapped, not looking up from his drawing.

'It's the twentieth to... to... today,' Nathan stammered.

'Yes, but this year Midsummer is on the twenty-second.' Oliver launched into a complicated explanation as to why it was a day later than usual.

Helen sighed. If this turned into one of their meandering conversations, they'd take longer to settle. Mercifully, no one had the inclination to argue with Oliver, and they soon lapsed into silence.

Wearily, she finished her tasks and climbed the stairs, leaving Dr Bingham to do his final round.

In her bedroom, she untied her apron and laid it on the bed, then undid the buttons of her uniform and slid out of it. She hadn't realised how hot she was until she felt the cool breeze through the open window. Noticing a movement outside, she went over and saw Richard Locke standing by the lake. He turned and, for a moment, seemed to look right at her. She ducked behind the curtain and watched him disappear into a copse of trees.

Helen stayed by the window a while longer. She was aware that the incline beyond the lake up to the manor offered a clear view of the bedroom windows on this side of Merewood Farm.

Had anyone ever stood on the sloped lawn and waited for a glimpse of Isabel Taplin? Perhaps hoping to watch her undress? Frederick Wintringham had clearly been besotted with the nurse. Maybe Richard Locke had, too.

After the departure of the rest of the hospital staff, Helen had her pick of the upstairs bedrooms. She'd chosen the room that was largest and offered a picturesque view of the lake even though she knew Isabel Taplin had once shared it with two other nurses.

She moved away from the window before removing her chemise and bloomers and plucking her dressing gown from the hook on the door. After picking up her soap bag, she left the bedroom barefoot. Dressed only in her robe, she padded across the corridor to the large bathroom, wondering if Dr Bingham ever heard her moving about from his office below.

Each evening, she felt the same surge of pleasure at having the upper floor to herself. Although she missed the camaraderie of the other nurses and the motherly care of Matron, she didn't miss the queue for the bathroom.

Lined up on the bathroom shelf were the little treats that she never tired of purchasing whenever she spotted something in the village. During the war, you were lucky to get a bar of coal tar soap. But on her recent visits to the chemist, she'd been able to buy tablets of lavender soap, sweet-scented talcum powder, rosemary shampoo and even a small bottle of scent.

When the hospital had been full, she'd barely spent a few minutes scrubbing herself with whatever soap she could find and occasionally rinsing her hair in beer. Now she could take her time, she relished her cleansing routine.

After soaking in the tub, she would wet her hair with warm water from a rose-patterned ceramic jug she'd acquired in France and slowly massage her scalp with foamy shampoo before gently washing the suds away. Then she'd dry herself with one of the large soft towels kindly provided by Dorothy Wintringham. She'd finish by patting on talcum powder and smoothing cream into her face. When she emerged, she felt less like Sister Hopgood and more like Helen.

But that evening, as soon as she opened the bathroom door, she knew something was wrong. She sensed it immediately.

The bathroom window was slightly ajar, though that wasn't unusual. The sink and toilet were as clean as she'd left them that morning.

Helen dropped her soap bag in fright when she saw what it was. The bath was occupied.

Lying in the water was a gleaming white skeleton. She couldn't stop the scream that burst from her as she stared in horror at the rotting yellow teeth and empty eye sockets.

What made the spectacle even more sickening was that someone had dressed the bones in hospital blues.

5

Helen leant against the door, trying to steady her breathing. She stared at the hideous figure in the bath. It was partially submerged, the skull resting on the back of the tub, grinning up at her.

She realised it was the skeleton that hung in Dr Bingham's office. What idiot had dressed it in hospital blues and laid it out in her bath? Her fear was replaced by anger. She would not tolerate this sort of behaviour.

A rap on the door made her jump.

'Sister Hopgood. Are you alright?'

It was Dr Bingham. She tightened the cord of her dressing gown and opened the door.

'No. I am not alright.' She gestured for him to enter. Albert Gates and Nathan Smith were at his heels.

Dr Bingham hesitated, then moved forward.

Helen pointed to the bathtub.

'Good God.' Dr Bingham stopped abruptly, and Albert stumbled into the back of him, his eyes wide.

'Bloody hell,' Albert said. 'Who's that?'

'B-b-b-' Nathan stammered convulsively. His eyelids flickered, and his facial muscles began to twitch.

Dr Bingham put a hand on his shoulder. 'It's nothing to worry about. I call him Yorick; you must have seen him hanging in my office. He died a long time ago of natural causes.'

'What's he doing in my bath?' Helen demanded.

'I've no idea,' said the doctor slowly.

The four of them stared at the skeleton, Nathan making hiccupping noises.

'What's going on up there?'

It was Morgan calling up the stairs.

This seemed to rouse Dr Bingham. He strode over to the bath and hauled the skeleton out of the water. Cradling it like a baby and dripping water across the floor, he marched out with it jangling in his arms.

Albert tugged Nathan's sleeve, and the pair followed him down the stairs. Helen stayed where she was.

'Is this someone's idea of a practical joke?' She could hear the edge to Dr Bingham's voice and guessed he was addressing Morgan. She didn't catch the reply.

Helen bent over the bath and removed the plug, watching the water drain away. The bathroom was her one luxury. A soak in the tub her only pleasure. Now it had been ruined.

She filled her rose-patterned jug with water, took it back to the bedroom and poured it into the basin on her washstand. She'd make do with a quick flannel wash.

After she'd dried herself, she sat on the bed to consider who would play such a cruel trick on her. Morgan was the most likely candidate. But would he have been able to get up the stairs unaided? And carrying a skeleton?

What were the alternatives? Either it was one of the other patients or someone from the manor. With so few staff, anyone could have walked in without being seen.

Whoever did it must have taken a set of hospital blues from the linen cupboard in the scullery off the kitchen and gone into Dr Bingham's office. What had possessed them to dress up the bones and put them in her bath?

Helen had used the bathroom after lunch that day but hadn't been upstairs since. Someone could have done it at any time during the afternoon. She'd ask Dr Bingham when he was last in his office. Surely, he would have noticed if his skeleton had been missing.

She dressed and went out onto the landing, pausing at the top of the stairs to listen. The sensation that she wasn't alone caused her to glance behind her along the hallway. Could someone be hiding up here in one of the empty bedrooms? She hadn't heard anyone come back up the stairs. Below, sounds were coming from the kitchen. Probably Kate setting out their dinner.

Previously, she'd shared the upper floor with eleven other nurses as well as Matron. Dr Bingham and the remaining patients used the large downstairs bathroom or the outside privy. It was fortunate that none of the men required bedpans, although David occasionally needed assistance.

Slowly, she opened the door of the bedroom next to hers. The curtains were drawn, and it smelt musty. Everything was still. She stepped inside and gazed around, then examined the two bedrooms on the other side of the hallway and, finally, Matron's old room at the far end of the house. The light layer of dust in each indicated none of the bedrooms had been disturbed for some time.

Feeling less tense but a little chilly, she returned to her room for a cardigan. Even when it was hot outside, the farmhouse remained cool, sometimes draughty.

Helen descended the stairs slowly, trying not to make a sound. The corridor was empty, and she guessed the patients had settled into their usual activities. For a few moments, she stood unseen by the door of the ward and listened.

'Can't see the point of it myself.'

She recognised Oliver Edwards' voice. His words irritated her. He seemed to be implying that it was a perfectly acceptable thing to have done if there had been a point to it.

'Perhaps someone thought it was funny,' Morgan was saying.

She didn't catch Oliver's reply as something touched her leg. Only just managing to stop herself from crying out, she looked down to see Chester, the farmhouse cat, rubbing his nose on her bare calf. He was a huge creature who liked to sneak in through the back door when Kate brought over their food.

Ignoring his persistent purring, she walked along the corridor, noticing Dr Bingham's office door was shut. When she tried the handle, it wasn't locked.

She opened the door and peeked inside. It appeared to be as normal – Yorick, now unclothed, was back on his stand, still dripping. She closed the door quietly and went to the kitchen, where Dr Bingham was waiting.

Kate had set out the dishes on the table. The smell of chicken casserole made Helen feel queasy, though she knew she had to eat something.

The cook at the manor prepared simple, wholesome meals based on Mrs Wintringham's instructions. Helen and Dr Bingham had the same food as the patients. Generally, it was soup followed by a stew or cutlet of some kind with potatoes and vegetables from the kitchen garden of the manor. For dessert, there would be fresh fruit and occasionally cream.

Dr Bingham was in the process of uncorking a bottle of red wine. Helen knew Joseph Wintringham had given him a case of claret from the cellar at Merewood Manor. The patients were not permitted to drink alcohol, and the wine was kept hidden in the doctor's office.

'Under the circumstances, I thought you could do with a glass.'

Dr Bingham showed Helen the bottle. 'I'm no expert, but I'm sure it must be decent if Mr Wintringham keeps it.'

'Thank you, Dr Bingham. That would be most welcome.' She smiled, thinking he could have been mistaken for a waiter. He'd removed his white coat and was wearing the suit he'd had on all day. He had a decent pair of shoulders, and his suits were all beautifully cut, giving him an air of authority.

'Please, call me Samuel. May I call you Helen?' He paused, then quickly added, 'Although perhaps not in front of the patients. I think formal titles would be more appropriate on the ward.'

'Of course.' She could imagine Morgan's reaction if they started to address each other as Helen and Samuel in front of him. 'I have to keep reminding Morgan not to address me by my Christian name.'

'That man is a nuisance.'

She noted his creased brow and wondered if he too suspected that Morgan wasn't as disabled as he pretended to be. Would he have been capable of putting the skeleton in her bath?

'Did you realise Yorick was missing?' She watched him devour his meal while she picked at hers.

He shook his head. 'He must have been there this morning when I finished my rounds. I was at my desk for some time writing letters and would have noticed if he wasn't on his stand. This afternoon, I walked around the estate. I'd just returned and was about to get my coat to begin my rounds when I heard you scream.' He looked at her with concern. 'How are you feeling?'

'Puzzled,' she replied. 'Why do you think someone did that?'

Although Oliver's comment had irritated her, she had to concede he was right. What was the point of putting a skeleton in her bath? Did someone want to scare her? They'd succeeded, but what now? Was it some kind of warning? She couldn't imagine why anyone would want to threaten her.

Samuel gave a rueful smile. 'I'm afraid that not all of our patients' ailments are physical. It could be the manifestation of an underlying psychosis.'

She considered this. 'Why me?'

'I think you know that, Helen.'

It felt strange to hear him use her first name. When she'd entered the bathroom, she'd wanted to wash away Sister Hopgood and spend the evening as Helen. But those feelings had drained away with the bathwater.

She tried to focus on Samuel's warm grey eyes and revive some of the feelings of attraction that had developed over the last weeks. It wasn't so much his looks that appealed to her, although he was undoubtedly a handsome man with his reddish-brown hair and strong, even features. What drew her to him was the care he showed to his patients. It was a shame that aspect of his character was often overshadowed by a pomposity of manner.

'I've seen patients become overly attached to their nurses. You've tended to these men for a long time and become embedded in their lives and thoughts.' He topped up his glass, but not hers. 'Surprising as it might seem, whoever did this may well hold you in high regard, though this can manifest itself in unusual ways.'

Helen took a sip of wine, enjoying the warm feeling in her throat. She'd been hurt that one of the men could have played such a mean trick, but what Samuel said was possible. 'This confirms what I already believed. Merewood Farm has become an unhealthy environment. I no longer feel I'm helping these patients to recover.'

He swirled his wine around the glass. 'Merewood Farm is a wonderful place to recuperate. But, alas, we don't have the resources we need. In these circumstances' – he gestured to their surroundings – 'we're limited in what we can offer our patients.'

The farm no longer felt like a wonderful place to Helen. When it had functioned properly as an auxiliary hospital, it had been real and solid. Now it had an artificial quality to it. It was neither a hospital nor a farmhouse. She felt like they were living in an imaginary world.

'Have you decided about the Royal Victoria?' she asked.

To her irritation, he looked at her blankly. Surely, he must have made a decision by now. 'The military hospital in Netley. You mentioned that you'd been offered a position there.'

'Oh, that. Yes. Much to think about.'

Exasperated, she took a gulp of wine. How often had he commented that they worked well together? She'd taken this to mean that he would welcome her joining him at the hospital. Yet he appeared not to have given the matter any thought.

After they finished their meal, she took their dishes over to the sink and told him she was tired and would retire early.

Samuel hastily stood up. 'Are you alright on your own? I mean, would you like me to accompany you? Just to make sure everything is as it should be. I could go up first and light a lamp if you'd like?'

Helen shook her head and picked up a candleholder from the sideboard. 'The mantle on the landing lamp is broken. It's light enough to do without it. This will suffice.'

Carrying the flickering candle up the staircase, the shadows heightened her sense of being in an unfamiliar place. Up until this evening, she'd enjoyed the solitude of the upper floor. Now she longed for the companionship of other nurses.

She tried to tell herself it was nothing more than a silly joke. She'd been at the farm for three years and had always felt safe, even after Isabel's death. But tonight, she experienced a sense of unease. Why had someone chosen to desecrate the private sanctuary of her bathroom?

Helen didn't believe in ghosts. If something sinister was going on at Merewood Hospital, there had to be a reason for it.

6

'Sister Hopgood.' Richard cursed his stupidity when he saw he'd frightened her. 'I'm so sorry. I didn't mean to startle you.'

His cottage was situated at the back of Merewood Manor, and he'd taken the track behind the kitchen garden to enter Gibbet Wood from the eastern side. She must have walked from the hospital, past the lake, and around the front of the manor to reach the woods from the south.

He appeared to have jolted her from whatever thoughts had been preoccupying her.

'It was inconsiderate after what happened to...' He'd been about to say what happened to Isabel there. But his reluctance to mention her name stopped him. They weren't far from where she'd lain underneath the conifers. The scent of pine would forever remind him of her cold body with those cruel ligature marks around that once-white neck.

Sister Hopgood seemed to take a moment to register what he'd said. Should he pretend he was talking about the prank instead? The story of her finding a skeleton in her bath had done the rounds of the manor and probably reached the village by now.

Then she gave a slight nod of understanding. 'I often think of her when I walk here.'

He fell into step with her. 'You're not afraid of the wood?'

She shook her head. 'It's a beautiful place.'

'Are you on your way to the village?' It was quicker to get to Greybridge by walking through the woods and joining the road on the northern side rather than going via the lanes that led away from Merewood Farm.

'Not today. I walk here to see the birds. I shall miss it.'

He raised an eyebrow. 'Gibbet Wood?'

She smiled. 'The countryside, the meadows, the farmland. And Gibbet Wood. A gibbet is a gallows, isn't it? Didn't they use to hang people here?'

'A gibbet was used to display the bodies of those executed. According to local folklore, the corpses were hung on a gibbet at the north entrance to the wood on the Greybridge Road so anyone going to or from the village would see them.' He pointed to the brow of the hill. 'To scare robbers from attacking travellers riding through the woodland.'

She grimaced. 'I wish you hadn't told me that. But I still love this place. Do you know there's a sparrowhawk nest in that conifer over there?' She pointed to a Scots pine. 'I've occasionally seen the female bringing food for the young. She appears to be a better hunter than the male.'

Richard tried not to show surprise at her knowledge. 'I've seen her. Female sparrowhawks are larger than the males and better hunters. They can kill a full-grown wood pigeon. She's been lurking around the pheasant pens on the outskirts of the woods.'

'Why do you keep the birds so close to the woodland?'

'It gets them used to their natural habitat. The chicks start off in an enclosed pen to protect them from foxes and other predators. When they're juvenile, they get moved to an open-topped pen so they can roost under cover of trees and shrubs.' He glanced at her quizzically. 'You study birds?'

'Only since I've been here. Apart from some field hospitals in France, this is my first real experience of the countryside. I wanted to make the most of it.'

'Where will you go next?'

'Probably back to London. Although I'm considering the Royal Victoria Hospital in Netley. I haven't applied for a position yet. I want to see the patients settled first. Perhaps I'll take a holiday after that.'

He noticed she said this almost apologetically.

'You deserve it. You joined up at the beginning, didn't you?'

She nodded. 'I never expected it to last so long.'

'None of us did. Have you always been a nurse?'

'I started my training in 1912. My mother died the following year, and I moved into the Nightingale School at St Thomas' Hospital. I was in one of the first units to be sent to France. October 1914.' She shook her head. 'Seems a lifetime ago.'

He grunted. 'It was.'

'Coming here...' She paused. 'It's not been easy, but it was better than being over there. I would have gone wherever they sent me. When I ended up at Merewood Farm, I felt I should make the most of the opportunity and enjoy rural life.' They'd taken a looping course through the woodland and were now strolling down the hill toward the lake.

As they walked, Richard observed the way she studied the wildlife around her. He hadn't expected that and suddenly wanted to know more about this enigmatic woman whose piercing green eyes weren't afraid to look directly into his.

She was striking in her way. Not pretty like Georgina. No, she was nothing like Georgina. Helen Hopgood had strength. Nor was she beautiful like Isabel – there'd always been a smile on those pretty pink lips, a smile that radiated from her aquamarine eyes. He rarely saw Sister Hopgood smile. Perhaps she had no reason to.

'I wanted to talk to you about Oliver,' Richard said. 'He's in pain. And the medicines don't seem to help.'

'He has a particular type of nerve pain that can be difficult to treat. I know Dr Bingham would like more time for his rehabilitation.'

'Merewood Hospital doesn't have any more time. You're aware of Mr Wintringham's plan to sell the farm?'

'Mrs Wintringham has indicated as much. Will you miss it?'

Her question took him by surprise. He suddenly realised he wouldn't miss Merewood Manor at all. He'd been appointed estate manager six years ago, taking up residence in one of the tied cottages in the summer of 1913. A year later, the country was at war.

Richard realised she was waiting for an answer and gestured to the countryside around them. 'Like you, I'll miss all this.'

'Not Merewood Farm?'

'What with the war, I haven't spent much time here.'

When he'd returned to Merewood Manor in April 1918, he'd had little appetite for his old job. Perhaps Frederick was right. Maybe a new manager could come in and turn the farm around. After all, it didn't need to make a profit. It simply needed to pay for itself. But Richard wasn't about to break his back trying. To his mind, it was a toy farm, not a real one. He had better things to do with his life than keeping the spoilt Wintringhams fed.

'Oliver's wife hasn't visited recently,' Sister Hopgood said.

He guessed she was trying to find out why. 'She wants a divorce.'

'Oh.'

He saw the look of dismay on her face. 'Oliver hasn't mentioned it to you?'

'No. I didn't want to risk upsetting him by asking about her.' She paused. 'He was often rude to her when she visited. Aggressive even. I think she became frightened of him.'

'That's not the real Oliver. She should understand that.'

'You've known him a long time?'

'We were at school together. Then we worked on the Kingsbury estate near Winchester. Oliver left to work for a racehorse owner, and I came here.'

'You joined the same cavalry regiment?'

'We started in the Hampshire Yeomanry and later got absorbed into another regiment. And then...' He shrugged. 'Our war was over.'

'I saw Oliver's notes when he first came to us. Submachine gun fire, wasn't it?'

'He saved my life. I took some shrapnel to the shoulder. Lost my horse.' Richard would never forget the sound the beast had made as it writhed on the ground. 'Oliver came back for me and took me up on his horse. We got caught in submachine gun fire. That was in the German offensive of March '18.'

She nodded. 'Oliver has been with us the longest. Morgan, David and Nathan came a month or so later. Albert joined us toward the end of the war – I think it was in early November. I remember he was here for Armistice Day.' She glanced at him. 'Did you arrange for Oliver to come to Merewood so you could be close to him?'

He nodded. 'We got shipped out of France and ended up in a crowded military hospital in London. I wrote to Mrs Wintringham, and she arranged a bed for Oliver at the hospital.'

Richard would always be grateful to her for that. The debt he owed his friend weighed heavily. He felt guilty that the shrapnel embedded in his own shoulder had been removed cleanly without much damage while the cruel machine gun fire had shattered Oliver's left forearm.

Sister Hopgood stopped by the lake and turned to look at him. 'Could you visit his wife and collect some of his clothes?'

The request took Richard by surprise. 'Why?'

'I'd like you to take him out somewhere.'

'Will the doctor allow it?'

'It's up to Oliver to decide if he's ready. We can't force him to stay here. Dr Bingham thinks he needs further rest and recuperation. However, I believe he should start to experience the outside world again. The first step in doing that is to wear normal clothes and not hospital blues. I'm afraid Merewood Farm is beginning to feel like a prison to him – one that he's reluctant to leave.'

Richard rubbed his chin, struck by her reasoning. The patients' uniform of blue flannel single-breasted jacket and trousers marked them out as convalescing servicemen, with their regimental caps and medals displayed on their left breast. But the war was over. It was time to get back into civvies.

'Where would I take him?'

'Anywhere. Just get him out into the world again. Although nowhere too stimulating. What would he enjoy?'

'We plan to run a livery stable together. I could drive him to see a few places I've had my eye on. No one can handle horses like Oliver. He's just not so good with people nowadays.'

'You think he could manage to run a stable with one arm?'

'I'll do all the physical work. And I can employ some stable lads to help. Oliver just needs to tell them what to do.'

'I wish you both well.'

'You don't think it will be too stressful for him? Going out and meeting people?'

He found himself on the receiving end of her cool gaze. 'I'll be honest with you, Mr Locke, I don't know. Perhaps we've reached the point where it's worth taking that risk.'

He felt stupid. She was right – and he should have seen it. Oliver wasn't making progress on the ward. All he did was sketch horses. And his conversations with the other patients could hardly be called stimulating. David Cowper might as well not be there.

'Thank you, Sister Hopgood. I'll do as you suggest.' He was aware of how oddly formal this sounded. Awkward even, like he was back in uniform, addressing a senior officer. But he wasn't good at expressing his feelings. And she'd provoked an unexpected emotion in him. He was touched by the way she continued to care for her patients – to the extent of trying to help them rebuild their lives before she moved on with her own.

He thought about this as they stood in companionable silence, watching a pair of swans leading a trio of cygnets across the water.

On the other side of the lake, Dorothy Wintringham and Georgina Vane sat in the wicker chairs he'd placed on the newly mown lawn earlier that day. Dorothy was chatting to David Cowper, and Georgina seemed to be having an intimate conversation with Morgan Jennings.

'You can call me Helen.'

This sudden invitation took him by surprise. 'Oh, yes. I will. And it's Richard, not Mr Locke.'

He saw curiosity in her eyes and felt an undercurrent of something intimate pass between them.

Then she said, 'I'd rather you continued to call me Sister Hopgood in front of the patients. Dr Bingham and I are trying to observe professional standards.'

The feeling of intimacy evaporated.

'Of course.'

As she walked away, Richard tried to imagine the slender frame hidden beneath that nun-like uniform.

She was a cool one, that was for sure. Once, he would have said cold, but his opinion had changed. As they'd talked, he'd sensed genuine warmth and compassion.

It made him realise what a fool he'd been over women in the past, prizing a pretty face above a good mind. That was a mistake he'd paid heavily for. Now his values had changed.

7

Helen watched Richard stride back to the manor. In the past, she'd found him to be somewhat distant and aloof. Although not unattractive, his dark shaggy hair and tall loping figure gave him a slightly sinister appearance. He had a touch of Heathcliff about him – perhaps it was the way he seemed so connected with the rural landscape.

Up close, she'd noticed the humour in his brown eyes and the warmth of his smile. It was clear he was concerned for Oliver.

She strolled around the lake to where Dorothy Wintringham was chatting to David. Unlike her husband, who'd grunt a monosyllabic greeting to the patients, Dorothy liked to talk to the men. She'd enquire about their lives before the war and try to find ways to help them adjust to their new situation.

The smell of newly cut grass hung in the air, and David appeared to be enjoying the summer scents and warm sunshine. Helen was pleased to see he was finally losing the grey pallor he'd had for so long.

'I'm sorry to interrupt, Mrs Wintringham. Before you return to the manor, I wonder if you'd have time to check the inventories I've made.'

'Of course, my dear. And I've told you before, call me Dorothy. I'll come and take a look now.'

Georgina, who'd been reading to Morgan, gave Helen a sideways glance from under her lashes. The woman clearly disliked her, though she had no idea why. She suspected it emanated from a possessiveness of Morgan. Perhaps she considered her a rival.

Georgina moved closer to Morgan and whispered something in his ear. The girl was pretty enough, having inherited her mother's violet eyes and gold hair, but she hadn't an ounce of sense. Poor Morgan must be desperate to put up with her simpering.

Helen smiled to herself as Morgan reached into his pocket and held out his cigarette case. Made of silver and engraved with the emblem of his regiment, it was the one valuable item he possessed, and she suspected he'd only offered Georgina a cigarette to show it off.

She hurried to catch up with Dorothy, who was striding across the lawn in patent leather brogues. While Georgina favoured frilly, girlish frocks, her mother wore simple but well-cut linen dresses that fashionably grazed her ankles. Her gold hair, lightly tinged with grey, was combed into a neat roll at the back of her neck. Dorothy's elegance made Helen feel ungainly, and she was conscious of the sound of her long uniform skirt swishing on the dry grass as she walked.

They entered the farmhouse through the patio doors and found Frederick Wintringham seated next to Oliver at the table. To Helen's annoyance, his dog, a golden retriever, was being petted by Albert and Nathan.

'Frederick. This is a hospital ward,' Dorothy remonstrated. 'The dog shouldn't be in here.'

'He's not doing any harm.' Frederick's blond head was bent over Oliver's sketch of Flame.

'Why don't you take the dog outside,' Helen suggested to Nathan. She knew he was fond of the creature and didn't want to spoil what little pleasure he had.

Nathan stood up. 'Come on, Dexter.'

The dog obediently followed him out to the patio.

As she entered her office, she heard Frederick say, 'I can't wait to see her face when I bring Blaze in here for you to sketch.'

Helen closed the door on their laughter.

'I apologise for my stepson.' Dorothy pulled up a chair. 'Now, I presume it's not the inventories that are concerning you, my dear?'

'I wanted to talk to you in private regarding the patients—' But before she could continue, Dorothy began to question her about Morgan.

'I appreciate some of what the men share with you is in confidence. However, I'd like to know anything you can tell me about Captain Jennings' background.'

Helen wasn't surprised by the request. It was obvious to everyone what was going on. Probably even to David Cowper.

'His father was a major,' she explained. 'Morgan joined his father's regiment, the Lancashire Fusiliers. He was made a captain at the start of the war and decorated for gallantry. I believe his parents have both died.' She didn't mention that Morgan had given her the impression he'd lost all the money he'd inherited following their death. 'He has a brother living in London.'

'And what do you know of his character?' Dorothy's sharp blue eyes were fixed on hers, seeming to search for any sign that she wasn't telling the whole truth.

She felt herself wilt under the forceful gaze. Dorothy Wintringham was a strong woman. And a good one, in Helen's opinion. She didn't want to lie to her.

'His friends describe him as generous and amusing company. While he's been here, he's done wonders in keeping the patients' spirits up. Even the more difficult ones.' By this, she meant Oliver Edwards. What she omitted to say was that from the conversations she'd overheard, Morgan was a womaniser who often drank to excess. But that had been in his previous life. Things were somewhat different now.

'You know why I'm asking? Georgina seems to have taken a shine to him.'

'It's not unusual for a young woman to develop feelings when ministering to an attractive man. Georgina doesn't have a nurse's training.' *And she's a silly girl with no intelligence*, Helen mentally added. 'I always kept an eye on my younger nurses to ensure they maintained a professional distance.' As she said this, the pretty face of Nurse Taplin flitted across her mind. She pushed the image away.

'I knew you'd understand the situation. My first husband, Georgina's father, wasn't the most reliable of men. He spent a lot of time at the racetrack, and when he died, we discovered we weren't as financially secure as he'd led us to believe.' Dorothy played with the sapphire ring on her left hand. 'I'd like to see Georgina happily married. To someone suitable, if you know what I mean.'

Helen knew exactly what she meant. Replace the word suitable with the word wealthy and you were left with the fact that Morgan would not be considered a desirable husband for her daughter.

When she visited the village, Helen often heard snippets of gossip about the Wintringhams. Dorothy had married Joseph Wintringham just before the war when she'd been in her mid-forties. Her first husband had died a few years earlier, leaving her and Georgina in impoverished circumstances. Joseph was a decade older than his bride and also a widower. His only son, Frederick, was known to have disapproved of the match.

When Frederick took a commission in 1916, he was predicted to have a glittering army career ahead of him. At the time, his stepsister, Georgina, had been betrothed to Patrick Wintringham, the son of a second cousin of Joseph's. The war changed all that.

Although Lieutenant Frederick Wintringham was honourably discharged, gossips said that honour had nothing to do with the minor injury he'd sustained to his hand. Meanwhile, Georgina's fiancé had been awarded medals for bravery on the battlefields of France. He'd returned a hero, called off his engagement, and recently married a colonel's daughter.

'I've persuaded Morgan to write to his brother, Harry,' Helen said, though by all accounts, Harry was little better than Morgan when it came to handling money. 'I'm encouraging him to go and stay with him for a while. Perhaps if a little distance is put between them, Georgina can decide on her true feelings for him.'

Part of her didn't want to deny Morgan his chance with Georgina. However, she respected Dorothy. And she also knew Morgan had been dependent on army routine and regulations to keep him in check. If he was to forge a life outside the military, he needed a strong woman to help him. Helen was certain that marriage to Georgina Vane would end in disaster for both of them.

'You're always so sensible. Yes, I think that would be for the best. Everything here has become too intimate.' Dorothy glanced out at the empty ward as she spoke. 'I heard about the skeleton in your bath. It seems normal codes of conduct are breaking down.'

Helen felt this, too. Merewood Farm wasn't a hospital any more. It was more like a convalescent home, though with hardly any staff and few patients. Uncertainty hung in the air, and this led to unrest and unusual behaviour.

'Dr Bingham had hoped that given more time, he'd be able to resolve some of the patients' ongoing issues. But...' Helen paused, wondering how frank to be. As usual, she opted for plain speaking.

'In my view, we've come as far as we can. I no longer feel I'm helping these men. My intention is to find suitable places for each of them so the hospital can close as soon as possible.'

To her relief, Dorothy nodded vigorously. Although she wasn't in charge of the medical staff, Dorothy was the commandant of the hospital and the Wintringhams' met many of its expenses. Helen needed her support to carry out her plans.

'I'm pleased to hear you say that. I've given it much thought and come to the same conclusion.'

Encouraged, Helen said, 'I'm going to ask Dr Bingham to write to St Dunstan's Hostel for Blind Soldiers and Sailors about David.'

'I've heard of their work. I'll talk to Dr Bingham and make sure he contacts them.'

Helen smiled. In recent weeks, she felt she'd gained a little more awareness of how to handle Samuel, but it wouldn't hurt to have the weight of the Wintringhams to fall back on. 'I get the impression he'd like to give David more time here.'

Dorothy sighed. 'I'm afraid there is no more time. My husband needs to sell the farm, otherwise we risk losing the manor. It's not as if David's improving. I think we've exhausted what we can do here.'

'I also intend to write to Albert Gates' fiancée. It may seem like I'm overstepping the mark, but—'

Dorothy held up a hand. 'You don't have to justify yourself to me, my dear. The sooner this place closes, the better. Between us, we need to make that happen.'

'I've begun posting the first inventories to the Red Cross, and they'll be sending vans in the coming weeks to take the equipment no longer in use. Most of it has been stored in the art studio.' Dorothy looked puzzled, and Helen added, 'Sorry, the south barn. Dr Bingham still calls it the art studio.'

Dorothy nodded in comprehension. 'That reminds me. When

Victor Protheroe was here, one of the patients painted a portrait of me. Do you remember he presented it to me when he left? I was touched that he'd chosen me as the subject.'

'Oh yes.' Helen couldn't recall the patient's name, though she remembered his picture had been rather good.

Samuel was convinced that painting was a form of therapy for soldiers with war neurosis, and Victor Protheroe's arrival at Merewood Farm had given him the chance to prove it. Never had shrapnel been so carefully removed from the arm of a patient. Samuel was determined the great artist would retain all his former dexterity as a painter.

During his stay at the hospital, they'd converted the south barn into a studio, and Victor had held painting lessons there.

'I left the portrait with Victor as he wanted to use it to encourage the other patients to try painting. Do you know what became of it?'

Helen shook her head. 'I suspect it's still in the south barn. I'll see if I can find it.'

* * *

'Are you alright, S-S-Sister,' Nathan stammered when she entered the ward that evening.

'Perfectly fine, thank you, Nathan,' Helen replied as she turned down his bed. Since the prank, all the patients had been anxious to show their concern for her. Apart from Oliver.

'Rotten trick to play on someone.' Albert was eyeing her cautiously.

'Yes, it was.'

'I'm sure no one meant any harm by it.' Morgan was lying on his bed, staring up at the ceiling.

She went over to him. 'Did you write to your brother?'

'Can't wait to get rid of me?'

'It was just a polite enquiry.' Helen turned and began to walk away, knowing he would call her back.

'Sorry, didn't mean to snap.'

She smiled and sank into the chair beside his bed, realising how tired she was. The patients had already dined, and once she'd folded down their sheets, she'd go upstairs to change before she joined Samuel in the kitchen.

'My brother's landlady returned my letter. I should say former landlady as Harry's done a bunk, owing two months' rent. She wants me to cough up.' Morgan sat up and reached over to his bedside cabinet for his cigarette case. 'Fat chance of that.'

Helen groaned inwardly. 'Do you have any friends you can stay with?'

'Thing is, I've asked Georgina to marry me.' He looked at her apologetically. 'You'd have been my first choice. If I thought you'd have me.'

'I've suffered enough.'

He gave a bark of laughter. 'Yes. You probably have.'

'What did Georgina say?'

'She's keen but needs a bit of time to settle it with her family.'

'Do you care for her?' she asked.

Morgan threw out his arms in a dramatic gesture. 'I'm in love.'

'You said you were in love with Nurse Taplin.'

She watched his expression change and could have kicked herself. She didn't want the other patients to hear and start talking about Isabel. Albert hadn't been at the hospital then, but the others might remember that Isabel was murdered on Midsummer's Eve. Nathan definitely would. Helen was sure he'd had a soft spot for the nurse.

'I did love her. I'd have run away with her even though she had no money.' Morgan slumped back onto his bed. 'I wish I had.'

'Georgina doesn't have any money,' Helen pointed out.

'Her stepfather does. We need some Wintringham cash to help us get off on the right footing.'

Of course you do, thought Helen in exasperation. But it would take a long time to persuade Joseph Wintringham to bestow any of his wealth on his ninny of a stepdaughter and her waster of a fiancé. And time was what they didn't have.

She finished her round and climbed the stairs wearily. Even a soak in the bath did nothing to revive her. The evening air was muggy, and it felt like a storm was on the way.

Earlier, she'd been galvanised by her conversation with Dorothy. Lying in the bath, she felt like a lead weight. Something about this place was sapping her energy and replacing it with a debilitating unease.

It was time to close Merewood Hospital – and soon.

8

Samuel looked appraisingly at Helen as she entered the kitchen.

When he'd been in her bathroom, he'd spotted the array of fragranced toiletries she'd accumulated. God knows it wasn't easy to get hold of much in the way of perfume or other little luxuries out here in the countryside. It pleased him that she made an effort with her appearance before joining him for dinner. He'd often catch a whiff of lavender soap or freshly washed hair. Her feminine scent made a refreshing change from the odour of gas and carbolic soap that pervaded the hospital.

When he'd turned forty, he'd decided it was time he got married, and she was the right age for him. If he'd picked someone as young as Nurse Taplin, it might have raised eyebrows. At thirty-two, Helen was a more respectable choice.

Although not an obviously attractive woman, there was something compelling about her. She had a slender figure and thick, dark hair. Her green eyes were her best feature. Irish eyes? He seemed to think she'd told him her father was from Ireland. She had a direct way of looking at you, a cool gaze that could make her seem unapproachable. Yet he found it strangely exciting – sexual even.

'There's a little wine left, if you'd like some?'

She nodded. 'It reminds me of the red wine we used to drink in a café in the village of...' She paused. 'I've forgotten the name. It was in northern France near the field hospital where I was stationed before I came here.'

He vaguely remembered her arriving in August 1916. He'd always made an effort to greet the new nurses individually. It was something he was sure they appreciated. After that, he hadn't taken much notice of her. He was aware of her efficiency. She'd always been diligent, working her way up to senior sister. When Matron left, it had seemed natural for Helen to assume command. While the others had been quick to pack their bags, she'd stayed out of a sense of duty to the patients, and he was grateful to her for that.

'I hope the men are behaving themselves.' He filled her wine glass. 'No issues with Morgan?'

'He doesn't bother me. I'm more concerned about David and Oliver. And I believe you are, too?' She ladled soup into their bowls.

He smiled. How well she knew him. 'Right as usual. I'm still unsure how to proceed.'

'I have a suggestion. Could you write to St Dunstan's Hostel for Blind Soldiers and Sailors? Ask if they'll take David?'

He frowned. 'The problem is he may not be blind.'

'I realise that. But as you've said yourself, it's difficult to know the best treatment. I think we're at the stage where we have to try every option.'

'He has a mother, doesn't he?' He tasted the lukewarm soup and reached for the salt.

'She's too frail to care for him. David used to look after her. When he joined up, she went to live with her sister in Romsey and his aunt can't cope with David as well. Wherever he goes, he'll need help. He won't be able to manage on his own.'

'I hoped, with the passage of time, the true nature of his condition would become more apparent. My feeling is, it's psychological rather than physical.'

'We're running out of time.'

'Mr Wintringham has assured me that nothing will happen until every patient has been found a suitable home.'

'From what I've heard, he won't be in a position to hold out much longer. He needs to sell Merewood Farm to pay his taxes.'

Samuel guessed she'd heard this from Dorothy Wintringham. He knew it to be true. Joseph would be forced to sell the farm if he were to keep the manor.

He sighed. 'It's a shame. This place has so much to offer.'

'Perhaps it did once. But we're beginning to lose the structure that made Merewood Farm a hospital.' She took a sip of wine. 'We can't stay here forever.'

He studied her closely. Did he detect a note of longing in her voice? And perhaps not just for the hospital.

'I think David and Oliver need more time here,' he replied. 'Merewood Farm is their best chance for rehabilitation. In the quiet of the countryside, the root of their problems might become clearer. If they were moved to more disruptive surroundings, I fear they'd deteriorate.' He noted her look of disappointment and hastily added, 'However, St Dunstan's could be an option for David.'

She took away their soup bowls and returned with two plates. 'I feel Oliver should start to go out. I've asked Richard Locke to take him somewhere.'

Samuel didn't like the sound of this. 'It's his temper that's the problem.'

'I admit, it's a risk. I'm afraid his wife has left him.'

'If only people had more patience. All Oliver needs is time to recuperate. The poor man has suffered enough.'

'So has his wife,' Helen replied. 'He was very aggressive when she visited. I think she began to feel afraid of him.'

Samuel toyed with the lamb cutlet on his plate. 'That's why I fear it's too soon for him to venture out. I'm worried something might trigger one of his outbursts and set him back. He's making progress here.' His voice held a conviction he didn't feel. And from the way Helen was looking at him, she wasn't fooled. Oliver had made little headway in the last six months. While the wounds of his amputated arm had healed, his neuropathic pain had got worse.

'Morphine is the only drug that seems to help,' she commented.

'It's of little value to Oliver in the long-term. I believe his problems stem from war neurosis. Undoubtedly, he experiences pain in his arm, but his psychological perspective could be magnifying that pain. It's something I used to discuss with Victor Protheroe.'

To Samuel, the spring of 1918, when Victor had set up an art studio in the south barn, had been among the most satisfying of his career. The war artist had combined his skills as a painter with his extensive studies of psychology to create a rehabilitation programme that had yielded surprising results.

'Weren't those paintings incredible?'

'Extraordinary,' Helen agreed. 'Oliver was a different man when he took part in Victor's art lessons.'

'I wish I could replicate them. Expressing emotions on canvas can help to dispel a private mental torment.'

'It's a tragedy Victor was so tormented himself,' Helen remarked.

'His own experience of the battlefields gave him an insight into the minds of his fellow soldiers. Alas, it proved too much for him in the end. And I think Nurse Taplin's death affected him badly.'

Samuel remembered his shock at hearing Protheroe had

thrown himself into the Thames. That had been in October 1918, only three months after the artist had left the hospital. Only four months after Isabel Taplin's murder. He sometimes wondered about that.

* * *

Helen undressed and lay on her bed, pulling the cover over her even though it was a warm night. What Samuel had said at dinner about Victor Protheroe had unsettled her.

Samuel had been so enamoured of the man, he'd failed to notice Victor's cocaine addiction. She'd seen enough drug users to know the signs.

At the start of the war, the army had given soldiers a gelatine-coated pill called Forced March that contained cocaine and cola nut extract. It was supposed to improve endurance, but soldiers took it to enhance their mood rather than their physical ability.

Even after the army tried to prohibit the sale of cocaine and opiates to servicemen, they were still readily available – just more care was taken by those who traded in them.

Helen always knew when one of Victor's parcels contained cocaine by the furtive way he opened the package. His artist friends kept him topped up with a regular supply. His mood swings had led her to wonder if he was somehow involved in Isabel's death.

When he'd asked if he could paint the nurse, Matron had quite rightly put a stop to it. Afterwards, Helen had speculated that he might have tried to persuade the girl to sit for him and then reacted badly when she refused. The police hadn't found any evidence against him. He'd been holding one of his art lessons on the afternoon of her death. But then, no one knew precisely when the murder had taken place.

These thoughts flitted across her mind, and she wished she'd drunk another glass of wine to help her relax. Slowly, she began to drift off, but the sound of a woman's laugh made her stiffen. She waited, then heard it a second time. It hadn't been her imagination.

Helen got out of bed and went over to the window. Was that a woman by the lake? She could have sworn she saw a figure dressed in white disappear into the copse of trees at the water's edge. Her skin pricked as her nostrils caught the sickly scent of a lady's perfume.

A tingle of fear passed through her until she realised the smell was coming from the jasmine climbing the farmhouse walls. Her breathing steadied, and she remembered the note under Morgan's pillow. It was probably Georgina Vane she could hear.

Helen chided herself for being so silly. She was only feeling unsettled because it was Midsummer's Eve, the anniversary of Isabel's murder.

She returned to bed and pulled the cover tighter around her. There wouldn't be many hours of darkness that night, and she tried to push thoughts of ethereal spirits from her mind. Did she seriously imagine the young nurse would rise from the dead to seek revenge on her killer?

9

Samuel observed Helen's pale skin and tired eyes as she entered his office. Was she still dwelling on the incident with the skeleton? Or had the storm kept her awake? He was vaguely aware of hearing thunder before drifting back off to sleep. It must have been in the early hours of the morning.

She hadn't eaten much at dinner the night before, and he was becoming concerned. He needed her fit and healthy for the role he had planned for her.

'What you said last night was true. We're starting to lose the structure and regulations that make this a hospital. Too many people come and go – it's disruptive for the patients. If I ran this as a private clinic, I'd insist on scheduled visiting hours.'

Samuel noticed Helen's look of surprise at his words. None-theless, she agreed it would be better for the patients to have a routine.

Encouraged by this response, he turned to address Richard Locke. He'd sent Kate to the manor with a note asking the estate manager to call on him at his earliest convenience. He was pleased by the man's prompt appearance in his office.

'This place is a medical establishment, and as such, it needs to be more secure. The Wintringhams walk in and out of here as if it's their own home.'

'What is it you think I can do about that?' Richard asked.

Samuel didn't like the man's surly expression. 'You manage the estate. Surely, it's your responsibility.'

'I'm not a receptionist. I can't monitor who comes and goes, and I can hardly tell the Wintringhams they're not welcome. They may not live here, but they do own Merewood Farm.'

'All I'm asking is that you look out for any trespassers. It's possible someone entered the premises without being seen and went into my office and Sister Hopgood's private living quarters.'

Richard turned to Helen. 'I'm sorry for what happened, but I doubt someone would bother to enter the hospital just to play a silly trick. It's more likely to be one of the occupants, though I will keep a closer eye on the place.'

'Thank you, Mr Locke,' Helen replied. 'You're probably right. I feel this is best dealt with by Dr Bingham and myself.'

Samuel didn't like the way Richard nodded respectfully at Helen and left the office without even looking at him.

'Insolent man,' he muttered, irked by Richard's lack of deference.

'I think this is something we're going to have to manage ourselves, Dr Bingham. In future, we need to discourage too much familiarity.'

He smiled. 'It's Samuel when we're in private. You're right, of course. We run this hospital, and it's our responsibility.'

He liked the way she'd said *in future*. It was a sure sign they were thinking along the same lines. Merewood Farm was too good to give up.

Samuel noticed her glance at Yorick as she turned to leave.

'Would you like me to get rid of him?'

Helen shook her head. 'As long as he stays here and not in my bathroom, I don't mind.'

He noticed the proprietary way she spoke of the bathroom. It was obvious she'd become attached to the place.

'I'll make sure of that.' He followed her out of the door, pleased by her no-nonsense attitude. She always stayed calm, a skill that would be vital if he was to get his venture off the ground. He had no doubt he needed her. The question was, in what capacity? Could they combine the personal and the professional?

In the kitchen, Nathan was holding the door open for Kate, who came in carrying a basket of bread. Chester took the opportunity to sneak in behind her.

'Bloody thing,' he muttered as the black cat headed straight for Nathan. Samuel tried not to touch the creature if he could help it and would shoo it out if no one was watching.

When the hospital had been fully staffed, a porter had taken food to the patients in their wards. Nowadays, unless one of them was poorly, they were encouraged to eat in the farmhouse kitchen. It was a way of nudging them into caring for themselves, and it worked well. Albert or Nathan would guide David from the ward to the kitchen and assist him during the meal. Oliver occasionally needed help cutting his food, and Samuel noticed he accepted it more graciously from one of his fellow patients than from Helen or himself.

'Where's Morgan? Breakfast has arrived,' he said to Albert, who was holding David's hand, guiding him to a chair.

Samuel took the basket from Kate and was setting it down on the table when he noticed Albert and Nathan exchange a nervous glance. He sighed with exasperation. The smell of freshly baked bread was making him hungry, but he could hardly tuck in until the patients had finished.

It was Oliver who replied. 'He's not here.'

Samuel gritted his teeth. 'I can see that. Where's he gone?'

Oliver shrugged. 'He wasn't in his bed when I woke this morning. And the door to the patio was open.'

Samuel studied the patients' wary faces. 'Did any of you see him go out?'

Nathan's facial muscles were twitching, and he gave a wobbly shake of his head. Albert's hand rose to scratch the sores on his cheek, and Helen reached out to stop him.

'He must have gone for a walk. One of his crutches is gone.' Oliver had pushed the teapot over to Nathan so he could pour a cup for David. But seeing the young man was shaking too much to get the tea into the cup, he stood up and went across to do it himself.

Despite it being warm and humid outside, the kitchen was cold, and Samuel saw Helen shiver. He indicated for her to accompany him, and when they were in the corridor, he closed the kitchen door behind him.

'Any idea where he's got to?' he said in an undertone.

She shook her head. 'I've never known Morgan to miss a meal.'

This was true. Morgan had the heartiest appetite of all the men. They walked down the corridor to the ward, where the patio doors stood ajar.

Morgan's bed hadn't been slept in. The sheets were rumpled, though not pulled back, indicating he'd lain on top rather than beneath them. His pyjamas were neatly folded under the pillow – Helen's handiwork. If Morgan had worn them, they'd have been strewn in a crumpled heap on the bed.

'It's not just the Wintringhams that come and go as they please. Now the patients are at it,' he grumbled. 'This is a hospital. We must have rules.'

Unseen, Chester had followed them out of the kitchen and took this moment to jump up onto Morgan's bed.

Samuel ran his hand through his hair. 'Even the bloody cat treats this place like home.'

'It is Chester's home.' Helen picked up the cat and placed him on the floor. 'He helps keep the rats and mice away.'

Samuel ignored this. 'Do you have any idea where Morgan might have gone?'

'There is something. It concerns Miss Vane—'

Before she could continue, Samuel heard someone calling his name and Richard Locke burst in through the patio doors. He was about to reprimand him for entering the ward without first checking with himself or Helen when he saw the expression on the man's face.

'Dr Bingham,' he panted.

'What is it?' Samuel suddenly realised Richard was soaking wet and trailing muddy water across the floor.

'There's been an accident. It's Morgan.'

Richard squelched out of the door, and Samuel dashed after him. Even when sopping wet, the man had a powerful stride, and he had to run to catch up. He looked back and saw that Helen had hesitated before deciding to follow.

Richard was making his way across the lawn in the direction of Merewood Lake. Samuel moved cautiously, afraid of slipping on the damp grass. He began to run faster when he saw the figure lying on the muddy shore. He thought he heard a muffled cry from behind him.

When he reached Morgan's body, he fell to his knees and gently turned the man's face towards him. Instinctively, he knew any attempt at resuscitation would be fruitless.

Samuel felt rather than saw Helen drop to the ground beside him.

'There's nothing you can do, Sister Hopgood. Morgan's dead.'

10

Richard had to stop himself from dragging Helen away. The woman was a nurse, for God's sake. How much death had she witnessed during the last five years? Instead, he leant down and helped her to her feet.

She seemed to be in a daze. 'Dead? Morgan?'

Bingham was still bending over the body, and Richard noticed the doctor's hair was starting to thin on top, unlike his own thick, dark mop. He cursed himself for having vain thoughts at a time like this.

'What happened?' Helen murmured.

'I was heading up to the manor when I saw something floating in the lake. I wasn't sure what it was at first.' Richard took a long breath. 'When I realised it was a body, I ran into the water and hauled him out.'

'What was he doing in the lake?' Helen gazed around. 'Where's his crutch and shoes?'

'Over there.' Richard pointed to a dense patch of rhodo-dendrons.

They turned to where the crutch was lying on the ground. The discarded shoes and socks next to it.

Bingham stood up, wet grass stains on the knees of his trousers. 'I fear he must have overestimated his capabilities and tried to swim in the lake. God knows what possessed him to do such a thing.'

Richard guessed the answer to that question was probably Georgina Vane. He stared down at Morgan's twisted body. The man looked so pathetic, his bare feet ridiculously white, jutting out from the sodden hospital blues clinging to his skin. So helpless. Nothing like the arrogant devil he'd been in life.

Helen was shaking her head. 'Morgan wouldn't go swimming. Not fully clothed. And not in the middle of a storm.'

Bingham removed his white coat and placed it over the body. Richard saw he was sweating profusely. It was still early, and the temperature was yet to rise above twenty degrees.

'I need to tell Mr Wintringham what's happened.' Richard couldn't risk Georgina stumbling upon the scene. Whatever he thought of her, she didn't deserve to see Morgan in this state. 'And we should inform the police. I can drive over to Winchester.'

Bingham nodded. 'I'll stay with Morgan until they get here. He's my responsibility.' Unsteadily, he sat down on the grass close to the body. 'Go back and tend to the patients, Sister Hopgood.'

'What should I tell them?' she asked.

'That there's been an unfortunate accident. Make sure they stay inside until the body's removed. I don't want them to see Morgan like this.' Bingham frowned. 'I hope the police won't want to interview the patients. It will be too distressing for them.'

Richard exchanged a brief glance with Helen before she turned to walk back to the farmhouse. He thought it likely the police would want to talk to the four men who effectively shared a room with Morgan. Not least, to ask them about his state of mind. Helen was right. He wouldn't have gone into the water in his hospital blues. Not if he intended to come out alive.

The smell of rotting vegetation filled his nostrils, and Richard realised it was coming from him. He had bits of pond weed clinging to his clothes. He took a quick detour to his cottage to change and arrived at Merewood Manor just as the family were finishing breakfast. He waited until Dorothy and Georgina had gone upstairs before joining Joseph Wintringham and Frederick in the dining room.

'Jennings? Dead? Bloody hell!' Frederick looked aghast but not displeased. 'Georgie's going to be furious.'

Joseph ordered his son to drive to Winchester to fetch the police, ignoring his protest that one of the servants could go.

Joseph Wintringham was a man used to having his commands obeyed. He didn't suffer fools gladly and, at over six foot tall with a broad frame, he'd been known to use his masculine physique to intimidate his business rivals.

Once Frederick had gone, Richard accepted Joseph's invitation to join him at the breakfast table and took the cup of coffee the housekeeper offered.

'Drowned, you say?' Joseph sat down heavily. He jerked his head in the direction of Merewood Farm. 'I'll be glad to get shot of that place. At least there's only four of them left now.'

Richard noticed he'd waited for the housekeeper to leave the room before making this callous statement.

He sipped his coffee. 'I'm afraid Georgina's going to be upset.'

Joseph seemed to brighten even more at that. 'Another problem solved. She was actually contemplating marriage to the man. Anyone with an ounce of sense could see he was a chancer, out for what he could get.'

Richard chose to remain silent.

Joseph drained his coffee cup and leant forward, causing the table to creak. 'I wanted to talk to you about the hospital. I've got a buyer for the farm, and I don't want to risk losing him.'

'Knight?'

Joseph nodded. 'He's offered me twenty-eight pounds per acre. We need to negotiate a few more details, but I think we can come to an agreement. I'll be frank with you, I'm not going to quibble too much. I've had little interest from anyone else.'

This didn't surprise Richard. Baden Knight owned a nearby farm with a few pastures adjoining the estate. Extending his farm made sense. On its own, Merewood wasn't large enough to appeal to a serious farmer. But it would do nicely for Knight.

'When do you think the sale will go through?' He was worried about Oliver. He still needed to find them a place to live.

'Soon. I don't want Knight to get cold feet. You know what he's like when it comes to the hospital.' He ran a hand over his closely cropped grey hair. 'I realise I promised it wouldn't close until all the patients had been found new homes. Nevertheless this is the last straw. Bingham has done a grand job, but enough is enough.'

He knew what Joseph was talking about. Baden Knight was a God-fearing man and lay preacher. Several times during the war, he'd visited the hospital to deliver sermons. 'Bugger off' had been one of the politer responses from the patients. Knight had labelled them all heathens and told anyone who'd listen that the doctors and nurses were all fornicators. His view that the hospital was evil had only been reinforced by Isabel Taplin's death.

Joseph said in a conspiratorial whisper, 'There's another thing. Clifford Knight is keen on Georgina. He may be dull as ditchwater, but he's a good match. With Jennings out of the way, she might start taking an interest.'

Richard knew little of Baden's son, Clifford. He vaguely recalled an earnest man in his mid-thirties, who'd accompanied his father to the hospital and read a few passages from the bible in a low measured voice.

'I agree it has to close. But I'm concerned about Oliver. I have to find a suitable livery stables with accommodation to house us both.'

'Start looking. Take whatever time off you need. And if you find a place that's above what you can afford, let me know. When I sell Merewood Farm, I'll be in a position to loan you the extra cash.'

Richard was taken aback. Joseph was a contradictory man. On the one hand, he could be callous, however, he could also be considerate.

'Thank you. That's kind of you,' he replied, though he had no intention of being beholden to anyone. When he left Merewood, he wanted to be his own master and provide for himself and Oliver.

'My wife's been discussing the patients with Sister Hopgood. She told me of your plan to go into business with Oliver. How's he going to manage with one hand?'

'He knows horses. I'll employ stable hands to do the physical work. Oliver will be able to do any training that's required.'

'Good. That just leaves Albert, Nathan and David. My wife and Sister Hopgood are capable women. Between them, they'll be able to get the men settled somewhere.'

'And Dr Bingham?'

'He keeps talking about needing more time. The man's dragging his heels. I don't want to force matters, but...' Joseph hesitated. 'I have to push things along. And I need your help.'

Richard looked at him enquiringly.

'The terms of my agreement with Knight will include various farm machinery that's no longer in use. I need you to find whatever we have and move it into one of the barns so he can view it. Preferably to the barn furthest away from the hospital.'

'I'd be happy to.' Richard rubbed his unshaven chin as he considered this. It was three years since the farm had been converted into a hospital, and the machinery was scattered all over the place.

'My wife has made a sensible suggestion. Sister Hopgood is compiling an inventory of hospital equipment to be returned to the Red Cross. Dorothy has offered your services to help her move the stuff to the south barn – the one they used as a painters' studio. At the same time, you can collect all the farm machinery and move it to the north barn. That way, Knight can see what he's getting.'

Richard smiled. 'Mrs Wintringham should have been a general. We'd have won the war faster.'

'I think you're right.' Joseph gave him a sly grin. 'And Sister Hopgood would make anyone an ideal right-hand woman.'

The comment surprised Richard, but he sipped his coffee and let it pass. They were still discussing plans for the sale of the farm when they heard a car on the gravel drive.

'What's going on? Why are the police here?' Georgina's high-pitched squeal came from the hallway.

Joseph rolled his eyes. 'This isn't going to be easy.'

Richard stood up. 'I'll deal with the police.'

'You get the easy job. Tell them I'll offer every assistance. And ask Bingham to liaise with my wife regarding funeral arrangements.' He sighed as he stood up. 'Once I tell Dorothy, she'll insist we give the damned man a decent burial. I've no doubt Jennings didn't have a brass farthing.'

At that moment, Dorothy entered the dining room, her daughter at her heels. Richard nodded to Joseph and made his escape. He didn't envy him the task of dealing with a hysterical Georgina. Facing the police and Morgan's dead body was preferable to that.

In the company of a sergeant and constable, Richard returned to the lake, where Dr Bingham was still sitting on the grass. A white sheet now covered Morgan's body; he guessed Helen had placed it there.

It was lunchtime before Richard walked back to the manor, intending to head straight to the kitchen for something to eat. He was stopped by Georgina, who was standing on the terrace looking down at the lake.

She gazed up at him with liquid eyes. 'You found him, didn't you?'

He nodded. 'I'm sorry.'

'How did he drown?' Her voice was a whine. 'I don't understand what happened.'

'Did you see him last night?' he asked.

'Don't be silly.' But she didn't meet his eye when she said it. Instead, she glanced back at the manor house. 'What am I going to do now?'

He sighed. Georgina wasn't grieving for Morgan. She was grieving for her lost opportunity to escape from Merewood Manor. She'd once told him how much she hated living in the Wintringhams' ancestral pile.

Richard scrutinised her bloodshot eyes and blotchy face. Had she been with Morgan last night? She'd be reluctant to say if she had, scared it would ruin her reputation and scupper any chances of finding another prospective husband. But he needed her to tell the truth.

It had occurred to him that a year ago, he'd found Isabel dead in the woods. Now he'd discovered Morgan's body. The police would think that suspicious. Georgina might be the only person who could tell them what happened.

When he'd first met her, he'd been taken with those unusual violet eyes and glossy gold hair. He'd responded to her flirtation, but the attraction had worn off fast. She was too needy. Too much of a child despite her thirty years. In his younger days, he might have overlooked her character. Now he was thirty-four, his attitude had changed. If he took a wife, she'd have to be a strong woman. Someone like Helen.

Was it possible Morgan had reached the same conclusion? It probably wouldn't have taken him long to realise a life with Georgina wasn't worth any amount of money.

Richard returned to the lake later that afternoon. The police had gone, along with Morgan's body, which had been transported to the local mortuary. He retraced his steps to the spot where he'd waded in and fished the man out.

That morning, something had given him the impression two people had been by the lake. Why was that?

He glanced around. It looked like someone had trampled through the rhododendron bushes, but that could have been Morgan on his crutch. Maybe he'd fallen over. Or perhaps it was just the storm lashing the branches. It had started raining at about one thirty in the morning.

He inspected the mud. That was it. He thought he'd seen footprints. Morgan hadn't been wearing his shoes, and the rain would have washed away any marks made by bare feet. Had he seen deeper imprints? From boots or shoes?

Morgan could have walked on the shore before taking his shoes off and going in. There was no way of telling now. If there had been any prints, Richard had obliterated them when he dragged Morgan's body out. Since then, Bingham and a dozen policemen had trodden in the mud.

11

'You found a skeleton in your bath?'

To Helen's surprise, Superintendent Townsend, a tall man of military bearing, had arrived at the hospital that morning requesting an interview with her. She hadn't expected Morgan's death to warrant the attendance of an officer of his rank. When he mentioned the incident with the skeleton, she understood why. Had he also made a connection with Isabel Taplin's death?

'Who told you about that?' The previous night, she'd dreamt of finding Yorick in the lake – when she'd waded in to drag the bones from the water, they'd turned into Morgan. The image of hospital blues clinging to white bones and then bare skin was lodged in her mind. A young nurse had floated around in the periphery of the dream, reaching out her arms to beckon Morgan toward her.

'Mr Locke mentioned it to one of my constables. It may have no bearing on Captain Jennings' death, but in the circumstances, I'd like you to tell me exactly what happened.'

Helen described her shock at finding Yorick in her bathtub.

'Who do you think did it?'

'I have no idea. Presumably, someone who found it funny.'

Although the patients couldn't hear their conversation – the superintendent had closed her office door before taking a seat – she was still reluctant to point the finger.

'Is there anyone here who would have been amused by that sort of trick?'

'If I'm honest, Morgan was the only patient I might have considered a practical joker. But...' She hesitated. 'Dr Bingham suggested the prank could have been the manifestation of a psychological problem.'

'Do you think Captain Jennings could have put the skeleton in your bath to gain your attention? To try to tell you he was planning to take his life?'

'It never occurred to me. Not at the time.' Only since they'd found Morgan's body had the thought struck her. Had she failed to recognise his cry for help?

Townsend took a small notepad and pencil from his top pocket and made notes as he spoke. 'Captain Jennings' body was found floating in Merewood Lake yesterday morning. We're presuming he drowned on Saturday night. When did you last see him?'

Helen calmed herself by reciting the facts. 'On Saturday evening, when I finished my last round at about seven o'clock. The patients had already had dinner. I went upstairs to my room to wash and change and came back downstairs at eight o'clock to have dinner with Dr Bingham in the kitchen. Sometimes I check on the patients again before I retire, but I didn't that day. I went up at around nine-thirty. I believe Dr Bingham was going to look in on the patients before he went to bed.'

'Do you have any idea why Captain Jennings might have left the ward and gone out that night?'

Feeling disloyal to Dorothy rather than Georgina, Helen pushed the note signed G across her desk.

'What's this?' Superintendent Townsend picked up the piece of paper.

'I found it the other day under Morgan's pillow. I pretended I hadn't seen it. When I was sorting through his belongings, I took it, intending to show it to one of your constables.'

The superintendent read the note aloud. *It's a full moon. Meet me by the lake. Usual time. G.* Do you know who G is?'

'I believe it's from Georgina Vane, Mr Wintringham's step-daughter. She and Morgan were having a romance. In my last conversation with Morgan, he told me he'd asked her to marry him.'

'Is it usual for patients to leave the ward at night?'

'No. It's not.' Helen took a deep breath. 'In hindsight, I should have spoken to Morgan about it. I... I...'

She trailed off, but the superintendent said nothing.

Feeling the need to fill the silence and to justify herself, she continued, 'Morgan is free to come and go as he pleases. He's really only here because he has...' She stopped, realising she'd been speaking in the present tense. 'Morgan *had* nowhere else to live. He couldn't have stayed here much longer. Mrs Wintringham and I are endeavouring to find suitable accommodation for the patients so the hospital can close.'

'Did Captain Jennings have any relatives?'

'A brother, Harry. I'd encouraged Morgan to contact him. On Saturday, Morgan told me he'd received a reply from Harry's land-lady saying his brother had left her lodgings owing two months' rent.' Helen pushed an envelope toward him. 'I believe this is the letter.'

Superintendent Townsend took it and scanned the contents. 'Do you think Captain Jennings took his own life?'

'He gave no indication that was his intention. I suppose if his meeting with Georgina hadn't gone well, he might have felt he had no other option. I hope he knew he could always come to me for help if he needed it.' Helen blinked back tears. 'Perhaps the prank was his way of asking for help.'

She hoped Townsend would offer some words of comfort. Instead, he watched her in silence. This time, Helen didn't feel able to continue, so she said nothing.

Eventually, the superintendent closed his notepad and tucked it into his top pocket, along with the letters she'd given him. 'Under the circumstances, I think it would be best if you boxed up Captain Jennings' possessions. Give them to Sergeant Newman, and we'll try to track down his brother.'

Helen nodded. Although part of her felt it was her duty to write to Morgan's relatives, she was glad to be relieved of the task.

'While you're sorting out Captain Jennings' belongings, could use your office? I'd like to speak to each of the patients privately.'

Helen had no choice but to agree, though she anticipated the effect this would have on the men. Agitation would cause Albert to scratch, Nathan to stutter and Oliver to lose his temper. And what of David?

'Could I suggest that Dr Bingham accompanies David Cowper?'

'The blind one?'

'Yes. I can go and fetch the doctor now, and perhaps you could speak to David first.'

'Thank you, Sister Hopgood.' Townsend stood up. 'No need to fetch him. I'd like a brief chat with the doctor before I start interviewing the patients.'

Helen opened the office door and went into the ward.

'Who's he?' Nathan jerked his head towards the superintendent, who was heading to Samuel's office.

'Superintendent Townsend of the Hampshire Constabulary. He'd like a chat with each of you in my office when he's finished speaking with Dr Bingham.'

'None of us knows when Morgan went out,' Oliver snapped.

'Then that's what you must tell the superintendent,' she replied reassuringly.

'What do you think happened to Morgan?' Albert scratched his cheek.

Helen had no desire to share her thoughts with the patients. 'I'm not sure. Perhaps he decided to go for a swim.'

'Bloody stupid thing to do,' Oliver growled. He was attempting to fill his pipe, which wasn't an easy thing to do one-handed. Helen knew better than to try to help him.

'I'm going to miss him.' Nathan spoke without stuttering.

She glanced at him. He was sitting still, and his facial muscles twitched slightly, but he seemed calmer than usual. Beside him, David slowly nodded his head.

Unrest usually exacerbated their symptoms. This was true of Albert, who was scratching compulsively, and Oliver looked about to explode. By contrast, Nathan and David were remarkably composed.

She went to Albert and gently took his hand away from his face. 'Stop scratching if you can.' She took the pot of cream from his bedside cabinet and smeared a small amount on his cheek.

After wiping her hands, she went over to Morgan's bed and reached underneath for the portmanteau case he stored there. It contained clothes and a few books. She pulled it out and placed it on the bed.

It didn't take long to empty Morgan's bedside cabinet and pack his few belongings. She was conscious of Albert, Nathan and Oliver watching her.

Albert came to stand beside her. 'Is his cigarette case there?'

She took another look inside the cabinet, even though she was sure it was empty.

'No, it's not.'

'He said it was the only thing of value he had left. It was his good luck charm. He managed to keep it with him all through the war.'

'I'll ask Superintendent Townsend if...' Helen tried to find the right words. 'If Morgan had it with him.' The thought of his sodden body lying in the mud brought tears to her eyes.

She picked up the pyjamas folded under his pillow and caught a whiff of the Player's cigarettes Morgan smoked.

'He was a brave man. I shall miss him.'

12

Dr Samuel Bingham was banging his fist on his desk in what Superintendent Townsend considered a futile gesture.

'I think this just proves we need more time.'

'More time for what?' Townsend wasn't impressed by this strange display. In fact, he found everything about the hospital quite bizarre. One doctor, one nurse and five patients.

'More time for my patients to get well again. What happened to Morgan was a tragedy. We should be running this place like a private clinic. But alas.' Bingham was now waving his hands around his office to emphasise the point. 'We lack the resources.'

'And that would have saved Captain Jennings' life?' Townsend chose his words carefully, trying to provoke a reaction. It worked, as Dr Bingham rushed to defend himself.

'I'm only a single doctor running a hospital with just one nurse. It's not enough.'

'You only had five patients. Now you're down to four.' He saw Bingham's face flush.

'It's not about the number of patients, it's about their complex needs. I'm well-read on the subject of psychology and can offer more to these men than a traditional doctor could.'

Townsend considered this. 'When I was informed of the tragedy, I was surprised to learn this place was still open. I was under the impression all the regional auxiliary hospitals had closed.'

'Merewood Farm is unique. Look around you.' Bingham was making futile gestures with his hands again. 'I don't mean inside the hospital itself, but outside. Look at the scenery, listen to the birdsong. The gardens, the horses, nature. It offers the perfect surroundings to recuperate from trauma.'

Townsend inclined his head. 'I take your point, Dr Bingham. Though, presumably, Mr Wintringham will want Merewood Farm back at some stage?'

'He's given up the idea of running it as a farm. I'm putting together a proposal I want to discuss with him.'

Townsend watched Bingham remove a handkerchief from his top pocket to mop his brow. Whatever this proposal was, it was causing the man to sweat. He decided not to push him on the subject. He got the impression it wouldn't be too difficult to find out what this blustering doctor had in mind.

'Let's return to the reason I'm here. When did you last see Morgan Jennings?'

Bingham described how he'd had dinner with Sister Hopgood and then gone into the ward at around ten o'clock for a last check before retiring to his room.

'What about Sister Hopgood? Did she go back into the ward?'

'Not that night. She was tired after the day's events and went straight up to bed.'

'Is this her usual routine?'

'Occasionally, Sister Hopgood will look in on the patients before retiring. I generally only do another round if one of the men feels particularly poorly. However, in the circumstances, I suggested she go up, and I said I'd check on the patients.'

'The circumstances of her finding a skeleton in her bath the previous day?' Superintendent Townsend scrutinised Yorick hanging in the corner.

'She told you about that? It was just a silly trick, though I believe it unsettled her and the patients.'

'Do you have any idea how this fellow' – he pointed to the skeleton – 'found its way to the upstairs bathroom?'

'Not the slightest.'

Townsend kept his eyes fixed on the doctor but didn't say anything. It was a tactic that usually worked. Bingham stared at him for a moment and then began to speak.

'Some of my patients have symptoms that could be considered types of psychosis. I can't discuss it with you, however, it's possible one of them did it to gain Sister Hopgood's attention. They're all highly dependent on her.'

'Perhaps it was Captain Jennings. Could it have been his way of telling her what he planned to do?'

'No. Absolutely not.'

Townsend was surprised by this reaction. 'But you've suggested it could have been a form of psychosis.'

'I can't believe Morgan would...' Bingham seemed to lose his way. 'He just wasn't that sort of chap.'

'Then what do you think happened to Captain Jennings?'

'It must have been an accident.'

Townsend considered this, then said, 'I believe a nurse was murdered here.'

Bingham began to sweat, and he could tell he'd unnerved him by this bald statement.

'Not here. In Gibbet Wood.'

'She worked here, though, didn't she? And was killed a year ago.

On Midsummer's Eve.'

Townsend heard the man's breath catch. Had he really not realised it was a year since Taplin's murder? He watched the doctor slowly exhale before replying.

'Nurse Taplin came to the hospital as part of a voluntary aid detachment a few months before her tragic death.'

'And her killer was never caught?'

'I think you should know that better than me.'

Bingham seemed pleased with this retort, and Townsend privately acknowledged the doctor had scored a direct hit. It still rankled that they were no closer to knowing who murdered Isabel Taplin. With a war on, they'd been short of officers. He'd never given up on the case, but he feared too much time had passed. You needed to catch a killer quickly – and they'd failed to do that. He decided to return to the death in hand.

'Could you tell me what each patient was doing when you made your final round on Saturday evening?'

The doctor replied that there had been nothing out of the ordinary. Nathan Smith had been reading, Oliver Edwards drawing, Albert Gates looking through the letters from his fiancée, and David Cowper playing with his clock.

'And you say Captain Jennings was lying on his bed. Where were his crutches?'

'Morgan slept nearest the doors that lead out to the patio. His crutches were leaning against the wall between his bedside cabinet and the doors. He was sitting up on his bed smoking.'

'In his hospital blues?'

Bingham nodded.

'What did you do after you left the ward?'

'I went to bed to read. My bedroom is further along the corridor. When we were at full capacity, the other doctors were given rooms at the manor, and the nurses and Matron took over the upper floor. I've always stayed here to be close to my patients.'

'And you didn't see or hear anything else after you retired? You weren't required to return to the ward?'

'I went to bed intending to read but fell asleep almost immediately. I think I heard the sound of thunder in the night, then drifted off and woke at around six-thirty. I didn't go into the ward until after Oliver told us that Morgan was missing. That was when we were preparing breakfast in the kitchen.'

Townsend asked a few more questions about the condition of the body when the doctor examined it at the lake.

'It looked like he'd drowned, but a pathologist will tell you for certain,' Bingham replied.

'Could Captain Jennings swim?'

'I've no idea. He had damage to his legs. He could walk with the aid of crutches, and there's no reason why he wouldn't have been able to propel himself in the water. He had power in both legs, and his arms were undamaged.'

'How strong was he?'

'He'd been walking by himself for a while now, albeit with the aid of crutches. He was slowly building up more muscle strength, though he would never have regained the power he once had. It took hours to remove all the shrapnel from his thighs, and he was left with extensive tissue damage. But the surgery was clean, and his wounds healed nicely.'

Superintendent Townsend nodded. 'I'd like to speak to the patients if I may. Sister Hopgood has kindly allowed me to use her office. She suggested you accompany one of them, a Mr Cowper?'

* * *

Samuel stood in the corridor for a few moments to gather his thoughts. He hadn't liked leaving the superintendent in his office, but he'd been desperate to escape. The way Townsend stared at him without speaking was most disconcerting. He could feel damp patches under his arms and detected the odour of sweat mingling with the starch of his shirt.

Had it really been a year since Nurse Taplin's death? The superintendent couldn't possibly think there was a connection.

When he entered the ward, the patients eyed him warily. Samuel was pleased to see they appeared well-kempt. He didn't want Townsend accusing him of neglect. Helen did a marvellous job of ensuring the men kept themselves clean, and she personally cut their hair, and in David's case, his beard.

She came over to him. 'I've told them that Superintendent Townsend wishes to speak to them. David is ready if you'd like to take him through to my office.'

'Thank you, Sister Hopgood.' He smiled gratefully. 'Efficient as ever.'

'Can't you tell that policeman we're not up to it?' Oliver snapped.

Samuel shook his head. 'Not in the circumstances. I'll stay here in the ward, and if you feel unwell or distressed at any point, ask the superintendent to fetch me, and I'll end the interview.'

Oliver grunted.

Samuel took David's arm, and when they entered the office, he was irritated to find Superintendent Townsend behind Helen's desk. He guided David into a chair and took the seat beside him.

The superintendent introduced himself and began his questioning.

'Did you hear Captain Jennings go out that night?'

To Samuel's surprise, David replied that he had.

'What time was that?' Townsend seemed as surprised as Samuel. He picked up his pencil and notepad.

David smiled apologetically. 'I'm afraid I have no idea. I have a small travel clock – I enjoy listening to it tick, but I can't see the face. It must have been late because everyone else was asleep. I can tell by the sounds of breathing and snoring.'

'What made you think it was Captain Jennings who went out?'

'I could hear his stick. He has two of them, but he only took one that night. I can tell by the tapping on the floor. He opened the doors to the patio and took his time going out so he didn't wake the others. If he rushes, he tends to fall into things. I believe he left the doors ajar to make it easier for him to get back in. He often went out at night.'

Samuel was astonished. David always appeared to be in a world of his own, staring out of the window. He'd never been sure if he was seeing something that was present or simply reliving the past. Yet, from what he'd just said, he was aware of what was going on around him for at least some of the time.

'Did you know about Captain Jennings' nocturnal outings, Dr Bingham?'

'No, I did not, though I can't say I'm surprised. Morgan could be insolent on occasion and seemed to think hospital rules didn't apply to him.'

Townsend turned his attention back to David. 'Did you hear anyone else go out, Mr Cowper?'

'No.'

'And you didn't hear Captain Jennings return?'

'No. I fell asleep at some point. I heard rain and thunder – I believe this was hours after Morgan had gone out. When I woke, I knew it was morning as the other patients were already awake and moving around.'

There wasn't much more David could tell them. And Samuel

suspected what he had said was of more interest to him than it had been to the superintendent. Although it may not have added much to what they knew already about Morgan's night-time prowling, it showed that David was more conscious of his surroundings than he'd suspected. Knowing this could help him find a treatment that David would respond to.

Samuel stood up and gently took David's arm. He felt stupidly proud of his patient. With his neatly trimmed beard and quiet manner, David looked like the schoolteacher he'd once been. And with Samuel's help, perhaps could be again.

As he led him from the room, Superintendent Townsend said, 'Dr Bingham, could I ask you to stay close by in case I need you?'

Samuel nodded. 'I'm not going anywhere.'

And he meant it. This was his hospital. Although only one ward remained, it was his ward.

13

'I know it was you. You were jealous because Morgan wanted me and not you.'

Richard had been about to enter the south barn when he recognised Georgina's shrill voice. He stopped, curious to hear who she was talking to.

'Don't be silly. You must realise the police have to investigate his death.'

He smiled at the contrast between Helen's clear, unemotional tone and Georgina's high-pitched screech.

'You think I had something to do with it?' Georgina sounded like she was working herself into hysteria.

'Of course not. It was a tragic accident. But the coroner will need to know all the facts.'

'My reputation will be ruined.'

'Calm down. I'm sure Superintendent Townsend will be discreet.'

He could hear Georgina sobbing.

'Would you like me to fetch your mother?'

'Leave me alone,' came the muffled reply.

The door to the south barn flew open, and Helen strode past. Richard expected her to return to the hospital, but she kept walking, either heading in the direction of the lake or further on to the woods.

He entered the barn and found Georgina staring hopelessly around her.

'Your mother sent me to lend a hand. What needs doing?' It was a silly question, as she clearly didn't have a clue.

To his embarrassment, she suddenly flung herself at him, wrapping her arms around his waist.

'Georgina.' He attempted to push her away, but she clung even tighter.

He fervently hoped Helen didn't reappear before he could untangle himself.

Taking her wrists in his hands, he backed out of her grasp. 'Georgina. Stop this and tell me what you're upset about.'

With a loud sniff, she loosened her grip and reached into the pocket of her dress for a handkerchief.

'It's that woman. Everyone thinks she's so perfect. Even Morgan liked her. I do my bit. I help, too.'

'Yes, I know you do,' Richard said, though he couldn't think of a single thing that Georgina did that wasn't motivated by self-interest. Even the care she'd lavished on Morgan had been for her own ends.

'It's all her fault.'

'Sister Hopgood? Why? What's she done?'

Georgina sniffed. 'She must have said something to that horrible policeman. How else would he know about my meetings with Morgan?'

Richard didn't answer immediately. He'd told Superintendent Townsend about Morgan's nocturnal outings and his suspicion that the man had been seeing Georgina in secret. He considered admitting this and defending Helen but knew it would rile Georgina even more.

'Tell Townsend the truth. If you lie, you'll only make it worse for yourself.'

'He thinks I had something to do with Morgan's death. Can't you help me?'

'How?' He wasn't sure what she thought he could do.

'We're friends, aren't we?'

Richard didn't like the sound of this. Or the way she was moving toward him again.

She lowered her voice. 'You could say I was with you that night.'

He shook his head in disbelief, wondering why she was so frightened of Townsend. 'That wouldn't do much for your reputation, would it?'

'But it would stop the police from questioning me. They wouldn't care that I was with you.' She bit her bottom lip. 'You used to like me.'

When he didn't answer, she glanced up at him from under her lashes and ran her fingers over his bare forearm.

'You used to want me.'

What a mistake that had been. Richard backed away.

She sniffed again. 'You don't come near me any more.'

He was silent. He knew better than to try to make polite excuses for his lack of interest. Georgina would only twist his words.

'You were jealous of me and Morgan, weren't you?'

Predictable as ever.

'I'm sorry for what's happened—' he began.

To his relief, the barn door opened, and Mrs Wintringham called, 'Georgina, are you in here?'

Dorothy appeared wearing a practical pinafore that covered her day dress while her daughter had on a frilly white frock totally unsuitable for clearing out a barn.

'Here, Mummy.' Georgina's expression changed instantly, and she skipped over to her mother, the coquettish pout replaced by a look of exasperation. 'Sister Hopgood was supposed to be showing me what to do, but she's disappeared.'

Richard stepped forward. 'I think she was called back to the ward. I'll see if I can find her.'

'Thank you, Richard. We'll start by sorting out the art studio so we can make some space for the hospital equipment.'

Knowing full well Helen hadn't been heading in the direction of Merewood Farm, he set off toward Gibbet Wood. When he spotted her, she was near the pheasant pens.

She smiled as he approached. 'I've just seen a fox. He was a fine-looking fellow with a bushy tail. I shooed him away.'

'He'll be back. Especially with this smell.' He wrinkled his nose. The birds were growing rapidly, and the pens were becoming rancid in the heat. 'I'll get a couple of my lads up here to clean the pens out.'

'I'm sure there'll be more than one predator watching to see if any of the pheasants try to escape.'

'We usually lose a few poults to foxes or birds of prey. Have you seen the sparrowhawk?'

'Not this morning, but I saw her catch a sparrow the other day. I couldn't believe how fast she was. She'd frightened it into leaving its cover and caught it in mid-air.'

'The speed takes your breath away, doesn't it?'

She nodded, then seemed to realise he probably hadn't come to find her to talk about birds. 'Sorry, were you looking for me?'

'I came to the barn to lend you a hand. I heard the row with Georgina.'

Helen gave a rueful smile. 'I found a note under Morgan's pillow. I think it was from her, arranging to meet him at the lake. I showed it to Superintendent Townsend.'

'I told him I'd sometimes seen Morgan out at night. And that I suspected he was meeting with Georgina.'

He saw the flash of relief in her eyes.

'That makes me feel better. I wasn't happy about giving him the note, but I had no choice. If she was with him, I hope she has the sense to tell the police.'

'I'm afraid sense is one thing Georgina lacks. From what she's said, she did see him that night. I certainly got the impression someone had been at the lake with Morgan.'

'Why?'

'When I went into the water to get him out, I noticed footprints by the shore.'

'A woman's?'

Richard frowned, trying to remember. 'I'm not sure. It all happened so quickly. It was only later I remembered seeing imprints in the mud as I waded into the lake. Perhaps I was mistaken. Or they could have been made by Morgan when he had his shoes on.'

'Did you see any marks made by his crutch?'

'I don't think so. But I'm not sure.'

They strolled down the slope to the lake, and Richard gazed at the shore. Since the storm, the weather had been hot and dry, and the mud was hard, showing no signs of disturbance.

Could Georgina have somehow enticed Morgan into the water and held him under? He couldn't imagine it. There'd been nothing wrong with Morgan's arms, and she wasn't strong. Perhaps it was just an accident. An invalid patient taking a swim. It was an easy assumption to make. But when he'd seen Morgan walking, there'd been power in the man's legs.

'I'd better get back,' Helen said, though she didn't appear to relish the prospect. 'Georgina will be hopeless on her own.'

'There's no rush, Mrs Wintringham is with her. They're going to clear out the art studio.'

Without urgency, they began to walk along the track toward the south barn.

'I was coming to ask you about Morgan's bed. When I heard Georgina's voice, I thought I'd better wait until she'd gone. Do you want me to move it into the barn or leave it where it is for now?'

He watched Helen's expression change as she considered the matter.

'I'm not sure. I'm worried about the effect it will have on the patients. On the one hand, it's not helpful for them to be faced with his empty bed. On the other hand, taking it away seems so final.'

'It is final,' he replied. 'Mr Wintringham has received an offer for Merewood Farm.'

'Really?' She seemed surprised. 'I got the impression the farm wasn't particularly successful.'

He smiled. 'It wasn't – not the way it was run. It cost more than it made. Baden Knight is a real farmer. He owns the estate to the east of Merewood. He'll amalgamate it with his existing operation.'

'Is he the preacher that used to come to the hospital?'

Richard nodded. 'The deal's nearly done.'

'In that case, we can't keep putting things off. You'd better move the bed into the barn.'

'Before I do, I'll take any farming equipment to the north barn. Knight wants to see everything he's getting as part of the deal. That leaves you the use of the south barn for the equipment that's to be collected by the Red Cross.'

She nodded. 'Dorothy informed me of the plan. Let's tackle the south barn together. You can remove anything that belongs to Mr Wintringham. And I'll help Dorothy sort out the remains of the art studio. She's keen to find a portrait that one of the patients painted of her. I haven't been in there since Victor Protheroe left, and I'd like to find it before it gets buried under the hospital supplies.'

'Sad business about Protheroe. His death affected Oliver badly.'

'Dr Bingham was upset too. He and Victor used to enjoy discussing psychology. How to heal the wounded mind.'

Richard couldn't help wondering that if Protheroe hadn't been able to heal his own wounded mind, how much help had he been to others? He'd heard rumours about the artist's drug taking. Oliver may have enjoyed his art lessons, but they hadn't provided any long-term benefit. Richard was keener to try Helen's proposal of getting Oliver out into the world again.

'I've thought about what you suggested and arranged to view some livery stables. I've asked Oliver to come with me.'

'How did he react?'

'He was apprehensive at first. Now he's had time to get used to the idea, he seems more willing to come along.'

'Good. I think it will lift his spirits. And give him something to work towards. I fear we've all languished here too long.'

'What about Morgan? I know you shouldn't discuss a patient's medical details. But in general, would you say he'd been languishing here, or was he getting better?'

She sighed. 'Both. His legs were improving, and he was able to walk more independently. However, he lacked mental stimulation. His reason for still being on the ward was lack of accommodation rather than anything else. If we could have found him a place in a home for disabled ex-servicemen, that would have been perfect. He could have continued his rehabilitation, and it would have given him more time to find somewhere permanent.'

'No one would take him?'

'I wrote to as many places as I know. They're all full to bursting point. There are a great many disabled ex-servicemen.'

Richard saw the frustration in her eyes and felt touched. In the past, her brisk efficiency had made her appear detached. Yet the consistent dedication she showed to the care of her patients humbled him. He wondered if her detachment was a shield against all she'd witnessed in the last five years.

'I think marriage to Georgina was his only hope.' They'd reached the south barn, and Helen whispered this last remark.

Richard paused before opening the door. 'Something went on between her and Morgan that night,' he replied in an undertone, before adding, 'Are you ready to face her again?'

She nodded. 'I am now Dorothy's here. She'll put a stop to any hysteria—'

As the words left her mouth, a high-pitched scream made them start in surprise. Richard yanked open the door and stumbled in, his eyes taking a few seconds to adjust to the dim interior after the bright sunshine.

Dorothy was standing at the far end of the barn, clutching her screaming daughter by the shoulders.

He strode over to where they were staring in horror at something propped up on an easel.

His breath caught when he saw what it was. The portrait on display had clearly been of Dorothy Wintringham.

Two long slashes crossed the canvas. But more grotesquely, two holes were gouged into the painting where her eyes had been.

14

'It's a warning. A threat. Someone's going to kill us. Just like they killed Morgan,' Georgina shrieked.

Helen wrenched her eyes away from the hideous portrait and took Georgina's arm. 'Come away. Both of you. Whoever did this is simply playing a nasty practical joke.'

'Joke? It's horrible,' Georgina whimpered.

'Please take your mother back to the manor. She's had a shock. I'll deal with this.' Helen removed the painting from the easel and turned it around so they weren't all staring at the gruesome image of Mrs Wintringham with her eyes gouged out.

'I'm fine.' Dorothy's voice was calm but quieter than usual. 'It was just a shock to come across it.'

'Someone killed Morgan,' Georgina whispered.

'His death was a tragic accident,' Helen replied without conviction.

'I don't believe it. Something happened to him. This place is cursed.' Georgina brushed her gold curls away from her face. 'I hate it here.'

'Let's go back to the manor, darling. You've had a terrible shock.'

Dorothy held her daughter's hand and led her away, murmuring to Helen and Richard, 'I'm sorry, she's still upset by Morgan's death.'

Helen nodded sympathetically, though it irritated her that, as usual, it was Dorothy looking after her daughter rather than the other way around. She often wondered how such a capable woman could have given birth to such a pathetic creature.

When they were out of earshot, Helen picked up the portrait and waved it at Richard, feeling a surge of anger. 'Who would do such a petty thing?'

He took the picture from her and held it up. 'Could it be one of the patients?'

The hideous image didn't improve upon second viewing. It was a cruel act, and Helen was astounded that anyone could feel such animosity towards Dorothy.

She instinctively shook her head. Mrs Wintringham had been nothing but kind to the men, and they'd always treated her with respect. Albert and Nathan, in particular, were almost reverential when they addressed her. David couldn't possibly have done it. Even putting his disabilities aside, this showed a rage she was sure he didn't possess. Oliver was another matter.

Richard put the portrait under his arm. 'Why don't you go back to the hospital? I'll take this away.'

'Will you show it to the police?'

She saw him hesitate. 'I'll talk to Mr Wintringham. See what he says.'

Helen gazed at the canvasses stacked against the wall and the dried-up tubes of paint in old wooden boxes. She'd never spent much time in the barn when it was an art studio. Samuel had described it as a vibrant, creative place. But after months of neglect, there was something sinister about it. Like the rest of Merewood Farm, it seemed to be slowly disintegrating.

'Do you believe in ghosts?' she asked, knowing what a ridiculous question it was. The barn's musty smell of dust and decay must be affecting her imagination.

Richard shook his head. 'I believe in retribution.'

She wasn't sure what he meant by this. 'Retribution?'

'If someone does something bad, they'll get their comeuppance.'

Helen wondered if he was thinking about Isabel Taplin. He'd been the one to find the nurse's body. And then, a year later, he'd discovered Morgan floating in the lake. She rubbed her temples, unsure what to do next.

Richard put a hand on her shoulder. 'Whoever is playing these tricks will pay. Let me deal with this.'

Feeling claustrophobic, she nodded and left the barn. Outside, she took long, deep breaths, though the air was still and warm rather than cool and refreshing.

In the privacy of her office, she rested her head in her hands. She stayed like that for some minutes, listening to the chatter of Albert and Nathan while she gathered her thoughts. Was Georgina right? Was Merewood Farm cursed? One thing was certain, it wasn't a suitable hospital for vulnerable patients. The ward had to close.

She stood up. It was time to take action. For the moment, she'd have to put the complex issues of David and Oliver to one side. Instead, she'd focus on Albert. Perhaps that problem would be simpler to solve.

In the ward, she went over to the open doors and saw David sitting on the patio. She asked how he was feeling.

'Enjoying the sunshine and the breeze. And the sound of birdsong,' he replied in his usual serene but distant manner. It was as though he had to make an effort to bring his mind back to the present.

Helen saw that Oliver had wandered down to the lake and was chatting with Richard. There was no sign of the portrait, and she wondered what had become of it. Of the remaining patients, Oliver was the only one to have spent time in the barn when it was an art studio. He also possessed a fiery temper.

It occurred to her that perhaps Richard had wanted to deal with the situation because he suspected his friend might have taken a knife to the picture. Could Oliver be responsible for the pranks? Or was she being fanciful? Would it even have been possible for him to have put the skeleton in her bath? Although he could have lifted the bones from their hook, it would have taken him some time to dress them in a set of hospital blues.

And she doubted his rage was strong enough to lead to murder. She'd seen Oliver snap at Morgan, though they'd never really argued. And he'd barely noticed Isabel Taplin. The pretty nurse had caused Nathan to stutter and Morgan to preen, but Oliver had seemed as oblivious to her charms as David.

She pushed these thoughts from her mind and went across to the table where Albert and Nathan were playing cards.

She placed a hand on Albert's shoulder. 'Have you written that letter to Emma yet?'

He shook his head, not meeting her eye. 'I need to let her go. Put her behind me.'

Helen strolled over to his nightstand and picked up the sheaf of letters. 'Shall I put these in the fire, then?'

'No.' Albert stumbled as he shot up from his chair.

'Th-th-that's not kind,' Nathan stammered.

She sighed, replacing the letters. 'You clearly haven't put her behind you, have you?'

'I just need more time.' Albert sat down again, his eyes downcast and his lips trembling.

She realised she'd been too harsh, but it was born of frustration. Did none of them realise there was no more time? Albert's reaction to her threat to burn the letters strengthened her resolve.

Helen picked up one of the envelopes and began to walk away with it.

'Don't,' Albert cried.

'I'll bring it back.'

She went into her office and made a note of the address at the top of the letter. Then she placed it back in the envelope and returned it to Albert's nightstand.

He was watching her every move. 'What are you going to do?'

'I'm going to write to Emma and invite her to visit you.'

'I don't want to see her.'

'Yes, you do. You just don't know how to ask her. That's why I'm going to do it for you.'

'I'm not ready,' Albert whined.

Helen ignored him and strode back to her office. She took a sheet of writing paper from her drawer and picked up her pen.

After writing a few lines introducing herself to Emma Perkins, she faltered. She considered how best to describe Albert's situation. After all, she wanted the young woman to come and see him for herself, not to break off the engagement.

She glanced out to where Albert was sitting. He was a pleasant-looking young man. He had curly brown locks that grew faster than any of the other patients' hair. She constantly had to trim his curls so they didn't reach below his collar. His cheeky grin made an occasional appearance, though more often than not, he looked pensive. His scars would have faded to resemble a smattering of freckles by now if he hadn't kept scratching them until they were red and sore. In her opinion, he just needed someone to restore his confidence and make him feel worthy of love.

After a few false starts, she finally signed the letter and folded it in an envelope. How Emma responded would depend on the strength of her feelings for Albert. At least they would know one way or the other.

Helen glanced up at the wall clock, wondering if she'd be able to walk to the village in time for the last post. To her irritation, the clock had stopped, though she knew she'd wound it up earlier that day. It was part of her morning routine. Her skin prickled when she saw it had stopped at eleven fifteen – around the time they'd found the slashed portrait.

'Sister Hopgood.'

She jumped at the sound of her name.

'I'm sorry. I didn't mean to startle you.' Samuel stood by the door of her office.

Why had she jumped? Her intuition always told her where he was in the hospital. Now even that was failing her. Everything in Merewood Farm seemed to be falling apart.

She cleared her throat. 'I'm sorry, Dr Bingham. I was a little preoccupied. What can I do for you?'

He hesitated, glancing into the ward. 'Perhaps you could come into my office for a few moments.'

'Of course.' She followed him into the hallway, assuming he wanted to speak to her out of earshot of the patients.

She hoped it was concerning David. Perhaps he'd heard back from St Dunstan's. Or it could be about the position at the Royal Victoria Hospital. With everything that had been going on, they'd spent more time discussing the patients' futures than planning their own.

Samuel ushered Helen into his office and pulled out a chair for her. She felt a flicker of irritation when her eye caught the skeleton grinning at her from the corner of the room.

Samuel sat behind his desk and picked up a sheet of paper. 'Superintendent Townsend sent me this. It's a copy of the autopsy report on Morgan.'

She noticed his hands were shaking slightly.

'The thing is...' He took a handkerchief from his jacket pocket and mopped his brow. 'The thing is...'

Helen tried to curb her impatience. She wanted him to get on with it but could see by his clammy complexion the report had upset him.

Samuel cleared his throat. 'The pathologist confirmed that death was due to drowning. However, he found evidence of alcohol and drugs in Morgan's body.'

15

Samuel felt uncomfortably hot and mopped his brow again. Helen was gaping at him.

'Drugs?' she repeated. 'He hadn't taken morphine for a long time. And where would Morgan get alcohol from?'

'It wasn't morphine. It was chloral hydrate.'

'Chloral hydrate? Are we missing any?'

Samuel took a sip of water. He tried to think of an excuse, though he knew there was no point. Superintendent Townsend would ask the same question, and he'd have to tell the truth.

He cleared his throat. 'I'm not sure.'

He waited for Helen to respond, but she just stared at him. No doubt, Townsend would do the same.

'I've given it to Nathan on occasion, only when he becomes too agitated to sleep. It calms him down. I'm afraid I haven't been as diligent as I should in keeping my records up to date.'

'When did you last administer it?' she asked.

'Not for months.' If he were being honest, he didn't have a clue. He decided to distract her with a question. 'In your view, was Morgan in poor spirits recently?'

Helen didn't answer immediately, and he was pleased to see she was considering the matter.

'It's difficult to say. He was generally an easy-going man. He clearly had his problems, financially, I mean. And his future was uncertain. I think he hoped Georgina Vane would provide a solution.'

'So you don't believe he killed himself?' came a low voice from the doorway.

They both jumped.

Superintendent Townsend shut the door behind him, pulled over a chair, and sat beside Helen.

Samuel was infuriated by his presumption and concerned about how much of the conversation he'd overheard.

'I wouldn't like to say that for certain,' Helen replied.

Samuel had to admire the way she was able to retain her composure. He cleared his throat and attempted to take control of the situation.

'Like all of the patients here, Morgan was still coming to terms with the trauma he'd experienced. He had good days and bad days, and it's difficult to judge how he would act in a fit of despondency.'

'Who has access to the medicine cabinet?' Townsend asked.

'I hold the key. It's always kept locked. Only I dispense the medicines.'

The policeman turned to Helen. 'You don't have access?'

She shook her head.

'There's no need for her to. I'm always on hand.'

'Did you ever see Captain Jennings go near the medicine cabinet?'

'No, never,' Samuel replied.

'The patients walk by Dr Bingham's office to get to the kitchen where they have their meals,' Helen said. 'They only go in when the doctor needs to talk to them privately.'

Townsend stretched out his long legs, and Samuel couldn't help but be impressed by the crease of his trousers. The superintendent's dark suit was immaculate, and he wore it well.

'Had Captain Jennings been in your office recently?'

'He came in once a week for a private consultation.' Samuel nodded to the examination couch. 'I saw him last Tuesday when I examined his legs and chatted to him about his future plans.'

'And what were his plans?'

'He wasn't too sure. I told him there was no rush. He was still healing.'

'And you're not certain if any chloral hydrate has gone missing from your supplies?'

The bloody man was actually admitting he'd been listening at the door. It was too much. Samuel took a deep breath.

'Sister Hopgood and I work under extremely trying conditions. We don't have the same resources a permanent hospital would.'

'Do the patients ever consume alcohol?' Townsend asked abruptly.

'Never. We allow them to smoke as it calms their nerves. Alcohol would have the reverse effect.'

Samuel was aware his breathing had become laboured. The room was airless and far too small for three people in this heat. He could smell perspiration, lavender soap and some sort of gentlemen's cologne. Unfortunately, the sweat was emanating from him.

'Where do you think Captain Jennings came by chloral hydrate and alcohol?'

'I have no idea.'

Townsend gazed around the room. 'Do you keep any spirits for your own private consumption?'

'I have a case of red wine given to me by Mr Wintringham. Sister Hopgood and I occasionally have a glass with our dinner. It's not served in view of the patients.'

'And where is this case of wine kept?'

'Locked in my cupboard.' He motioned toward it.

Townsend stood up and went over to the cupboard. He tried the handle, and the door opened to reveal a row of white coats.

'It's not locked now,' he observed. He pushed aside the garments and bent down to inspect a wooden box. 'How many bottles have you drunk so far?'

'Sister Hopgood and I have shared two bottles.' He avoided meeting Helen's eye, aware that she'd only shared one of those.

'Then there should be ten left.' Townsend began to remove the bottles from the case.

'That's correct.'

'There are only nine.'

Samuel hurried across to the cupboard and Townsend stood back to let him count for himself. 'There should be ten.'

'You agree that a bottle is missing?'

Samuel put the wine back and closed the cupboard door. He nodded his response before returning to his desk and slumping into his chair.

Ignoring the superintendent, he looked at Helen. 'Do you think Morgan took it?'

'It would be the type of thing he might do,' she admitted.

He nodded slowly, thinking of the man's insolent grin. An unexpected wave of grief washed over him. 'I hope he enjoyed it.'

Helen gave a sad smile. 'So do I.'

For a brief moment their eyes met, and Samuel felt warmed by their shared remembrance of Captain Morgan Jennings.

Superintendent Townsend had moved across to the medicine cabinet and was trying the handle. Samuel couldn't remember if he'd locked it or not. To his relief, it didn't open.

Townsend came over to his desk and held out his hand. 'Key.'

Samuel bit his lip, furious at this terse command. He had no choice but to reach into his desk drawer and fish out the key. He placed it in the superintendent's palm.

Townsend raised an eyebrow. 'Is that where you keep it? In an unlocked desk drawer?'

'No, superintendent, it's not. It's usually kept hidden in my bedroom. However, I've been checking the drugs in the cabinet in preparation for your visit.'

'Show me the choral hydrate.'

Samuel went to the cabinet and pointed to a collection of tiny bottles.

'I don't keep a large quantity. It's in individual phials. I generally only prescribe a small amount at any time. Just to aid sleep. Therefore, I've had no need to request any further supplies recently.'

Townsend closed the door of the medicine cabinet and locked it. He returned to his seat, still gripping the key in his hand.

'What's the state of mind of the remaining patients? Have any of them shown signs of aggressive behaviour?'

Samuel was taken aback by the question. 'No. Why would they?'

'I haven't had the opportunity to tell Dr Bingham about the damage to Mrs Wintringham's portrait if that's what you're referring to,' Helen said.

'It is. Mr Locke was showing the painting to Mr Wintringham when I arrived at Merewood Manor. Mrs Wintringham and Miss Vane are extremely upset by the incident.'

Samuel rubbed his eyes as Helen explained what had happened in the barn that morning.

'I don't believe any of my patients would do such a thing. I suggest you look in the direction of Merewood Manor.'

'Is there anyone in particular you suspect?'

'It strikes me it could be the act of a hysterical woman.'

'Miss Vane? Do you think she could have put the skeleton in Sister Hopgood's bath?'

Samuel inclined his head. 'It's a possibility. Or it could be a disgruntled employee. One who's about to lose his job.'

'Mr Locke?'

Samuel nodded in what he hoped was a confident manner. Townsend's penetrating gaze and Helen's surprised expression were making him feel extremely uncomfortable.

'I don't think it can have been Mr Locke. I was talking with him outside when we heard Miss Vane scream.' Helen paused. 'Though I suppose it depends on when the portrait was damaged.'

'No one seems to have seen the painting since last year,' Superintendent Townsend remarked. 'Which makes it difficult to ascertain when someone took a scalpel to it.'

'A scalpel?' Helen exclaimed.

'A scalpel was found in the barn with fragments of paint on it.'

Samuel shrank into his seat as Townsend suddenly stood up and placed the key on the desk in front of him. 'In future, I suggest you take greater care in securing your drugs and keeping your records up to date. I'm going back to Merewood Manor. I'll return tomorrow to talk to the patients again. You may want to prepare them.'

He stalked from the room without waiting for a response.

Samuel couldn't help thinking there was a touch of the showman about the superintendent. He stood up and slammed the office door closed. 'That man is overstepping the mark. I'm tempted to report him to his superior officer.'

Helen didn't respond immediately. When she did, she said, 'Do you think Oliver could have taken a scalpel to the portrait? I can't see any of the other patients doing such a thing, but Oliver does have a temper.'

'It's probably someone from the manor who feels aggrieved by the Wintringhams.'

'Maybe,' she replied. 'Though I think it's unlikely to be Mr Locke. Georgina is a possibility. She was in a hysterical state.'

Helen's defence of Richard Locke irked him.

'I don't know who it was,' he snapped. 'I'm more concerned about keeping the patients calm under this intolerable pressure. The sooner we can sort out more resources, the better. A psychologist would be ideal.'

Samuel saw Helen's confusion and wished he could confide in her. But it was too soon. He needed more time to set his plans in motion. All he could do was pray that she'd understand how important it was to keep the place going and show everyone that Merewood Farm was a place of healing.

16

'I haven't done anything wrong,' Georgina Vane shrieked.

Townsend exchanged an exasperated glance with Sergeant Newman. 'No one's suggesting you have.'

The two men were seated on an elegant but uncomfortable sofa in the Wintringhams' drawing room. Georgina sat on the opposite couch, her mother by her side.

'You think I killed Morgan. I loved him. Why would I hurt him? We were going to be married.'

'Calm down.' Dorothy placed a hand on Georgina's knee. 'We seem to be going around in circles, superintendent. My daughter's told you she met with her fiancé that evening and that he was perfectly well when she left him.'

'I appreciate that, Mrs Wintringham. But I need a little more detail. Miss Vane, you say you met Captain Jennings at the lake at ten thirty. How long were you with him?'

'I don't know. About an hour, perhaps a little longer.'

'And what did you and Captain Jennings do? Did you go for a walk or stay by the lake?'

Georgina sniffed and dabbed her eyes with a handkerchief. 'We walked around the lake and talked.'

'It wouldn't have taken more than fifteen minutes to walk around the lake. Did you keep walking around it?'

'We sat down and talked,' she snapped.

'Is that all you did? Just talk?'

'We might have kissed.' Georgina spoke into her handkerchief, avoiding looking at her mother.

'What do you mean you might have? Don't you remember?'

'Yes, we kissed. He was my fiancé, after all.'

'I'm not here to judge you, Miss Vane. I'm just trying to establish what happened that night.' Townsend exchanged another glance with Newman. It was evident by the girl's blushes that she and Morgan had done more than kiss. 'What did you and Captain Jennings discuss?'

'Our forthcoming marriage.'

'What about it exactly?'

Georgina flushed again. 'I told Morgan my stepfather wasn't thrilled at the prospect of our engagement and that it might take him a while to get used to the idea.'

'And your stepfather's blessing is important to you?' Townsend asked, knowing full well it was Joseph Wintringham's money that was important.

Dorothy Wintringham intervened at this point. 'Superintendent, I'm sure you're aware that Captain Jennings was not a rich man. My husband had his reservations about the match.'

'Did you share those reservations?'

Dorothy glanced nervously at her daughter. 'Yes, I did. I didn't want Georgina to rush into things.'

At this, Georgina began to sob.

Townsend indicated to Newman that he should take over the questioning.

'Miss Vane,' the sergeant said in a fatherly tone. 'I know this is upsetting for you, but can you tell me if you and Captain Jennings had been drinking that evening?'

'No, we had not.'

'Captain Jennings didn't bring a bottle of wine with him? Perhaps to celebrate your engagement.'

'No.' Georgina sniffed.

'Do you think he could have had a drink before he met you? Did he seem at all inebriated?'

'He was perfectly sober. He hadn't been drinking. I would have smelt it on his breath.' She blushed again. 'We talked. I kissed him goodnight and returned to the manor. I was in bed before midnight as I heard the clock chiming.'

'You left Captain Jennings by the lake?'

'Yes. He offered to walk me back to the manor, but I didn't want him to tire himself out.'

Townsend guessed she hadn't wanted to be seen out with Morgan at that time of night. He decided that was probably all they were going to get out of Georgina for one day.

'Thank you, Miss Vane,' he said. 'We won't take up any more of your time.'

'I hope you'll treat what my daughter's told you in the strictest confidence.' Dorothy Wintringham's polite smile didn't hide the steel in her eyes.

'Of course, Mrs Wintringham.' Townsend had the feeling it would be unwise to cross this lady. 'Perhaps I could ask you about the damaged portrait you found in the barn. When was it painted?'

'Last year. I think it was in September, shortly before Mr Protheroe left. It was done by a young patient who gave it to me when he was discharged. I meant to bring it up to the manor, but Mr Protheroe asked if he could keep it in the art studio to show his students. I rather lost track of it after that.'

'And you have no idea what could have prompted someone to have taken a scalpel to it?'

'None whatsoever.'

'Whoever did it killed Morgan.' Georgina's voice rose. 'They're trying to hurt us. They wanted to stop my marriage, and now they're threatening Mummy.'

'I'm sure that's not the case,' Newman said reassuringly. 'I don't think you have anything to be afraid of.'

Townsend rose from his seat. He had no time to pacify a hysterical young woman. He'd leave that to her mother. He thanked Mrs Wintringham for her hospitality and hastily left the room, Newman at his heels.

In the hallway, a butler appeared by their side and showed them out. Townsend had a strong suspicion he'd been listening at the door.

'What do you think, Newman?' He lit a cigarette as they strolled down the driveway.

'With a voice like that, I'm surprised Jennings didn't drown her.' The sergeant raised his hands to the sides of his head. 'My ears have never been subjected to such abuse.'

Townsend laughed. Newman's cauliflower ears, the result of one too many rugby scrums, were a running joke at the station. But there was nothing wrong with the man's hearing or his mind. Though he was nearing retirement, he still had the nose of a young bloodhound when it came to sniffing out liars.

'You think she drowned him?' he suggested.

Newman shook his head. 'Can't see it. But then why would anyone kill him? Chap sounds harmless to me.'

'Perhaps they didn't. Maybe it was an accident. Jennings steals the wine, gets a bit jolly and goes for a swim.'

'Wine laced with choral hydrate?'

'Hmm. That does muddy the waters, no pun intended. I pity the coroner who gets this case.' Townsend stared down at Merewood Farm. 'There's something not right about that place. And my intuition tells me it's Bingham.'

'Not the saintly Sister Hopgood?'

'Not unless they're in it together.'

'Who's that with Bingham?'

Townsend turned to see where Newman was pointing. The doctor was strolling along the lane that led to the village, chatting to a tall man of around sixty.

He squinted and recognised the craggy features and shock of grey hair. 'Baden Knight. Owns the neighbouring farm. Rumour has it he wants to buy Merewood Farm from Wintringham. The land, at least. I've also heard his son, Clifford, has taken a shine to Miss Vane.'

'Perhaps he's deaf.' Newman gave a theatrical shudder and put his hands to his ears again.

They watched Bingham and Knight hastily move to one side as a car came up the lane and drove past the hospital, heading in the direction of the manor. Following its progress, they saw Richard Locke pull up outside his cottage in a battered Vauxhall-D. Oliver Edwards was in the passenger seat.

'What do you make of Locke?' Newman asked. 'He found Isabel Taplin's body too, didn't he? What was he doing in the woods that day?'

'The matron was concerned when Taplin didn't turn up for her shift. She sent Sister Hopgood to ask Locke to search for her. He found her body in Gibbet Wood. There was nothing to connect him to the girl. And I can't see why he'd want to harm Jennings.'

'What about the damage to the portrait? He's losing his job. He might have a grudge against the Wintringhams,' Newman suggested.

'It's possible,' Townsend conceded. 'Keep an eye on him.'

* * *

Richard brought the car to a halt outside his cottage and turned off the engine. 'Why don't you come in? We can talk about the stables we saw in Andover.'

'I'm tired. I need to get back to the ward,' Oliver replied.

Richard tried to hide his exasperation. His friend had seemed like his old self when he'd been with the horses. But on the journey home, he'd become morose.

'I think the one in Andover deserves a second viewing. Are you feeling up to another trip out?'

'At least it gets me away from that bunch of imbeciles. Albert and Nathan aren't exactly scintillating company, and David might as well not be there. Is there a pub nearby where I could get a pint?'

'I'm not sure beer is a good idea. I'll see if I can find a restaurant and treat you to a decent lunch.'

Oliver grunted. 'Have you been talking to Sister Sanctimonious and Dr Do-Gooder about me?'

Richard was getting fed up with his constant nasty comments. Earlier, when he'd mentioned Joseph Wintringham's offer of a loan, Oliver had snorted, saying, 'How Lord and Lady Bountiful love to patronise us.'

'Sister Hopgood must have told me that alcohol wasn't allowed at the hospital,' Richard began diplomatically, then his frustration got the better of him. 'Why are you so bloody rude about everyone? God knows they don't deserve it. You never used to be so unkind.'

Oliver's shoulders slumped, and he stared down into his lap. When he looked up, his eyes were wet.

Richard leant over to the passenger seat and put an arm around his friend's shoulder. 'Talk to me. Tell me how I can help.'

'I try to stop myself. I know I'm being cruel. I just get so bloody angry.' Oliver hit the stump of his left arm against the door, then waved it at Richard. 'This is not what I wanted. This is not how my life was supposed to be.'

'It will get better, I promise.'

'My bloody arm won't grow back, will it?' Oliver snarled. Then he seemed to deflate. 'I'm sorry. It's not your fault—'

'It is my fault. If you—'

'No.' Oliver almost shouted the word. 'It's not your fault. I'm glad you're alive. I'm glad I'm alive. I realise we're the lucky ones. But sometimes it doesn't feel like that.'

'We are the lucky ones. Once we get our own stables, we'll be in control. Just us and the horses. No one telling us what to do.'

Oliver nodded. 'That sounds good.'

'In the meantime, why don't you move in here with me?' Richard jerked his head toward the cottage. 'It's small, but it will do until we can sort out the stables.'

'I need a bit more time at the hospital first.'

Richard ran his fingers through his hair in frustration. Time was running out. 'With patients you consider imbeciles?'

'I'm sorry I said that. They're not so bad.' Oliver glanced at him and smiled. 'Bingham's a pompous twit, though.'

'True,' he replied with a grin.

Oliver laughed, and they got out of the car.

To Richard's dismay, Frederick was trotting along the lane on Blaze. He was uneasy about the friendship that had sprung up between Oliver and the arrogant young man.

Oliver began to fondle the horse's ears, and he told himself it was Blaze rather than his owner that was the draw.

'How did it go? Did you see anything you liked?' Frederick asked.

'The one in Andover had most to offer,' Oliver replied. 'Good paddocks, a stream running through it and plenty of space for cross country.'

Richard gritted his teeth. Why couldn't Oliver have said this to him?

'That's what you need,' Frederick agreed. 'I think I should turn Merewood Farm into a livery stables. It's what my mother would have wanted. She was considered the finest horsewoman in Hampshire.'

Richard had heard about the first Mrs Wintringham's prowess in the saddle, although he suspected calling her the finest horse-woman in the county might be an exaggeration. He also wondered how Frederick knew what his mother would have wanted as she'd died giving birth to him, and Merewood Farm hadn't been built until a year after her death.

Frederick dismounted, and the pair continued their conversation as they strolled down the lane to the hospital. Richard watched them with growing unease. He told himself he should be glad Oliver was at least discussing the future, even if it wasn't with him.

But his fears were justified when he saw Frederick take a hip flask out of his pocket and hand it to Oliver.

17

'What did happen between you and Morgan that night?' Richard had been reluctant to let Georgina into his cottage, but it was that or leave her crying on his doorstep.

'Nothing. Why does everyone keep asking me that?'

'Because he's dead,' Richard retorted, handing her a cup of tea. He expected this to provoke a fresh wave of tears. Instead, her temper flared.

'Well, he wasn't when I left him. He hadn't been drinking, and he certainly hadn't taken any drugs. I would have known. He was perfectly fine and in good spirits.'

'Even though he knew your stepfather wasn't going to cough up any money?'

'I told him I just needed a bit more time. Mummy would be able to bring Joseph around.'

'So why was he in good spirits?'

'Because I made him happy. Just like I used to make you happy.' She pouted.

Richard wished he'd never asked. 'What do you want, Georgina?'

'For us to go back to the way we were.'

He shook his head.

'Joseph likes you. If we were to marry, he'd give us some money.'

'I don't want his money.' *And I don't want you*, he mentally added.

'Is this because of her?'

Richard wasn't sure who she meant and decided not to ask. 'I'm leaving here soon.'

'Take me with you,' she pleaded.

He felt sorry for her. Too sorry to lie. 'The only person I'm taking with me is Oliver.'

Richard bundled Georgina out of the door before the trickle of tears became a flood. He watched her walk around the back of the manor to the kitchen garden before he headed in the opposite direction to the front of the house. Helen often took a mid-morning walk, and he was hoping they might arrive at the entrance to Gibbet Wood at the same time. His hand rested on the pair of field glasses tucked in his pocket.

He cursed when he ran into Frederick leading Blaze down to the lake, a shotgun slung over his shoulder. It was ironic the injury to the man's hand had been the reason for his discharge from the army. It was thought it would affect his ability to fire a rifle, yet Frederick spent most of his day shooting at rabbits, pheasants or pigeons, commanding Dexter to fetch his quarry. He wasn't a particularly good shot and never took on hunters, such as foxes or birds of prey.

'Is that policeman still around? I don't like the way he keeps turning up at the manor,' Frederick moaned.

'Not yet, though I believe he plans to talk to the patients again.' He was concerned about the effect this would have on Oliver.

'Turns out Jennings was an alcoholic and a drug addict. I told Georgie she's had a lucky escape.'

Richard could imagine how well this comment would have been received. 'I don't think Morgan was a drug addict—'

But Frederick was in full flow. 'I'm not surprised the man drowned. Probably three sheets to the wind.' He gave a nasal laugh as he led Blaze over to the lake. Dexter bounded into the water, scaring a pair of moorhens.

Richard thought this was rich, considering how much wine Frederick was known to drink at dinner, not to mention the hip flask.

'Nasty business with the portrait. Probably one of those half-wits.' Frederick motioned to the hospital.

'They're not half-wits,' he growled.

'Didn't mean your friend. Never known a chap to have such a way with horses. In fact, I think I'll take Blaze to see him now. He's been a bit skittish recently.'

Richard worried how Oliver would cope with visits from Frederick and Townsend in one morning. However, the thought of Bingham's reaction to a horse turning up on his ward gave him some satisfaction.

He watched Frederick tug a reluctant Blaze away from the lake and start toward the hospital. Had the young man been too quick to blame the patients for the damage to Dorothy's portrait? Frederick had never warmed to his stepmother, though she'd always been kind to him, particularly when he was discharged from the army.

But then Frederick had never shown much affection for anyone except Isabel Taplin. Apart from her, he hadn't come close to marriage, even though he was considered to be handsome. Of course, he had an obnoxious personality, but the Wintringham money would be enough for some females to overlook that.

Richard knew Frederick had been at Newbury races on the day of Isabel's murder. If the police hadn't verified this, he'd have suspected him of a jealous attack.

His thoughts returned to Helen, and he hurried up the hill when he spotted her by the pens.

'Hello. Are you checking on the pheasants?' she asked.

He wondered if she'd been waiting for him. 'I caught a fox pulling at the fencing. Probably the fine-looking fellow you saw the other day.'

'You can't blame him for trying. All those plump birds just out of reach.'

'He'll have his chance soon enough. They'll be released once the shooting season begins.'

'Poor things. Bred only to be hunted.'

'It's not something I enjoy. But Merewood is famous for its pheasant shoots, and Mr Wintringham likes to keep up the tradition. I prefer to see birds in the wild that can fend for themselves.'

'Birds like her.' Helen peered up at the sky. 'I think she's got something.'

They followed the path of the sparrowhawk until she swooped down into her nest in the Scots pine. She appeared to have a small bird in her beak.

'You can see her more clearly through these.' Richard took the field glasses from his pocket.

She put them to her eyes and squinted. 'I can't see much.'

'Keep watching until you get used to them,' he advised. 'She's to the left of the nest.'

Helen adjusted her focus, then exclaimed, 'I can see her! She's got two... no, three chicks. She's dishing out the food between them.'

It was rare to find someone who shared his love of nature and he enjoyed seeing her delight. When the sparrowhawk flew off, she turned to him with a smile that reached her eyes and made her look much younger.

'Thank you. I've never seen anything like that before.'

'We arrived at the right moment. If we stay a while, we might see the male bring in food as well. This is my usual spot.'

He took off his jacket and laid it on a patch of grass. She hesitated, then gathered the skirts of her uniform and lowered herself to the ground.

'The male usually flies in from that direction.' He pointed to the east as he sat down beside her.

Helen watched for a while before handing him the field glasses. 'I can't be too long. I have to get back to the hospital. Things are unsettled since...'

Richard guessed what she was reluctant to say. 'Mr Wintringham told me the pathologist found drugs in Morgan's body.'

She nodded. 'Chloral hydrate.'

'Do you think he took it on purpose?'

'It wouldn't have been difficult for him to have taken the phial from the medicine cabinet. He could have found the keys. But...'

'You're not sure?'

She gave a slight shrug. 'Perhaps it's because I don't want to believe he was in that frame of mind. I could certainly see him stealing a bottle of Dr Bingham's wine. But drugs?'

'Unless he was depressed.' Richard's encounter with Frederick had made him think about Isabel. 'Could Morgan have had something to do with Nurse Taplin's death? It was exactly a year since her murder.'

They weren't far from where she was killed, though he didn't say this to Helen. All around them, the bramble was in flower as it had been that day. The thickets of white and pale pink flowers reminded him of Isabel. The scents of summer and the hum of bees had filled the air, signifying new life, while she'd lain cold and grey on the woodland floor.

'Funnily enough, one of the last things he said to me was that he'd been in love with Nurse Taplin and would have run away with her even though she had no money.'

Richard grunted. 'I doubt she'd have had any desire to run away with him. He didn't have much to offer, did he?'

She shook her head. 'I think he hoped marriage to Georgina would solve his financial problems.'

'She did meet him that night. Apparently, she told him she needed more time to persuade her stepfather to cough up some money.'

Helen looked at him sharply. 'How do you know that?'

'She told me.' He wondered what she'd think if she knew what else Georgina had said to him. He wasn't about to tell her. 'She believes someone killed Morgan to prevent their marriage.'

Helen gasped. 'I can't imagine anyone would go to those lengths.'

'Neither can I.'

'Had Morgan been drinking when she saw him?'

'She says not. She said Morgan was his normal self, and someone must have forced alcohol and drugs on him later.'

'I think that's highly unlikely. Does Superintendent Townsend know all this?'

He nodded. 'Georgina can't keep a secret to save her life. She didn't stand a chance against him. I expect he only had to look at her, and she blurted it out.'

'I can picture it. Is she alright?'

He detected a note of amusement mingled with her sympathy.

'I think the superintendent had a pretty good idea of how the interview would go and let Dorothy sit in. She had to mop up Georgina's tears as usual. And persuade Townsend to be discreet about the matter.'

'Georgina was Morgan's last hope.' Helen sighed. 'I don't want to dwell on it. Tell me, how did your outing with Oliver go? He was quiet when he came back.'

'Good.' Richard tried to sound optimistic. 'We have some obstacles to overcome. In time, he'll regain his old confidence.'

He wondered who he was trying to convince. Oliver's frustration and bitterness had shocked him. Sometimes he caught glimpses of his old friend, then he'd disappear to be replaced by someone Richard wasn't sure he liked. The furious slashes across Dorothy's portrait came into his mind. Could Oliver be capable of such an act? He wouldn't have believed it before. But he had to acknowledge his friend had changed.

'With your support, I'm sure he'll cope,' Helen said. 'He's lucky to have you.'

Richard tried to smile. In truth, the obligation he felt towards Oliver was beginning to weigh on him. 'Once he's around horses, he'll be fine. He loves them, and they love him. They know the real man.'

'You can see the affinity he has from his drawings,' she commented. 'I've never seen such detail in a sketch done purely from memory.'

Richard nodded. 'He just needs to feel brave enough to return to the real world instead of relying on his imagination.'

Helen smiled. 'The same could be said of all the patients. They need to feel brave enough to leave the security of the ward and restart their old lives. I wondered if you might be able to help.'

'How?'

'I have a favour to ask. Well, two, actually. I believe Nathan is getting a little better. What he needs is to be more active and mentally stimulated. Do you have any jobs he could help with around the estate? Nothing too taxing, or...' She paused. 'Nothing he might fail at. I want him to start to feel more confident in his abilities.'

Richard was absurdly pleased by the request. He told himself it was because he was keen to help the patients. Deep down, he knew it was because he wanted to win Helen's approval.

'I'll supervise him and make sure he's not overwhelmed by anything. I could do with a hand moving some of the farming equipment to the north barn. Let me check with Mr Wintringham first, though.'

'Thank you. I also wanted to ask if you'd act as chauffeur. Albert's fiancée, Emma Perkins, is coming to visit tomorrow. And Leonard Gates, his father. Would you pick them up from the station? It will save them from having to wait for a cart. You know what it's like in the village. The taxi man is never around when he's needed.'

He was touched when she explained about the letter she'd written to Miss Perkins. 'Of course. As long as they're happy in an ex-army vehicle. It's got a few dents and scrapes.'

His old Vauxhall motorcar would have been an elegant sight when it was first manufactured. Five years and a war later, Richard had spotted it in a scrap yard and picked it up cheap. He'd bought or made new engine parts and got it running again.

'I'm sure they won't mind.'

'I'd be happy to help. I hope for Albert's sake the meeting goes well. What about you?' he asked in what he hoped was a casual manner. 'Have you made any further plans for the future?'

She shook her head. 'We've been too preoccupied with the patients. I intend to talk to Dr Bingham about a place at the Royal Victoria Hospital. He's been offered a post there and might be able to influence my application for a residential position.'

Did she have feelings for Bingham, he wondered. They'd been living side by side in the hospital for some months now. It wasn't inconceivable they'd developed feelings for each other. Her tone didn't indicate any great passion, but she wasn't the type of woman who wore her heart on her sleeve.

He wasn't jealous, he decided. It was just that Helen Hopgood was far too good for that fool of a doctor.

18

'I don't want to see Emma.'

Helen took Albert's hand from his face and reached for the cream. 'You must stop scratching. You'll make your skin worse. Try to think of other things.'

'Is she coming? I don't want to see her.'

He was working himself into a state. Townsend's visit of the previous day had already caused unrest, and Albert's panic would likely have a further unsettling effect on the patients.

'It's just your father coming to visit.'

'Not Emma?' Now he sounded disappointed.

'No, not yet.' Exasperation had led her to lie. In the last few days, Albert had scratched his arm until it bled, and she'd covered it with gauze to stop him from touching it. Changing the dressing would be difficult as it was stuck to his skin with dried blood. Helen gave a sharp tug on the gauze, causing Albert to yelp in pain and Nathan to wince. 'I'm sorry, it's better to get it over with quickly rather than prolong the pain by taking it off slowly.'

Is this what we're doing here? Prolonging the pain? It certainly felt like it.

Later that morning, Dorothy appeared in Helen's office, closing the door behind her.

'Have you told Albert that his fiancée's coming?'

Helen shook her head. 'I decided against it. I've said it's just his father visiting today. He's getting himself worked up.'

'I don't suppose Superintendent Townsend's visit helped.'

'He questioned the patients and made them all feel like they were under suspicion. Even David. Yet none of them knew what Morgan was up to, I'm sure of it.'

'He did the same to us at the manor. Georgina's in a terrible state. It's my feeling Morgan acted on impulse. He took the drugs and wine and decided to go for a swim when he was intoxicated. He probably went into the water knowing the risks. Perhaps he felt like he was putting his life in the lap of the gods.'

'You could be right,' Helen replied, without conviction. If it had just been the red wine, she might have believed Dorothy's theory. It was the chloral hydrate that troubled her. It didn't seem Morgan's style. 'One good thing to come out of all this is that it's made Albert more inclined to leave.'

'Would you like to bring his father and fiancée up to the manor?' Dorothy asked. 'I'm happy to offer them hospitality there.'

'No. I think it would be best if Albert's in familiar surroundings. I've cleaned up his grazes and tried to make him as presentable as possible.'

'What time are they coming? I'll send Kate over with some cakes and get her to brew a pot of tea.'

'Thank you, that would be helpful. Richard is picking them up from the railway station at three o'clock. I'm going to meet them outside and take them into the kitchen. Then I'll fetch Albert and leave them to it.'

Dorothy raised an eyebrow. 'You're not going to stay?'

Helen frowned. 'It depends how Albert reacts when he sees Miss Perkins. If things go well, I'll slip away, but I won't go far.'

'Good luck, my dear. I think you're doing the right thing.'

'Before you go, could I talk to you about Nathan?'

'Of course. Is it my imagination, or does he seem to be getting a little better?'

'You've noticed it too? Yes, I think he's ready to take the next steps. I've asked Richard if he has any jobs for him and he said he'd be happy to supervise Nathan moving equipment into the north barn. I wondered if your gardener would consider giving him a few odd jobs too.'

'I'm sure Gulliver wouldn't mind another pair of hands. I'll have a word with him. The boy has no family?'

Helen shook her head. 'He never knew his mother. She died shortly after his birth. His father died of influenza during the war.'

'Poor lad. We'll see what we can do for him. He's such a pleasant young man and nice looking when he isn't fidgeting. What about David?' Dorothy asked. 'Have you seen any improvement in his condition?'

Helen considered this. 'It's difficult to tell. He gives the impression of being locked inside his own thoughts. In fact, he's more aware of what's going on around him than you might think. I'm no psychologist, that's Dr Bingham's area, but I get the impression David's protecting himself. He's suffered and has seen others suffer and wants to retreat from the world. Nathan sometimes acts in a similar way, which is why I want to get him out of the hospital. He needs to start looking outward rather than inward in the way David's done.'

'You're a good woman, Helen. And an intelligent one. In my view, you're as knowledgeable about what's best for the patients as Dr Bingham is.' Dorothy rose and went over to the door. 'More so, in fact.'

Helen began to protest but Dorothy was gone. Feeling more optimistic, she returned to the ward to cleanse Albert's face and apply a little more cream, giving him strict instructions not to touch his skin.

'What time's my father coming?' he asked, not for the first time that day.

'At around a quarter past three, if his train gets in on time. Mr Locke is going to fetch him from the station. I'll come and tell you when he arrives.'

It was just before three when Richard pulled up in the old Vauxhall. Helen felt a flutter of nerves on Albert's behalf as she went into the yard to greet Miss Perkins and Mr Gates. Richard helped them out of the car and told them he'd be back at five to run them to the station. He gave Helen a conspiratorial wink as she showed them into the kitchen.

Kate had set out the tea things on the table, and though it wasn't exactly homely – you could tell not much cooking went on there – it felt a little more cosy than usual. The smell of freshly baked fruit cake helped to disguise the odour of the gas pipes.

'Sister Hopgood. I'm Emma Perkins. Thank you so much for writing to me.' The young woman had a pretty smile and warm brown eyes.

Helen felt reassured by her composed manner and neat appearance.

'I'm glad you came. Although I have a confession. I haven't told Albert you're here. You'll appreciate that anxiety can make his condition worse.'

Emma nodded. 'Your letter helped me to understand Albert's reluctance to see me. We used to be so close. I hope...' Her lip trembled. 'I hope I don't upset him.'

Albert's father, Leonard, looked anxiously from Emma to Helen. He was a widower of about fifty who'd visited the hospital many times before. On each visit, he'd been unsuccessful in trying to persuade his son to come home with him.

'I don't know what to say to the boy.' He'd removed his hat and was rotating it in his hands.

'Just chat about everyday things that are going on at home. It's important to make Albert feel he can return to his old life. He's made himself believe that he's somehow abnormal and won't fit in any more. He thinks he'll be a burden to you.'

'He fought for his country,' Leonard said gruffly. 'He could never be a burden.'

Emma took his hand, and they sat down at the kitchen table, their faces tight with tension.

'Try to relax if you can,' Helen advised, offering a silent prayer as she went to fetch Albert from the ward.

'Your father's here. I've shown him into the kitchen.'

Albert's head shot up. 'Why can't he come in here? He usually comes in here or in the garden.'

'Because you can talk more privately in the kitchen. And Mrs Wintringham has sent over some cake. I thought your father might enjoy a slice with his cup of tea.'

The fingers of Albert's right hand went instinctively to his left forearm, and he began to scratch.

Helen took hold of his hand and led him into the hallway. He started to sniffle, and she was aware he was becoming agitated. She handed him a clean handkerchief and told him to try to stay calm and not scratch or sniff if he could help it.

Taking a deep breath, she opened the kitchen door and gave him a gentle nudge inside.

Emma stood up, and Albert let out a wounded cry. He tried to back away, but Helen blocked his path.

Placing her hands firmly on his shoulders, she propelled him inside and pushed him down into a chair. She felt a tremor run through him.

'Miss Perkins, why don't you pour the tea.'

Emma smiled at Albert and picked up the teapot. Helen noticed the young woman's hands were trembling and was relieved when she spoke in a normal, friendly tone. 'It's nice to see you, Albert. You're looking well.'

'Good to see you, lad,' Leonard said. 'Mr Barlow, your old schoolteacher, was asking after you the other day. He's planning to retire soon. Said he's had enough of running around after little tykes like you.' He gave a forced laugh.

Emma managed to giggle more naturally. 'I don't blame him.'

Helen gave them a nod of encouragement. She kept her hands on Albert's shoulders, gently massaging them.

Leonard began to tell his son about the gas oven he'd had installed and how Emma was helping him to cook some new dishes.

'I can do more than fry eggs and bacon now.'

Albert managed a faint smile. 'I miss your eggs and bacon,' he muttered. 'And your fried bread. Never get fried bread here.'

Helen felt his shoulders drop and slowly removed her hands. She stayed for a few minutes, listening to them chat about the meals Mr Gates could now cook, then silently stepped out of the room.

Back at her desk, she craned to listen for any sounds coming from the kitchen. She was exasperated to see her clock had stopped again, though she supposed it prevented her from repeatedly looking at it.

Helen wasn't sure how much time had passed before she got up and crept to the kitchen. Feeling self-conscious, she pressed her ear to the door. Leonard was telling Albert about a stunt he'd seen in a Charlie Chaplin film. Emma giggled and suggested they all go to the cinema together. When Albert replied that he'd like that, Helen let out a small sigh of relief.

She returned to her office and didn't venture back to the kitchen until she heard Richard's car in the courtyard. Albert's face fell when she told them that Mr Locke was waiting to run them to the station.

'Already?'

'We'll come again soon,' Emma promised. She and Mr Gates stood up.

'You can come home whenever you feel up to it, son. Your room's just as you left it.'

Albert rose and went over to his father. 'Thanks, Dad. Look after yourself.' Tentatively, he hugged him but made no move towards Emma.

'I'm nearby if your father needs anything.' Emma leant forward and gently kissed Albert on the cheek. He coloured and mumbled something unintelligible.

They went out to the yard, and Richard opened the doors of the car and helped Emma and Mr Gates in. He gave Helen an enquiring glance and she winked in response.

There was a grin on his face as he got into the driver's seat. She and Albert stood in the yard and waved until the car was out of sight, then returned to the kitchen.

'Why don't you help me clear up?' she suggested, thinking Albert might need time to digest all that had happened before going back to the ward.

He nodded, his brow creased as he picked up the cups and took them to the sink. He looked preoccupied rather than happy.

'I'm sorry I didn't tell you Emma was coming.'

'It was good to see her.'

Helen was content to see he wasn't scratching and didn't say any more.

That evening, she took more pleasure in her bath time routine than she had since the discovery of the skeleton. She sank into the warm water with the satisfied feeling of finally having made some progress. Over dinner, she'd tackle Samuel about David.

When they were seated at the kitchen table, she served the cold supper of game pie and salad and asked if he'd heard back from St Dunstan's.

Samuel hesitated before reaching for his knife and fork. 'It's not good news, I'm afraid. They don't feel they'd be able to help him. I understand their concerns. David is probably better suited to a quieter, more secluded environment.'

If Samuel had deigned to share one of his bottles of wine with her that evening, Helen would have taken a large gulp. It felt like they were taking one step forward and two steps back. What annoyed her most was that he didn't appear upset by the news.

'Have you decided if you'll accept a position at the Royal Victoria?' she asked, irritation making her speak more plainly than she might have otherwise.

'I have so much more to do at Merewood Hospital before I can consider moving on.' He smiled at her and corrected himself. 'We have more to do here, I should say.'

Helen didn't respond. She didn't know how to. What did he mean by that? All that was left to do was to find suitable homes for the remaining patients. She was striving to make that happen, yet he seemed to be doing nothing.

Lying in bed that night, her irritation grew. Samuel had given her every indication he wanted their friendship to continue once they were away from this cursed place. His remarks had certainly led her to believe she formed part of his future plans. But it wasn't clear what those plans were, and Helen wasn't sure if she cared any more.

She found herself wishing she could have spent the evening

with Richard instead. It would have been nice to discuss the afternoon's events with him.

She turned onto her side, listening to a pair of tawny owls call to each other in the darkness. The sharp 'to wit' of the female was answered by the wavering 'too woo' of the male. She found the noises comforting.

Recently her sleep had been disturbed by visions of Morgan lying dead on the shores of the lake. A young nurse knelt by his side, wiping mud from his face with a scarf.

Helen didn't believe in ghosts, but there was no getting away from the fact that something sinister had invaded Merewood Hospital. As the sound of the owls lulled her to sleep, she felt a fresh resolve.

With Dorothy and Richard's help, she was going to find homes for the remaining patients and see to it that the hospital closed for good. Whether Samuel liked it or not.

19

'You want to buy Merewood Farm?'

Samuel had expected surprise, but Joseph Wintringham's reaction was closer to shock.

He coughed. 'Yes.'

'Why?' Joseph stood by the window, legs apart, hands on hips, staring at him as if he was mad.

'I want to run the hospital as a private clinic.' Samuel wished he'd remained standing instead of taking the chair offered. He felt like he was in a schoolroom rather than a study, and his words had sounded childlike.

'It's not a hospital, man. It's a farm.'

Joseph regarded him with what he considered to be an intrusive stare, and he tried to summon a more authoritative tone. 'It's been a hospital for three years. I admit it needs some renovation, but I believe I could transform it into a sanatorium to treat patients with physical and mental ailments. Specifically, ex-servicemen suffering from war neurosis, although it wouldn't be confined solely to those types of patients.'

'Out here? In the middle of Hampshire?' Joseph turned to the window. 'There's nothing but woods and fields.'

Samuel smiled and followed his gaze. 'That's what makes it the perfect location. A place to retreat from the turbulence of life and take time to heal. It's what the patients will be paying for, along with the rehabilitative therapies I can provide during their stay. When they leave, they'll be ready to enter into normal society once more.'

'These patients would pay for their treatment?'

'That's correct. However, I hope in time to be able to accept a few charity cases.'

'How will you run it?'

Samuel answered through gritted teeth. This barrage of questions was starting to vex him, though at least Wintringham finally seemed to be taking him seriously.

'I'd employ a small team of staff to begin with. As my clinic grows, I'll be able to hire more nurses and additional physicians. I'd particularly like to engage the services of a psychologist.'

'You're aware I already have an interested party? A buyer who wants the whole farm, the barns and the equipment.'

'I want the whole farm. Eventually, the plan would be to run it as a smallholding with the patients helping to tend to the animals as part of their therapy. I'm thinking of a few cows, some chickens and maybe a horse. Not dissimilar to how Merewood Farm used to be run. This wouldn't be immediately. I'd need to establish the sanatorium first and give it time to grow at a sustainable pace.'

Joseph raised his hand to his chin. 'You really think you can make it work?'

'Would I be investing my own money if I didn't?'

'I'll be frank with you, Bingham. I'm surprised you even have the money. You don't strike me as a rich man.'

Samuel flushed at Joseph's impudence. 'I choose to live a simple life, caring for others,' he replied, cringing at how pompous he sounded.

'Which is admirable, but that kind of life doesn't usually pay enough to enable someone to buy a farm.'

'I have some money from my parents and a little saved of my own.' Samuel felt his anger rising. He hadn't expected to be subjected to this level of scrutiny.

'What are you offering?'

'The same as Knight. Twenty-eight pounds per acre, I believe?'

'You've been talking to him?'

Samuel didn't reply. It was true that on his walks, he'd engineered a few encounters with Baden Knight and managed to steer the conversation around to the purchase of the farm.

To his frustration, Joseph ended the conversation by striding from the room, saying he'd think about it. Samuel remained in the study, wondering if he should have spent more time preparing for the meeting. Had he played his hand too soon? Last night's dinner with Helen had unnerved him. He felt he was in danger of losing her, and that had pushed him into action.

He wanted to take her into his confidence, but he had to wait until he'd secured Merewood Farm. He was more convinced than ever that he needed Helen to make his sanatorium a success.

He finally rose from his chair and went into the hallway, where he encountered Frederick Wintringham, his retriever at his heels.

'You can't bring any more bloody invalids here. Just get rid of the ones you've got and get out,' Frederick snapped. Then he strode out of the front door, the dog scampering after him.

Either his father had just told him of Samuel's offer, or Frederick had been listening at the door. He suspected the latter.

Samuel hurried out of the manor. He slowed once he reached the lake, stopping to admire the building that would soon be his. It was too ornate for a farm anyway, with its decorative red brick façade and those charming arched windows. The jasmine was in flower, and the white blooms looked glorious in the sunshine against the red backdrop.

The sound of gunshot nearby told him that Frederick had gone in search of some poor defenceless creatures to vent his anger on.

Instead of going through the kitchen, Samuel approached the hospital from the patio outside the ward. He'd expand this area, he decided. At present, the flagstone flooring was wide enough for about a dozen chairs. He'd have tables, too. He remembered Helen once suggesting the patients could play table tennis there. He'd dismissed the idea at the time as too frivolous for a military hospital. But it might not be a bad notion for a sanatorium if it were kept in in the barn.

And he'd have more plants. Gulliver did his best, but the beds were too plain. He'd like to see more colour, though he supposed the border of French lavender and rosemary was practical.

Dorothy Wintringham and David Cowper sat side by side in wicker chairs on the patio. He glanced into the ward and was surprised to find it empty.

'Good afternoon, Dr Bingham.' Dorothy placed the book she'd been reading to David on her lap. 'Doesn't the lavender smell glorious? And look at all those bees.'

Samuel tipped his hat at Mrs Wintringham. 'Delightful. Where is everyone?'

'Nathan and Oliver are helping Richard Locke in the north barn. I believe Albert has walked into the village.'

'On his own?' He felt uneasy. This was unlike Albert.

'He was keen to post a letter to his father,' David commented.

Samuel hurried in to find Helen and was disappointed to see that she wasn't in her office. He guessed she was still sorting out hospital supplies in the south barn.

He considered going in search of her but decided to take advantage of the quiet to work on his plans for the sanatorium. He needed to generate interest in what he had to offer. That meant raising his profile within the medical profession.

With the money he already had, he could afford to keep the four remaining patients there. They'd provide the material for the case studies he intended to submit to medical journals.

Albert would be a good one to start with. Samuel could describe how the young man had been badly injured when he'd arrived and how he, as a skilled physician, had patched up his wounds. His focus would be on the psychological impact of Albert's injuries, his fixation on his scars, and how their healing had been accompanied by incessant scratching.

Nathan was another interesting case. Physically, he could be considered healed, though mentally, there was still some way to go. His war neurosis had presented itself in the form of stammering and twitching. However, the constant motion appeared to be abating. His speech was also better. Samuel would attribute this to the healing properties of Merewood Hospital and his own expertise in psychology. Nathan could definitely be seen as a success story.

David and Oliver were another matter. But that was all to the good. They had problems that couldn't be fixed overnight. Could he use them as examples to encourage families to entrust their loved ones to his long-term care? It would certainly help his cashflow to have secure monthly payments for around half a dozen patients, for say a year, at least.

Oliver was an intriguing subject, although assessment was difficult due to his temper. His phantom limb pain was genuine, Samuel was sure of that. And there were plenty of men out there who'd lost limbs during the war. How many of them were suffering in silence? He'd write an article on phantom limb pain and its effects on a person's character.

Morgan was the only patient he wouldn't mention. He'd have

made an interesting study, but considering the outcome, he wouldn't attempt to tell that story.

And what of David? He was the trickiest case. Samuel hoped that Helen would never find out he'd lied to her. But it really hadn't been worth writing to St Dunstan's. As worthy as that organisation was, David was a special case. He was better off here at the hospital until they could get to the root of his problem. Only then could Samuel begin to work on his case study.

He started to draft a paper on Albert, detailing the shellfire that had caused the young man's injuries. Then he described his difficulties adjusting to his new physical appearance and his reluctance to let his fiancée see him.

After a while, he stopped writing and leant back to think. Daydream, to be more precise. He envisaged a prestigious future for himself. When people mentioned his skills as a doctor, the term 'pioneering' would be used.

Samuel's eyes began to droop. He'd had a restless night, disturbed by the strange call of some night birds. They really did make peculiar noises – quite sinister sounds that could distress his patients. As he drifted off to sleep, he wondered if it would be possible to track the birds down and shoot them. Frederick liked killing things. When the young man was in a better mood, he'd ask him about it.

Samuel woke with a start when he heard the clock in the hallway chime. His brain was fuzzy, and the remaining wisps of his dream were disintegrating. Something about a young woman in a blue dress with a red cross on her pinafore floating into the air with outstretched wings.

He stood up, rubbed his back and wandered down the corridor to the ward. To his surprise, it was still empty. This wasn't good enough. It was after five. The patients should be resting, not working. He'd have talk to Helen about their routine.

David was still sitting outside, though Mrs Wintringham had gone. He strolled over to the door.

'Would you like to come in now, David?' he called.

He received no answer. It was a beautiful evening, and the view across the lawn to the lake and Gibbet Wood was a feast for the eyes. But could David see it? That was the question. And where were his thoughts? Was he in the present or the past?

He went outside to David's chair. 'You can stay out a little longer if you prefer...'

The words died on his lips. Something was wrong. David wasn't moving.

Samuel felt his body go rigid. There was red. Blood. All over David's lap. It was coming from his wrists.

Blood covered his hospital blues. He could smell it – cold and metallic. And there was another smell. Urine.

Samuel knew he had to act fast but was paralysed.

You're a doctor, for Christ's sake, he told himself.

He needed to bind the man's wrists quickly. They were gaping open – blood was dripping.

But Samuel couldn't move except to raise his hand to touch David's neck. It was too late. He was dead.

20

Richard stood by Merewood Lake watching the police flitting around the farmhouse. He'd spent the night worrying about Oliver and Helen, even though Superintendent Townsend had assured him that an officer would be stationed outside the hospital.

Townsend and Newman had returned that morning to interview everyone on the ward. No doubt, they'd find their way to the manor next.

'That's another one gone.' Frederick raised his shotgun to his shoulder, giving the cruel impression he'd just fired it at David.

'First Morgan and Mummy's portrait and now this. We're all in danger.' Georgina began to cry as Richard had known she would.

Neither man made any move to comfort her. The three of them stood in ghoulish contemplation of what was happening at the hospital. Richard felt embarrassed at this blatant display of morbid curiosity, but like Frederick and Georgina, he'd been desperate to know what was going on.

'Poor David. He was so sweet,' Georgina simpered. 'Evil spirits took his innocent soul.'

Richard didn't recall her ever making an effort to talk to the

man or read to him. Morgan was the only patient she'd paid atten-
tion to.

He scratched his unshaven chin. 'What reason could anyone
have to kill Morgan or David?'

'Does there have to be a reason?' Georgina replied. 'The curse is
forcing them to do it.'

'Two down. Three to go. Once they've all gone, I think I'll move
into Merewood Farm.' Frederick marched away, his shotgun over
his shoulder and Dexter at his heels.

Richard watched him go, deciding to talk to Townsend about
him. He didn't like whatever was going on in that young man's head.

Georgina followed his gaze. 'Freddie never got over that nurse.
He was weird before that, but he was worse afterwards. I think he
wants revenge.'

'Revenge on who?'

'He doesn't know. That's the problem. Everyone was so besotted
with that girl. You included.'

He didn't bother to deny it. 'You think he's doing this?'

'No, of course not. It's one of their own.' She motioned to the
hospital. 'Or the curse is making them do it to themselves.'

Richard had no answer to this. He wondered how plausible it
was for two men to commit suicide in such a short space of time. It
could be said that all the remaining patients were in a sorry state.
Oliver included. But had David even been capable of cutting his
own wrists?

He felt Georgina's hand on his arm. 'I don't want to stay here. It's
too horrible. Let's go back to your cottage.'

The suggestion alarmed him. 'Don't be silly.'

'I'm not being silly,' she said shrilly. 'You used to like me. Why
don't you like me any more? Is it her?' She gestured towards the
hospital. 'Sister Perfect?'

Richard sighed and turned away. He wasn't going to have this conversation.

'I sometimes think you hate me. I think everyone hates me.'

'I don't hate you, Georgina.' It was true. He looked into her violet eyes and felt nothing but pity.

'Prove it to me.' She pushed her body against his.

'What?'

She ran crimson painted fingernails along his forearm. 'Take me back to your cottage and show me you don't hate me.'

He was surprised at how much the idea repelled him. It hadn't been so long ago he'd responded to her teasing with an eagerness he felt ashamed of. He examined her pretty features and let his gaze fall to her neat figure. There was no stirring of desire. Yet when he was with Helen, his eyes were constantly drawn to the curve of her neck, and he couldn't stop thinking about the body beneath that nun-like uniform.

'I'm leaving here soon, Georgina. It wouldn't be fair.'

'It would if you took me with you.'

'You know I'm not going to do that.' He didn't want to hurt her, but there was no point in lying.

She bit her lip, and said with a tremor, 'That was your last chance. Clifford Knight won't say no to me.'

Richard watched her go, feeling pity and relief, before turning his attention back to the farmhouse. He wanted to go and see Helen but guessed the police wouldn't welcome a visitor at this time. Then he saw Oliver come through the patio doors of the ward. He waved, and Oliver started to stroll toward him.

Richard hurried around to the other side of the lake to greet him.

'Are you allowed out?' he asked.

'The superintendent has already questioned me. I'm free to go.'

Oliver gave a bitter laugh. 'Not sure where he thinks I have to go. I'm a lamb to the slaughter.'

Richard's skin prickled. 'What do you mean?'

'Do you believe Morgan's drowning was an accident? That at least would have been possible. You can't imagine David slashed his own wrists.'

'Do you think you're in danger? Why don't you come and stay with me at the cottage until we get the stables sorted? You'll be safer there.'

Oliver gave another laugh. It was a sinister, hollow sound. 'Who am I afraid of?'

Richard wasn't sure what his friend was asking. Did he suspect a person? Or, like Georgina, did he think an evil spirit lurked at Merewood Farm? Whatever was going on, Helen was right. The hospital had to close. And soon.

'I don't know who you have to fear. I suppose the person you imagine is responsible,' he prompted. 'Who do you think could be doing these things?'

Oliver shrugged. 'Whoever has the clock, I suppose.'

'What clock?'

'David's clock. It's missing.'

Richard ran his fingers through his hair in frustration. Was his friend suffering from shock? Or was there really a missing clock? 'Come with me to my cottage. We can talk there. I'll make up a bed for you.'

Oliver shook his head. 'I need to get back to the ward. I have a drawing to finish.'

With that, he turned and walked towards the hospital.

Richard had to fight the urge to stop him. He wanted to drag him away from that bloody place. But Oliver was a grown man, and he couldn't make him do anything he didn't want to.

Later that evening, he felt a surge of relief when he heard a light tap on the cottage door. He was in the kitchen, washing at the sink, and didn't bother putting a shirt on before he went to open it.

To his embarrassment, it wasn't Oliver. It was Helen. She'd only ever been to his cottage once before. It was when she'd come to tell him that Isabel was missing. He wondered if she was remembering that now.

'Oh, I'm sorry. I've disturbed you.' She was blushing and averted her eyes from his bare chest.

'Come in. Please.' He held open the door and took a step back, ushering her into the parlour. She was wearing a pink cotton sundress, and beneath her straw hat, her hair looked like it had been freshly washed. As she passed, he could smell soap and shampoo. 'Stay here. I won't be a moment.'

He dashed into the kitchen and picked up his work shirt. It smelt of sweat, and he discarded it in favour of a clean white shirt drying on the wooden rack in the scullery.

He returned to the parlour to find Helen gazing at his bookshelf. She had one of his books in her hand, and he was curious to know which it was.

She turned and held up *Hampshire Days* by W. H. Hudson. 'I have a copy of this.' She opened the book at the first chapter. 'His studies of birds are so detailed. His description of how a newborn cuckoo manages to roll unhatched eggs out of the nest is quite chilling.'

Richard nodded. 'I've seen them do it myself. The cuckoo will get rid of newborn chicks as well. The parents continue to feed it. They seem to have no idea it's killing their real offspring.'

He stood awkwardly, unused to having visitors. He was also unaccustomed to seeing Helen in normal clothes. On their recent walks, they'd become more relaxed with each other, but that familiarity wasn't present this evening. He felt like a clumsy teenager, and it occurred to him that he might look like one too, standing there gawping at her in her pink dress.

'Sit down.' He gestured to an armchair by the unlit fire. 'Would you like something to drink?'

'No thank you.' She replaced the book and took a seat. 'I just needed to get away. To talk to someone. Someone who's not a policeman.'

He lowered himself into the armchair opposite. 'It's terrible about David. What do you think happened?' He stopped, realising he was being insensitive. 'Sorry, I'm sure Townsend asked you that.'

She nodded. 'He wanted to know if David could have done that to himself.'

'And could he?' It was a question he had to ask.

'Physically, he was capable, although inflicting those wounds would have been difficult for anyone, let alone someone who couldn't see what they were doing.'

'Are you sure he was blind?'

'Yes, although we didn't understand why. I can't imagine how he could have got hold of a scalpel.'

'A scalpel?' Richard thought of the gouged portrait of Dorothy Wintringham.

'It was found at his feet. Dr Bingham occasionally uses them on the ward. I suppose he could have left one behind by accident, not that I've ever seen one lying around.'

'I spoke to Oliver earlier.' Richard wasn't sure whether to mention his friend's strange behaviour. 'He said something about a clock that's gone missing? I wasn't sure what he meant.'

Helen's eyes narrowed. 'David had a little gold travel clock he used to play with. I didn't know it was missing. Dr Bingham volunteered to sort out David's things.'

'When did you last see it?' Richard wondered how Oliver knew about the clock.

She frowned. 'I'm not sure. Probably the evening before he died. He used to wind it up before he went to bed. He liked to listen to it ticking.'

'You didn't see him with it yesterday?'

'I don't think so. I didn't notice. He could have had it with him in the morning. I hadn't seen him since lunchtime because I was in the barn.' She bit the nail of her thumb. 'Did you see anyone? In the afternoon, I mean? You were back and forth between the two barns.'

This was true. Oliver and Nathan had worked in the north barn for most of the time while Helen had been in the south barn, and he'd moved between the two.

'I saw Albert walking into the woods. He had a letter in his hand. I don't usually see him out on his own.'

'He's written to his father saying he wants to come home.'

He noticed her face soften as she said this.

'I saw Dorothy reading to David,' he continued. 'Joseph joined them at one point, and Georgina passed the hospital on her way to the village. She never walks through the woods; she always goes by the lanes. Frederick was in the fields between the two barns shooting rabbits.'

'Did you see David moving around at all?'

He shook his head. 'He was sat outside whenever I looked over. I didn't notice when Dorothy left him. Where was Bingham?'

'He called at the manor after lunch and then spent the rest of the afternoon in his office. He was the one who discovered David.'

'Didn't he see or hear anything? He must have been there when it happened.'

Helen shook her head. 'He says not.'

Richard could sense their unspoken thoughts hanging in the air.

'Why now?' he asked.

'What do you mean?'

'Why would two men suddenly decide to take their own lives in the space of a week?'

'Because the hospital is closing. And they have nowhere to go?'

Richard shook his head. 'I don't believe it.'

Helen regarded him with those cool green eyes and then said softly, 'Neither do I.'

21

Helen stood on the patio outside the ward, her eyes drawn to where David had died. His blood had been scrubbed from the flagstones, but a dark patch remained.

She saw Richard on the other side of the lake, probably going up to the pheasant pens. Why had she put on her most flattering dress and gone to his cottage last night? It hadn't been to talk. She'd gone because she'd wanted him to comfort her. She'd hoped he would hold her in his arms and tell her everything would be alright.

Instead, they'd skirted around each other like a couple of teenagers. Their awkwardness had only diminished when they'd talked about the murders. And she was certain that's what they were.

She'd come away feeling more afraid than when she'd arrived. He'd walked her back to the hospital, and a police officer had greeted them. Townsend had promised that one of his men would be there all night, and Richard had said she could come to his cottage whenever she wanted. But she'd still spent a sleepless night thinking about David.

Helen went over to his bed and began to strip the linen. She wanted to do it while the patients were having breakfast. The tragedy of his death had taken them all by surprise. Obviously, the violent nature of it was traumatic for everyone. They were still reeling from that.

What was unexpected was the loss of the man himself. David had rarely spoken. He'd sat quietly, listening. And perhaps observing, in his way. Yet somehow, his presence had made an impression.

Helen hadn't realised before how likeable David had been. He'd possessed a serenity that was reassuring.

With Albert making plans to leave, it was Nathan that worried her the most. He'd miss David, and staying on the ward would be a constant reminder. She'd have to talk to Dorothy about him again.

Then there was Oliver. She'd hoped for a little more enthusiasm after his day out with Richard. Although he'd seemed in good spirits when he returned, his mood had rapidly deteriorated. Helen could have sworn she'd smelt whisky on his breath when she helped him take his shoes off. Perhaps Richard had thought one drink wouldn't do his friend any harm. She'd been reluctant to mention it to him when they'd talked in Gibbet Wood.

In the privacy of his cottage, Richard had told her how afraid he was for Oliver. She could understand his fear. She felt it herself.

Last night, she'd suggested to the patients they might like to move to another room. Even have rooms to themselves. Samuel had looked appalled at this, as she'd known he would. He seemed to be determined to retain the hospital structure. She'd ignored him. It wasn't as if they were short of space. But the men had displayed a strange reluctance to leave the ward or each other. It was understandable they felt safer together. She'd lain awake, wishing for the company of Matron and her team of nurses.

As usual, Helen didn't need to turn her head to know that

Samuel had entered the ward and was watching her. She carried on stripping the sheets.

'Helen, I'm reluctant to move David's bed out. We don't want the patients to feel more unsettled than they already are. This is their home.'

She turned to face him. 'With respect, Samuel, this is not their home. This is a hospital ward. A temporary hospital ward.' Her nerves were shredded, and she didn't care about his seniority. 'My priority is to find suitable places for the patients and close this place as soon as humanly possible.'

His pained expression exasperated her. Surely, after David's death, he didn't think they could stay there any longer.

After a short silence, he said, 'Could you come to my office? I have some news I want to share with you.'

Helen piled the crumpled linen on the bed and followed. Once she was seated, he closed the door and clasped his hands together. This was a sure sign he was about to make one of his pompous statements.

'David's death has come as a huge shock to us all. No one could have known the extent of the poor man's torment.'

She rubbed the back of her neck, feeling a dull ache across her shoulders. 'I wish St Dunstan's had felt able to take him. It could have saved his life.'

Samuel gave one of his annoying coughs and looked down at his hands. 'The thing is...' He hesitated.

She grew impatient. He clearly had something to get off his chest, and she wished he'd get on with it. Did it concern David?

'Did you tell Superintendent Townsend about David's clock? Oliver seems to think it's missing,' she said.

'Not yet. I'll mention it later. The thing is... I've spoken to Joseph Wintringham regarding the hospital. Buying it.'

She had no idea what he was talking about. 'Buying what?'

'The farm. I intend to buy Merewood Farm.'

Her incredulity must have shown as he quickly began to explain. She listened wide-eyed as he described a private sanatorium with psychological therapies, fee-paying patients, and wealthy families seeking help for their sick relatives.

When he'd finished, she blurted out the question foremost on her mind.

'How can you afford it?'

It was probably an ill-mannered thing to say, but it hadn't occurred to her that Samuel would have the kind of wealth needed to open a private practice.

'I have some money put by,' he replied vaguely. 'I know it's a lot to take in. The reason I'm telling you all this is because I'd like you to stay here with me.'

'Stay? What do you mean?'

'Between us, we can establish our own sanatorium. We'd be in charge. There'd be no hospital board to answer to. We could make a real difference.'

'I thought you intended to take a post at the Royal Victoria Hospital. I was going to apply for a position there myself.'

Samuel raised a hand in a dismissive gesture. 'I've had enough of hospital life. I have more to offer than just patching up patients. In my sanatorium, I'll be able to rehabilitate them, give them a chance to lead a more rewarding life. I want Albert, Nathan and Oliver to stay too. I can help them.' He rubbed his eyes. 'I wish I could have helped Morgan and David as well.'

'Don't you think these patients have been in hospital for far too long already?'

'This wouldn't be a hospital. It would be a sanatorium. A place where they could heal and grow. They'd be able to help on the farm, tend to the animals, nurture plants in the garden, listen to music or paint in the studio.'

'I see.' It was all she could think of to say, though she wasn't sure she did see. Could Merewood Farm be transformed into the sanctuary Samuel described?

'I've taken you by surprise. I wish I could have told you sooner, but there's been so much to arrange. Think about it. That's all I ask. Give it some serious thought before you come to a decision.'

'I will.' Helen rose, feeling desperate to leave his office.

She returned to the ward and finished stripping David's bed. Then she dragged the laundry bag to the kitchen and left it by the back door to be taken to the manor for washing. As she moved around the farmhouse, doing her usual chores, she realised she was looking at it with different eyes.

After depositing the last laundry bag by the back door, she slumped into a chair. Chester took advantage of her lethargy by jumping on her lap and purring loudly. She stroked his ears and gazed around the kitchen. Only it wasn't a kitchen. No meals were ever cooked there.

Merewood Farm wasn't a farm. It wasn't a hospital. Could it be a sanatorium? She had no idea. That was the problem. How could she make a decision when she felt like she was living in a pretend world?

Should she take Samuel's proposition seriously? Until this morning, her goal had been to get the patients settled and then find herself a new position. Was that still what she wanted?

He'd sounded sincere in his desire to create a wonderful place for healing. But he must realise the hospital would always be tainted by Morgan and David's deaths. Perhaps Isabel's too.

Helen now understood Samuel's strange remarks and what had been driving him all this time. It made her wonder just how far he would go to achieve his ambition.

22

'I'm interested to learn how the farm was managed before the war. You kept a few cows and chickens back then?'

Samuel had taken some pleasure in the look of surprise on Richard Locke's face when he'd asked if he would give him a tour of the estate.

Richard nodded. 'A small herd just to supply produce for the manor. The cows were sold when Merewood Farm became a hospital, and the chickens got moved. They're next to the kitchen garden at the manor now.'

Samuel listened as they walked and couldn't deny Locke knew his stuff, particularly when it came to animals and birds. His descriptions of how pheasants were reared for shooting had been most informative.

Richard appeared even more surprised when Samuel asked if he could help him sort out the farming equipment in the north barn. Helen had found him a pair of blue overalls, and he rather liked his appearance in them. It felt like childhood dressing up – putting on a new uniform and becoming a different person. Today, he was a man who wasn't afraid of honest manual labour.

In truth, it was a way to escape from the hospital and Townsend's incessant questions. Did the man seriously think he could have had anything to do with David's death? It was absurd. But is that what people were thinking? Even though Locke was being civil enough, he could sense an underlying hostility.

Doctors didn't kill people. Well, apart from that Crippen chap, and his was a crime of passion. And he hadn't been a real doctor. Doctors didn't kill their patients. At least, not often.

David's death sickened and puzzled him in equal measure. It couldn't be linked to the portrait, surely? That's what Townsend was implying. He might have abandoned his scheme if it hadn't been for Helen. He'd shared his dream with her – asked her to be part of it – and she hadn't said no.

Samuel stood in the centre of the north barn, listening to the doves cooing in the rafters. He enjoyed the physical exertion of the tasks, although he wasn't keen on being told what to do by Locke. He gazed at the assortment of machinery, sacks of feed and crates of goodness knows what. It smelt like a farm. An odd aroma that seemed to be a mixture of rust and earth. It felt like he was finally taking practical steps to put his plan into action. Soon, all this would be his.

A feeling he was being watched crept over him. A glance toward the door caused a flash of fear followed by irritation. Superintendent Townsend was standing there.

'Dr Bingham. Perhaps I could have a moment of your time. In your office.'

Samuel had no choice but to accompany him down the dirt track that led back to the hospital.

'I've told you everything I can, superintendent,' he said when they were seated and Townsend had closed the door. His questions made Samuel feel like a failure. Like he was personally responsible for David's death. There was nothing more he could tell the man.

They'd been through it all a dozen times. How he'd found the body. What he'd been doing that afternoon.

'No, you haven't.' Townsend regarded him through narrowed eyes.

He felt his face flushing. 'I can assure you I have.'

'What about your correspondence with St Dunstan's Hostel for Blind Soldiers and Sailors?'

He felt a mixture of relief and alarm at the question. 'What about it?'

'Sister Hopgood told me you'd written to the hostel asking if they could take Mr Cowper. You didn't mention that when I asked you to tell me everything you could regarding his situation.'

'I didn't think it was relevant. It relates to his medical care, and it's private.'

'I'll decide what's relevant. Why wouldn't they take Mr Cowper?'

'He didn't fit their criteria. There was no physical proof he was blind.'

'Did you think he was blind?'

'I... I'm not certain. It could have been a physical manifestation of a mental problem.' Samuel wished he was wearing his white coat rather than the ridiculous blue overalls. He needed the authority of being Dr Bingham.

'I see.' The superintendent leant back. 'Could I see the correspondence?'

'I'm sorry?' Samuel was beginning to sweat. Townsend seemed to have an uncanny ability for sniffing out lies.

'The letter. The reply you received from St Dunstan's.'

'I'm not sure where it is.' He racked his brain to think of some valid reason why it wasn't possible to show it to him.

Townsend regarded him with a disbelieving stare. 'I can wait while you find it.'

Samuel resented the way the man scrutinised him like a he was specimen in a laboratory.

He gestured hopelessly at his desk. 'I don't have it to hand. I have a great deal of correspondence.'

Townsend glanced around the spartan office. 'It's not a huge room. Perhaps I can help you search for it.'

Samuel grew angry. 'I threw it away.'

'You threw the letter away?' Townsend raised his eyebrows. 'You seem to take as much care of your patients' records as you do to securing your medicine cabinet.'

'That's uncalled for.' Samuel stood up. 'I'd like you to leave.'

'Not until I see that letter. Or should I pay a visit to St Dunstan's and see what they have to say? I'm sure they keep records of the correspondence they receive regarding vulnerable ex-servicemen.'

Samuel was silent for a few moments while he weighed up what to do next. He was still standing up and was starting to feel idiotic.

Finally, he sat down and said, 'I didn't write to St Dunstan's.'

Townsend stared at him for a few moments before speaking. 'Why did Sister Hopgood tell me you had?'

'I confess, I'm guilty of leading her to believe I'd acted upon her suggestion to contact them. However, I personally felt that the hostel wasn't the best solution for David.'

'And what did you consider the best solution to be? Did you want Mr Cowper to stay here at Merewood Farm – as a patient of your private sanatorium?'

Samuel had been wondering if Joseph Wintringham would mention his offer to Townsend. 'Yes, as a matter of fact, that's exactly what I thought.'

'Unfortunately, Mr Cowper's treatment here doesn't appear to have been entirely successful.'

'His was an extremely complex case. I can assure you that I did all I could to help him.'

'You say Mr Cowper gave no indication he was planning to take his own life?'

'None whatsoever. He was an extremely placid gentleman.'

'Taking a scalpel to your wrist is a violent act for anyone, let alone a placid gentleman. Cutting both wrists seems an unlikely scenario in the circumstances.'

Samuel had no answer to this. He wiped his wet palms on the trousers of his overalls.

'Do you have any idea where Mr Cowper would have acquired a scalpel?'

'It's a hospital, there are scalpels everywhere.'

'In reach of suicidal patients?'

'No, of course not. They're kept in those drawers.' Samuel pointed to the oak chest in the corner of his office.

'What about the one used to deface Mrs Wintringham's portrait?'

'The south barn is full of medical equipment to be collected by the Red Cross. There may well be some surgical instruments stored in the boxes there. Sister Hopgood has been making inventories. She would have the details.'

'Could I see where you keep your scalpels?'

Samuel went over to the chest and opened the top drawer. An array of medical instruments lay on the cushioned interior.

'Are they all there?'

'It would appear so. I don't count them.'

'It seems unlikely that, given his condition, Mr Cowper would have made his way to the south barn on the off-chance he might come across a scalpel there. Far easier for him to search your office, though even that wouldn't have been a simple matter.'

Samuel nodded. He couldn't deny it.

'You say you were here all afternoon.'

'No. Not all afternoon. As I've already told you, I called on Mr Wintringham after lunch. My office was empty then.'

Samuel didn't like the way Townsend was looking at him.

'Mr Cowper was with Mrs Wintringham on the patio when you returned from the manor?'

'That's correct.'

'Mrs Wintringham said that Mr Cowper didn't have his clock with him when she was reading to him. Presumably, it would have been by the side of his bed on the ward?'

'I should think so.'

'The clock is now missing. You were the only person in the hospital after Mrs Wintringham left, and you discovered Mr Cowper's body. Do you know where the clock is?'

Samuel ground his teeth. 'No, I do not.'

'And it hasn't been found?'

'Not that I'm aware.'

'When did you last see the clock?'

'I have no idea. David often had it in his hands when I talked to him. It's like Albert's letters and Oliver's sketch pad. They're items you become so familiar with you cease to see them.'

Townsend gave an unpleasant smile. 'When it comes to your patients, there's a lot you seem to have stopped seeing.'

23

Richard spotted Helen heading into the south barn and hurried down the track. When he entered, he found her gazing at the assortment of beds, screens, trolleys and cabinets haphazardly stored there.

All traces of the art studio had been removed, and the agricultural machinery taken to the north barn. To his credit, Bingham had done a thorough job of getting the north barn sorted, no matter how ridiculous he'd looked in his overalls.

Helen smiled as he entered. 'Perfect timing. Now we have more room, would you help me to arrange things into some sort of order?'

'Of course.' No overalls for Helen, he noted. She wore her usual blue uniform and white apron, her glossy brown hair hidden beneath a white muslin cap. He thought longingly of the pink sundress she'd worn to his cottage.

'The beds will need to go into the vans first. Could you help me move them nearest to the doors? Followed by the cabinets, then the trolleys and screens.'

Between them, they lifted a bed frame and carried it over to the space she'd cleared.

'Mr Wintringham tells me Bingham has put in an offer for Merewood Farm.'

Helen nodded. 'Samuel has asked me to stay on and manage the sanatorium with him.'

It's what he'd feared. And her use of Bingham's first name irked him. 'I thought you wanted to leave.'

'So did I. But I promised Samuel I'd consider his proposition.'

Richard didn't like the sound of this. 'After everything that's happened?'

'I don't know. I think Samuel is right. The surrounding country-side does make this the perfect setting for a sanatorium. I'm not so sure about the farmhouse.' She shrugged. 'It's not an ideal hospital, though I suppose it could be converted into a private clinic.'

'What's to be done with all this stuff?' He indicated the medical equipment surrounding them. 'Will it stay if Mr Wintringham accepts Bingham's offer?'

She shook her head. 'It all belongs to the Red Cross. They want it back. If Samuel does buy Merewood Farm, he'll have to start from scratch.'

'Where's he getting the money from?'

'That's what we'd all like to know. Dorothy told me his offer took Mr Wintringham by surprise. Samuel's certainly never given me the impression he's wealthy enough to consider setting up his own practice. He's a senior doctor, but it doesn't pay that well. Until recently, I thought he was considering taking a position at the Royal Victoria Hospital.' Helen sank onto an upturned crate.

Richard found another crate, checked it was solid enough to hold his weight, and pulled it over to sit beside her.

'Does Bingham want to keep Oliver here? He doesn't have the money to pay for residential care in a sanatorium.'

'Samuel wants to treat some patients for free. Oliver would be one of them. He believes Merewood Farm is still the best place for him. If Oliver leaves, he may not be able to cope with life outside.'

'He's not making any progress here.'

'His moods do seem to be getting worse,' Helen agreed.

This was precisely what Richard was afraid of. 'I'd like him to come and live with me.'

'It's up to Oliver. He can leave at any time if he feels ready. Does he want to?'

'I think the thought scares him.' Oliver had spoken disparagingly of everyone at the hospital and the manor. Yet even now, after David's death, he seemed reluctant to leave the ward.

'If Merewood Farm is converted into a sanatorium, it might be able to offer him the type of rehabilitative treatment he needs.'

Richard could hear the doubt in her voice. 'Is he safe? Are you safe?'

'I don't know.' Her usual placid tone was tinged with anxiety and her cool gaze replaced by a look of uncertainty.

'Was David's clock ever found?'

She shook her head.

'And Morgan's cigarette case hasn't been seen since he died?'

'I couldn't find it when I packed up his belongings. He could have had it with him at the lake and it fell into the water.'

'I suppose so.' He eyed her cautiously. He wasn't sure whether to tell her what had been lurking at the back of his mind.

She must have picked up on his hesitation. 'What is it?'

'Isabel Taplin's brooch was missing. Do you remember?'

She nodded. 'One of the nurses said it was pinned to her scarf. I can't ever recall seeing it, but then she wouldn't have been allowed to wear it when she was on duty.'

'It was a grey pearl in a twisted silver setting.'

'You seem to know it well.' She sounded almost jealous.

'The police gave the estate workers a description and asked us to keep an eye out for it in the woods and on the lanes to the village.'

'It was never found, was it?'

He shook his head.

She bit her lip. 'You think whoever killed her and took the brooch could be the same person who murdered Morgan and David and took the cigarette case and the clock?'

'It's just a theory. I always thought Victor Protheroe might have killed Isabel. But he's dead.'

She nodded. 'I must admit, so did I. He wanted to paint her portrait. Isabel was keen, but Matron put a stop to it. You can't permit that sort of intimacy between a nurse and patient; it wouldn't be right.'

Her puritanical tone amused him. Richard doubted the famous artist would have taken as much notice of Matron's authority as Helen had.

'I'd heard he was a drug addict. Do you think he killed himself because of guilt?' It was the conclusion he'd come to.

'I've often wondered. He certainly had his demons, though that's hardly surprising given his time in France. When he was in one of his black moods, he'd take cocaine. It didn't help.'

Richard was anxious to raise the subject that was concerning him most. He tried to frame a subtle question, then realised she'd know exactly what he was trying to say and decided to be frank.

'Do you think Oliver could be violent? I wonder if I'm too close to see him clearly. He was always a good man. He saved my life. If he hadn't...' He paused. 'It's my fault he lost his arm.'

Helen held up her hand. 'Do you know how many times I've listened to men attempting to make sense of what happened to them? Questioning why they survived when their brother, father, uncle, nephew or best friend was killed. The war caused Oliver to lose his arm. Not you.'

'He gets so angry.' After their trip out together, it had been clear how frightened Oliver was of the future. 'I worry that his frustration might have led him to hurt someone.'

'The war trained men to hurt people. Perhaps it's within all of us if sufficiently provoked. But why would he?' She brought her hands to her face to massage her temples. 'Why would anyone? I've no idea what's happening here. Should I be afraid? Or has it just been a run of bad luck.'

'Someone put a skeleton in your bath, someone attacked Dorothy's portrait – and someone murdered Morgan and David.'

'We don't know when the damage to the portrait occurred. It could have been done months ago by someone who's since left the hospital.'

'Or it could have been done deliberately for Georgina and Dorothy to find – by whoever murdered Morgan and David. I'm getting Oliver out of here. It will be best for him and everyone around him. I don't want him to be one of Bingham's charity cases.'

At first, he thought she was going to argue. Then she said, 'I'm going to speak to Dorothy about finding a position for Nathan at the manor. Albert has already written to his father saying he'd like to go home, and I'm helping him with the arrangements.'

'What about you? Will you stay?'

'I'm not—'

A loud cry from the farmhouse made them both spring up from their seats.

'What on earth?' he spluttered.

It was a woman's scream. Could it be Georgina?

Helen was already out of the barn and making her way up the track. At the kitchen door, she stopped abruptly on the threshold. Richard almost ran into the back of her.

He saw immediately what had brought her to a standstill. A red gelatinous liquid was spreading across the kitchen floor. By the rich, fruity smell, it was tomato soup.

Kate was standing in the centre of the kitchen, a black tureen rolling on the ground at her feet. She was staring in horror at a dead bird lying on the kitchen table. Its head lolled to one side, and its wings were grotesquely outstretched.

Helen let out a low wail. 'It's the sparrowhawk.'

24

'How could anyone hurt her?' Helen stepped cautiously around the tomato soup to bend over the dead bird. Even as she said it, she felt foolish. After the deaths of Morgan and David, what did a bird matter? But seeing the fragility of the once-powerful sparrowhawk made her want to weep.

When a frightened-looking Albert and Nathan appeared at the door, she heard Richard tell them to take Kate back to the manor. Albert stood gawping while Nathan was quicker to react, gently ushering the maid out of the kitchen door.

'Out. I'll deal with this,' Richard ordered, and Albert stumbled after them. Oliver had been standing behind them in the corridor. He gazed impassively at the bird and then turned to go back to the ward.

Helen couldn't stop staring at the sparrowhawk. She felt Richard's arm around her shoulder and leant into his solid body, allowing herself to be comforted. It was what she'd wanted when she'd gone to his cottage on the evening after David's death – for him to assure her everything would be all right. But he couldn't make it right and nor could she. All they could do was try to keep the patients safe.

'I'm sorry,' she heard him murmur.

Helen straightened up and pulled away. 'What happened to her? Could Chester have done it?'

Richard went over to inspect the dead bird, lifting each lifeless wing. 'There's no sign of injury. No claw or teeth marks.'

'Then how did she die?'

'I suspect she ate something poisonous.'

'And flew in here?' Fury was rising within her.

He gazed at the soup on the floor, seeming unwilling to answer.

'It's happening again, isn't it? Another trick.'

'Some cruel bastard's idea of a joke.'

Helen wanted to pick up the stack of plates on the sideboard and smash them on the stone floor. She took a long, ragged breath.

'First the skeleton in the bath, then Morgan dies in the lake. After Dorothy's portrait is slashed and the eyes gouged out, David's wrists are cut. Does this mean someone else will die?'

'I'm going to show the police.' Richard picked up the sparrowhawk gently and carried it to the door. He turned to look at her. 'I'm sorry,' he said again.

Helen went over to touch the bird's head, then squeezed Richard's arm. He was the only one who could understand what the sparrowhawk had meant to her.

Through the kitchen window, she watched him walk across the yard, the bird in his arms. Then she straightened her apron and began to fill the sink. In the scullery, she found a mop and set about clearing up the spilt soup.

As she worked, she chastised herself for letting a dead bird affect her so much. God knows she'd seen worse than that over the years. But when she came to scrub the kitchen table, she couldn't stop her tears from falling into the suds.

Once the table was clean, she took bread from the basket and found a lump of cheese in the larder. She made sandwiches and took them through to the ward just as Albert and Nathan came in through the patio doors.

'Is Kate feeling better?' she asked.

Nathan nodded. 'We walked with her to the manor. I told Cook what had happened, and she's taking care of her.'

'Thank you, Nathan.'

'It was only a dead bird.' Oliver looked up from his sketch. 'I can't see what all the fuss is about.'

Helen placed the sandwiches on the table and glared at him. 'Did *you* put it there?'

'No, of course not,' he snarled. 'Do you think I could manage to kill a bird single-handed?' He waved the stump of his left elbow at her. Then, with his right hand, he tapped the ash from his pipe and took out his tobacco pouch.

She thought about her conversation with Richard that morning. Could Oliver's temper lead to violence? She'd been on the receiving end of his harsh tongue. The previous night, he'd sat up late, sketching compulsively and sworn at her when she'd tried to persuade him to go to bed. In the end, she'd left him to it as he wasn't disturbing the others.

Helen turned to Albert and Nathan. 'I'm afraid it's only sandwiches for lunch. Do you know where Dr Bingham is?'

Nathan shook his head. 'We haven't seen him since breakfast.'

She went to her office and sat at her desk for a long time, her head resting in her hands.

'Are you alright, Sister?'

Albert was standing in the doorway, shuffling from foot to foot. He was holding an envelope.

She managed a forced smile. 'I'm fine. Just tired. What's that you've got there?'

'It's a letter to Emma.' He blushed. 'I've told her I still love her and I'd like to take her to the pictures when I get home. I'm going to walk into the village to post it. Nathan's coming with me.'

This time, Helen's smile was genuine. 'I'm sure she'll be delighted.' She rose from her chair. 'I'll come with you as far as the manor. I need to call on Mrs Wintringham.'

At the manor gates, Albert and Nathan took the path up to Gibbet Wood while she walked across the lawn, hoping to catch sight of Richard. She wondered what he'd done with the sparrowhawk.

The maid informed her that Mrs Wintringham was in the garden with her daughter. Helen's heart sank. She'd come to discuss Nathan and had no desire to do so in front of Georgina.

She'd was about to leave a message when Dorothy appeared in the hallway, Georgina in tow.

'Why did Richard have to bring it here? It was horrible,' Georgina wailed. 'It's probably cursed.'

So the sparrowhawk had made a trip to the manor.

'Don't worry, Georgie.' Frederick came out of the drawing room and mounted the stairs, swinging his shotgun over his shoulder. 'I'll be taking this to bed with me. If anyone tries to pull any tricks around here, it will be the last one they play.'

Helen wished she had a shotgun.

Georgina didn't appear reassured by this. 'I'm going to my room to lie down. I feel sick.'

Dorothy touched her forehead. 'You don't look well, my dear. Shall I ask the doctor to call in?'

'No,' Georgina practically screamed. 'I just need to rest.'

'I can come back later,' Helen murmured. She watched Georgina scurry up the stairs and had a good idea what was wrong with her.

'Sorry, my dear.' Dorothy swung around. 'Come and tell me what happened this morning. I've yet to hear a coherent account.'

In the drawing room, Helen described the discovery of the bird on the kitchen table. As she talked, she felt some of her tension lift. Merewood seemed a less frightening place when you were sitting on an elegant sofa surrounded by gilt-framed paintings and vases of fragrant roses.

'I'm sorry Georgina was upset,' she said. 'I didn't know Richard was going to bring the bird here.'

'You're the one who should be upset, my dear. Not Georgina. She has a tendency to overreact. It's funny, she wasn't like it as a child. You'll find it hard to believe, but she was a delightful, happy-go-lucky little creature.' Dorothy gave a shrug of resignation. 'Things change. She adored her father and was devasted when he died. As you know, he left us in financial difficulties, and it was hard to protect his memory. Discovering he wasn't what she'd believed him to be had a shattering effect.'

Helen's thoughts turned to her own father – his promise of a family holiday in Kent and her mother's reaction when she'd discovered they'd be living in a caravan and picking hops. Then that long trek back to the railway station carrying their suitcases.

'You lost your own father at a young age, I believe?' Dorothy said.

'That's right. I was twelve.' Helen had never seen her father again after they'd left the hop farm. She didn't know if he was still alive and didn't care. Even at such a young age, she'd realised he'd only begged them to stay because he was desperate for the money he hoped they'd earn for him.

'It must have been difficult for you and your mother. Georgina and I had our hard times. I hoped marrying Joseph and coming to Merewood Manor would bring her some stability. Unfortunately, she has a habit of choosing unsuitable men. Then, because they let her down, she thinks bad things always happen to her. I'm hoping Clifford Knight might change that.'

'She's been through a lot recently,' Helen said diplomatically. 'Superintendent Townsend's questioning probably hasn't helped.'

'I know he's only doing his job, but he can be heavy-handed. He virtually accused her of murdering poor Morgan. It's increased her paranoia.'

'His visits unsettled the patients too.'

Dorothy frowned. 'And now this business with the bird. Who was in the hospital at the time?'

'Albert, Nathan and Oliver were in the ward. I'm not sure where Dr Bingham was. They said they hadn't seen him since breakfast. I was in the south barn for most of the morning with Richard. Do you know what he's done with the bird?'

'He's taken it to the police station. He wants them to test it for poison. Whoever's playing these tricks has a cruel sense of humour.' Dorothy reached out and patted her hand. 'Given what's happened, would you like to move out of the hospital and come here? No one would blame you if you did.'

'Thank you, Dorothy. I'd like that very much. But not yet. The patients are too vulnerable. I can only leave the hospital once they're settled. It's what I came to speak to you about. How's Nathan getting on? He seems much improved. Even after what happened this morning, he stayed calm and was able to take care of Kate.'

'Indeed, he was.' Dorothy's eyes twinkled. 'Young Kate has been singing his praises. As have Gulliver and Richard.'

'Are there any permanent jobs going here at the manor? I think he'll thrive if he has employment and a place to live. He just needs some stability.'

'I've already spoken to my husband, and he's agreed I can hire Nathan as an undergardener. Believe me, we're as anxious as you are to close the hospital. What's happening with Albert?'

Helen told her of his decision to return to his father. And to resume his courtship of Emma.

'We're nearly there.' Dorothy's smile was almost triumphant. 'And what about you, my dear? Have you given any more thought to your future? I hope you're not considering Dr Bingham's ridiculous scheme?'

'I was.'

'But not any more?'

'No. Not after this morning.'

'What will you do?'

'I'm going to apply for a position at the Royal Victoria Hospital.'

'Have you ever contemplated marriage?'

Helen smiled. 'I'd have to give up nursing.'

Dorothy tutted. 'Ridiculous, isn't it? I thought the war would change all that. In my opinion, a married woman has infinitely more experience of dealing with intimate matters...' She waved a hand. 'You know what I mean. But never mind all that. You deserve to be looked after for a change. Perhaps by a loving husband?'

Helen guessed she was hinting at Richard. Before she could think of a non-committal response, the door swung open, and Joseph Wintringham burst into the room.

'Bloody Knight's pulled out of the deal. Can you believe it?'

'Why?' Dorothy asked.

'He's been listening to village gossip and got himself into a state about the hospital. He thinks the place is cursed and says his workers will refuse to come here. Bloody superstitious claptrap.' Joseph suddenly became aware of her presence. 'Sorry, Sister Hopgood. I do apologise, I didn't realise you were here.' He gave her a polite nod. 'You may as well tell Bingham the farm is his if he wants it. Because no one else does.'

25

Samuel's meeting with Joseph Wintringham had been brief. And his jubilation short-lived.

Frederick had accosted him as soon as he'd left Joseph's study. 'The sale won't go ahead, you know.'

Samuel had to resist the urge to tell him to go to hell. 'Your father and I have agreed terms, and his solicitor is drawing up a contract.' Diplomatically, he added, 'I'm sorry if the idea of the hospital becoming a sanatorium displeases you. It will be a peaceful place, and I can assure you it won't have a detrimental effect on Merewood.'

Frederick glowered at him. 'You're a fool.'

Georgina was standing at the foot of the stairs, listening to their conversation. To Samuel's alarm, she looked like she was about to faint.

He crossed the hall and went over to her. 'Are you feeling ill, Miss Vane? You look rather pale.'

Despite the warmth of the morning, she gripped her shawl around her. Her lips trembled. 'You only want a sanatorium so you'll have more patients to kill.'

'Good grief, Georgie. That's a bit much,' Frederick said but still gave a snort of laughter.

Deciding that further conversation with either of them was futile, Samuel made for the door.

His morning didn't improve when he returned to the hospital. Finding Helen in the kitchen, he grabbed her hand and dragged her into his office, coming to an abrupt halt when he saw Superintendent Townsend was seated behind his desk. The bloody man didn't even get up when they entered.

'Good morning, Dr Bingham. Sister Hopgood said you wouldn't be long, so I decided to wait.' He gestured to a chair. 'Please, take a seat.'

Samuel couldn't believe the temerity of the man. His office reeked of Townsend's cologne.

'Would you like me to close the door?' Helen had pulled her hand away and was edging out of the room.

Samuel didn't want to be left alone with the policeman. 'Please stay, Sister Hopgood.' He forced a smile. 'We have no secrets.'

Townsend smiled back. 'Is that so? Have you told Sister Hopgood that you didn't write to St Dunstan's about David Cowper?'

'I... I... told you that in confidence,' Samuel spluttered.

Helen stared at him, then sank into a chair. 'I don't understand. You told me they said David wasn't a suitable candidate.'

Samuel's loathing for the superintendent reached new heights. He knew Townsend had done this to see how he would react. He hated the way the man was watching him. Even worse was the look Helen gave him.

Resisting the urge to run from the room, he tried to placate her. 'He wasn't a suitable candidate. I did try to explain that to you. It wasn't worth wasting their time. David was better off here with us.'

She pursed her lips and said nothing.

Townsend suddenly stood up. 'I'd like to take another look in your medicine cabinet if I may.'

He stiffened. 'Why?'

'Just give me the key.' Townsend held out his hand.

Samuel bit back a retort and took the key from his drawer. His face flushed as he realised he'd left it there after his last conversation with the superintendent. It clearly hadn't been hidden away as he'd said it was.

Rather than handing Townsend the key, he unlocked the medicine cabinet himself.

The superintendent peered inside. 'Do you keep morphine?'

'A small quantity, about six vials.'

'*About* six vials? Or exactly six vials?'

Samuel pointed. 'As you can see, there are six vials here.'

'You're not aware of any missing?'

'No. Why do you ask?'

'Because the sparrowhawk that found its way onto your kitchen table had been poisoned with morphine.'

Samuel heard Helen gasp. He avoided looking at her and regarded Townsend with what he hoped was disdain.

'As you can see, it did not come from my medicine cabinet.'

'Can you tell me what you were doing on Wednesday morning? I've been informed that no one saw you between breakfast and late afternoon.'

Samuel sank back into his chair. 'I was walking around the estate. You already know of my intention to buy Merewood Farm. I wanted to inspect certain areas more closely.'

'Which areas?'

'The field where the cows were kept, the barns and the old chicken coop. I'd like to re-introduce some farming elements once my sanatorium is up and running.'

'Have you and Mr Wintringham agreed terms for your purchase?'

Samuel nodded. 'I was about to share the wonderful news with Sister Hopgood.'

He turned to Helen, but she avoided his gaze, staring down into her lap.

'Do you still have three patients on the ward?' Townsend asked.

'Albert Gates, Nathan Smith and Oliver Edwards,' Helen replied.

'And will they remain here as patients?'

'My hope—'

Samuel was interrupted by Helen.

'Nathan is going to start a new job at the manor and will be given accommodation in the servant's quarters once a room has been prepared.'

'Nathan can stay here and still do odd jobs at the manor. There's no need for him to leave,' Samuel muttered.

She ignored him. 'Leonard Gates, Albert's father, is coming on Friday to take him home.'

'This is the first I've heard of Albert leaving. It's too soon,' he protested. 'The poor chap still has a fixation with his skin. I need more time with him. When was all this arranged?'

'Albert has been more receptive to the idea of going home since Emma's visit. Leonard is going to come and collect him so he doesn't have to travel on the train on his own.' She turned to Townsend and said, 'Emma is Albert's fiancée.'

'There's no need for him to leave just yet.' Samuel knew Townsend was watching this exchange with interest. Maybe even enjoyment. He gritted his teeth. 'I'm writing a case study on Albert's condition. It's an important piece of work.'

'Albert will be going home on Friday with his father.' Helen's tone left him in no doubt hers was the final word on the matter.

Samuel could sense her anger and wondered if he'd ever be able to persuade her that he'd acted in David's best interest. Given what had happened to him, it was unlikely.

26

Richard laid his jacket on the ground so Helen could sit down. Elsewhere on the estate, the earth was hard and dry and the grass brown. There had been little rain in the last week. Only the dense woodland was cool and damp.

'The sparrowhawk was given morphine.'

Richard could hear the anger in Helen's voice.

He nodded. 'Townsend told me. He wanted to know what poisons we use in the gardens. I told him just arsenic for the rats. I put it inside crevices that the birds can't get to.'

'Who do you think's doing this? Could it be Frederick? He likes killing things.'

'He would have shot the bird. Although I've never known him to aim at a hunter. He admires them. And he's not a very good shot. He takes on easy prey like rabbits and pigeons. A fox or hawk would be too fast for him. He's not quick off the mark.'

'Perhaps that's why he chose to poison her?'

'He's a sick bastard, whoever he is.'

'Or she.'

He glanced at her. 'You think it's a woman?'

She shrugged. 'I suppose I'm becoming suspicious of everyone.'

'Me too. Everyone but you.'

She looked at him curiously – a slight smile hovered on her lips. 'You don't suspect me?'

'Oliver told me the bird wasn't on the table when he went into the kitchen to get a glass of water at around half past eleven. Kate brought over the lunch an hour later. Someone put it there while we were in the barn.' He moved his head closer to hers. 'Besides, I know you would never have harmed that bird.'

'And neither would you,' she whispered.

The kiss came naturally. Richard didn't have to think about it, he just leant forward and put his lips to hers. His hand reached up to touch her hair and found that damned white cap in the way. He wanted to rip it from her head. And as for that starched apron. He thought of her in the pink sundress instead.

They sprang apart when they heard the rustle of leaves nearby. Helen laughed, and Richard was relieved to see a squirrel eyeing them cautiously before darting forward to grab an acorn lying at their feet.

He was embarrassed by the fear he'd felt at the noise. He supposed it was nothing to be ashamed of under the circumstances.

'We need to get away from here,' he said.

She nodded. 'Albert and Nathan are almost settled. Albert's father is coming tomorrow. Dorothy says she'll make sure Nathan's room is ready at the manor so he isn't left behind without Albert. They've become close.' She took his hand. 'That just leaves Oliver.'

'He's coming to live with me, even if I have to drag him to the cottage.' Richard hoped Oliver would see that he couldn't remain on the ward after Albert and Nathan had left. 'It's you I'm worried about. You can't stay there with Bingham.'

'Dorothy has arranged a room for me at the manor.' Helen looked thoughtful. 'Do you think Samuel...?'

Richard shrugged. 'You don't believe Morgan and David committed suicide, and neither do I. He lied to you about David. And who else knew where the portrait of Dorothy was? Not many people could have put that skeleton in your bath or the sparrowhawk on the table.'

Helen nodded slowly, then said, 'I have to get back.'

Richard cupped his hand behind her head, resting his fingers on the long muslin cap, and pulled her face towards his. The kiss began slowly, almost relaxed, then became more intense, more heated.

He breathed heavily. 'Don't stay at the farm tonight. Come to my cottage.'

She stood up. 'I can't. Not while the hospital still has patients.'

When they left the wood, he saw Townsend and Newman standing by the lake. Beyond them, Bingham was talking to Oliver on the patio outside the ward.

Despite the policemen's presence, Richard wanted to bundle Oliver and Helen into his car and drive them as far away from Merewood as possible.

* * *

'Do you still think it's the good doctor?' Newman asked.

'He's hiding something.' Townsend watched Bingham usher Oliver Edwards back into the ward.

'What about Sister Hopgood?'

He shook his head. 'She's beginning to turn against him. I almost felt sorry for Bingham. You don't want to be on the receiving end of one of her stares.'

'I get the impression she's started to look elsewhere.' Newman indicated to where Helen and Richard were strolling side by side, their hands almost touching. They were coming out of Gibbet Wood. 'Is she in danger?'

Townsend wished he knew. 'Not from Bingham. I think he wants her too much. But...'

'But it might not be Bingham?'

He nodded.

'How about young Frederick Wintringham?' Newman was now looking toward the manor. 'He told Richard Locke he wanted to move into Merewood Farm. If you ask me, he's as barmy as his step-sister. And he had a thing for Isabel Taplin, didn't he?'

'When we interviewed him at the time, he told us he wanted to marry her, but his father wasn't keen.'

'He definitely didn't kill her?'

Townsend shook his head. 'I checked his alibi myself. He was at Newbury races and didn't get back until after her body was found. I spoke to several racehorse owners who spent the afternoon with him and one who stayed out drinking with him until about ten o'clock that night.'

'What time did Isabel Taplin go missing?'

Townsend knew the events of that day by heart. He'd gone over them often enough. 'She left the hospital at two o'clock that after-noon. One of the nurses said she was wearing her favourite dress with a scarf around her neck that was pinned with a brooch. A grey pearl thing. The nurse said she'd never seen Isabel wearing the brooch before. We assume she must have been meeting someone.'

'A man? Maybe he gave her the brooch.'

'Seems likely. No one saw which direction she went off in. It was a warm afternoon, and some of the patients were in deckchairs on the patio. They would have seen her if she walked across to the lake or up into Gibbet Wood.'

'Perhaps she walked into the village by the lanes.'

'That's what we thought. She could have decided to return by taking the shorter route through the woods. The only thing is, no one in Greybridge saw her that afternoon. It's a small village, and she was pretty enough to turn heads.'

Newman considered the red brick walls of the farmhouse. 'Not many places to go around here. She could have walked along the lane in the opposite direction, which would have taken her up to the manor. And if she went passed the back of the house, she could have entered Gibbet Wood from the eastern side. Who was home that day?'

'Dorothy Wintringham and Georgina Vane spent some time with the patients by the lake and then returned to the manor. They said they were in the garden reading for most of the afternoon. Joseph Wintringham was in his study and then joined them in the garden before going up to his bedroom to change for dinner. They dined at about eight o'clock that night.'

'Could Joseph have done it? You said he didn't want his son to marry the nurse. Presumably it was because of money.'

Townsend nodded. 'Wintringham isn't as rich as he used to be. Taxes might force him to sell the manor. Can't see him murdering a nurse over it, though. It's not as if there are many heiresses out there for Frederick to marry. And there's no indication Taplin was keen enough on him to say yes if he did propose.'

'And Locke found her body?'

'Taplin didn't show up for her shift at five o'clock. Matron was worried and asked Sister Hopgood to find Richard Locke and get him to search for her. He discovered her body in Gibbet Wood at about seven thirty that evening.'

'Could there be a connection with the patients? Perhaps Frederick wants his revenge.'

'He certainly made a fuss afterwards. Kept turning up at the police station demanding we investigate some poor bloke or another that he'd decided was a suspect. There was nothing in any of it. The interesting thing is, when we told him that, he seemed relieved.'

The lines on Newman's brow deepened. 'Why?'

'I got the impression he was trying to find out if she'd been seeing someone else. It's an obvious assumption to make, isn't it? Beautiful young woman killed by a spurned or jealous lover.'

'And you didn't find one?'

Townsend shook his head. 'It seems she toyed with men. Liked the attention, but the other nurses said it was no more than that.'

'What about the artist? Victor Protheroe.'

Townsend grinned. 'He liked painting women. But that's all he enjoyed doing with them. He was more attracted to the masculine form, if you get my drift. Besides, he was holding an art class that afternoon. It's possible he sneaked off into the woods afterwards, though we couldn't find any evidence of it.'

'You never found a credible suspect?'

'Not one. We interviewed the patients and staff at the hospital, the family and servants at the manor and half the village. The theft of the brooch could indicate it was a random attack.'

'There was no sexual assault?'

'No. A straightforward strangulation. Her own scarf was used. Someone pulled it tight round her neck.'

'If it was a random attack just to steal the brooch, the killer could be long gone.' Newman frowned. 'But where had she been that afternoon?'

'If we knew that, we might have some clue as to who murdered her.'

27

After lunch, Helen waited in the yard until Richard pulled up in his battered Vauxhall car and Mr Gates got out.

She ushered Leonard into the kitchen, where Dorothy and Joseph had joined Samuel and the patients to give Albert a send-off. Kate had cleared away the lunch plates and brought out a Victoria sponge for afters. Nathan was helping her set out cups and saucers on the table.

Helen couldn't help feeling exasperated by Samuel's sulky expression. Everyone else was pleased Albert was finally going home – even Oliver was less moody than usual.

After introducing Leonard to Dorothy and Joseph, Helen slipped out of the kitchen and went to the ward where Richard was waiting.

He smiled at her. 'Well done.'

'What for?'

'This.' He pointed to the suitcases that stood beside two of the beds. 'You helped them to reach this point.'

She gave a rueful smile. 'I haven't been able to persuade Oliver to pack any of his belongings yet.'

'I told you, leave him to me. Your work is done.' He leant forward and pressed his lips to hers.

'Not on the ward,' Helen said before she could stop herself. Then she laughed and shook her head. 'Perhaps this isn't a ward any longer.'

'As soon as the last patient leaves, this is officially no longer a ward. And Merewood Farm ceases to be a hospital,' Richard declared.

She allowed him a quick kiss before presenting him with Albert's case. 'Put this in the car.'

He saluted. 'Yes, Sister Hopgood. I'll collect Nathan's when I come back from the station.'

He headed for the kitchen, and she was about to follow when she became aware of someone watching her. A pair of large violet eyes peered in through the patio doors.

'I thought something was going on between you and Richard,' Georgina commented. 'Lucky you.'

Helen blushed. 'Have you come to say goodbye to Albert?'

Georgina ignored the question. 'I always choose the wrong men. Except Morgan.' She gazed at the space where his bed had been. 'I miss him.'

Helen went over to her. 'So do I. He was a brave man.' She wanted to say he was a good man, but that wasn't strictly true. 'The patients miss him too.'

She nodded. 'He was kind to them. And to me.'

Helen held out her hand. 'Everyone's in the kitchen having tea and cake. Why don't we join them?'

Georgina backed away. 'I can't come in. This place is cursed.' With that, she hurried away.

Helen was about to close the doors when Frederick Wintringham barged in, shotgun over his shoulder. Dexter trotted around the ward, sniffing the beds. Normally she would have shooed him out and taken a mop to the floor. Now there didn't seem to be any point.

'On your own?' Frederick glanced at the empty beds. 'Have all the patients gone at last?'

'I hope to be able to close the ward by the end of the day,' she replied.

'About bloody time.' He gave her an apologetic look. 'Not that I'm blaming you. Dorothy told us how much you've done to help them. It's that bloody doctor who's been dragging his heels. If I have my way, this hospital won't re-open in any shape or form.'

She didn't reply. In truth, she felt the same. Merewood Farm's days as a hospital were best left in the past.

He regarded her with a curious expression. 'What do you think happened?'

The question unsettled her. 'To Morgan and David, you mean?'

He shook his head. 'Isabel. Was she seeing someone? I thought... I thought she had feelings for me.' He looked like a bewildered child. 'Perhaps I was wrong.'

'Nurse Taplin was a lovely young woman. She had many admirers, though I don't think she had a boyfriend.' Helen saw the flicker of relief in his eyes and pushed memories of Isabel's flirting from her mind.

'She didn't favour anyone in particular?' His attempt at indifference failed miserably.

'I wasn't in Nurse Taplin's confidence,' she answered truthfully. 'As far as I'm aware, she concentrated on her nursing duties. You must remember things were very different then. There was little time for socialising when we had so many patients to care for.'

This wasn't strictly true. Some of the nurses had gone to dances in the outlying villages and formed friendships with the locals. She remembered Matron reprimanding Isabel on more than one occasion for being late for her shift.

'Yes, of course.' Frederick sounded doubtful but gave a curt nod and strode out. Dexter took a last sniff around, then charged after him.

Helen closed the patio doors before anyone else could intrude. She returned to the kitchen to find Samuel finishing some sort of speech.

'I'm sure you'll all join me in wishing Albert well in his new life. We're going to miss his presence in the hospital.'

She exchanged a glance with Richard. Didn't Samuel realise that by this evening, there would be no hospital?

When it was over, Oliver, who'd been listening impatiently, slapped Albert on the back. 'Best of luck, mate,' he muttered, then quickly retreated to the ward.

Helen noticed Richard pick up a cup of tea and slice of cake and follow him.

The rest of the gathering went out into the yard, and Albert mumbled his thanks when Joseph Wintringham handed him an envelope, saying it was 'A little something to help you get back on your feet'. Joseph then strode off in the direction of the north barn, clearly feeling his duty was done.

When Albert's hand instinctively rose to scratch his face, Helen took it in hers and squeezed it.

'No more of that.'

'Thank you, Sister Hopgood. For looking after me.'

'It was a pleasure. It's time for someone else to take care of you from now on. Don't give Emma any trouble now, will you,' she chided with a wink.

He gave one of his rare cheeky grins. 'I won't, I promise. I know I'm lucky she stuck by me, and I'll try to make it up to her.'

'Good. Then you'll be just fine.'

'Write to m-m-me,' Nathan stammered. Although his speech was much improved, his symptoms returned when he became stressed or emotional. His facial muscles were beginning to twitch, and Helen feared Samuel would use this as an argument for him to stay longer.

Albert gave Nathan a hug. 'I will. Take care of yourself, mate.'

Richard reappeared and held open the rear door of the car. She hoped he'd had more luck persuading Oliver to pack his case than she had.

Helen stood in the yard with Dorothy, Nathan and Kate, waving at Albert and his father until the car was out of sight. Samuel had already disappeared inside.

'When Mr Locke comes back, he's going to take your belongings up to the manor,' Helen told Nathan.

'In the meantime, why don't you go up to the house with Kate, and she can show you your room?' Dorothy suggested.

Helen could sense Nathan's nerves and noticed Kate give his arm a playful tug.

'They make a pretty couple, don't you think?' Dorothy said as she watched them go.

Helen smiled. 'I only asked you to find him a job. You didn't have to provide a girlfriend as well.'

Dorothy laughed. 'I like to encourage young people. What about you, my dear? Would you like to come back to the manor with me now?'

'I need to help Richard get Oliver settled in the cottage first.'

Dorothy pulled a face. 'Good luck with that.'

Helen returned to the kitchen and began to pile dirty cups and saucers into the sink. She was curious to know where she'd be sleeping at the manor but hadn't liked to ask Dorothy. Would she be sharing with one of the maids? Hopefully, she wouldn't be there for long. That morning, she'd received a letter inviting her for an interview at the Royal Victoria. She should tell Samuel the news.

She placed the last cup on the drainer and went into the corridor, wiping her hands on her apron. Samuel's office door was open, but he wasn't at his desk. She could hear him in the ward, talking to Oliver. Was he going to try to convince him to stay? Helen hesitated, then went back to the kitchen. It would be easier to tackle Oliver when Richard was around.

When she heard the car pull up outside, she went out into the yard. Richard wasn't even out of the driver's seat before she began to question him.

'How was Albert at the train station? Did he seem nervous? He's been here a long time. I hope he wasn't too overwhelmed by everything.'

Richard held up his hand to stop her. 'He was fine. In fact, he seemed to be looking forward to the train journey.'

He must have noticed her frown as he asked, 'What's the matter? I thought you'd be pleased.'

She gave a sad shake of her head. 'I can't help thinking I should have acted sooner. Been firmer with Albert and got him out of here before now.'

'Sister Hopgood, you cannot be responsible for everyone.' He drew her toward him. 'It's time you started thinking about yourself. And your future.'

Helen felt the heat rise between them and pulled away. 'Your next task awaits. Nathan has already gone to the manor with Kate. He knows you're bringing his suitcase up in the car.'

'How's Oliver?'

'Samuel's been speaking to him.'

He groaned. 'Persuading him to stay?'

Helen shrugged. 'I'm not sure.'

There was no sign of Samuel in his office or on the ward. Oliver was sitting at the table, pencil in hand, working on a sketch of Frederick's horse, Blaze.

Richard picked up Nathan's case. 'I'm taking this up to the

manor. When I come back, we can sort your things out.'

'If you say so,' Oliver replied, without looking up from his drawing.

Helen saw Richard's troubled expression and watched him trudge down the corridor with the case. She picked up the empty cup and plate on the table and headed to the kitchen. The door to Samuel's office was still open and he wasn't at his desk. As she washed up, she heard the car start and drive away. In the silence that followed, she realised it was just her and Oliver left in the hospital.

When she returned to the ward, he shot her an inquisitive glance.

'Do you think we'll get out of here alive?' he asked in a dreamy voice.

Startled, she walked over to him, unnerved by his indifferent expression. His apparent lack of fear contradicted the brutality of his words.

She forced a smile. 'I don't believe in silly curses, and I'm sure you don't either. Nevertheless, the ward has to close. You will go and stay with Richard, won't you?'

'Probably. What about you? Are you deserting him, too?' Oliver nodded in the direction of the corridor. She presumed he meant Samuel.

'I've applied for a position at the Royal Victoria Hospital in Southampton.'

'I mean now. You won't stay here alone with him, will you?'

'Mrs Wintringham has offered me a room at the manor. I can sort out the remaining inventories from there.'

'Good.' He turned back to his drawing, and she knew the conversation was at an end.

She went over to Albert's bed and began to strip the sheets, wondering if she'd been too quick to suspect Oliver of killing the sparrowhawk. He was a difficult man to fathom.

Helen removed the linen from Albert and Nathan's beds, deciding to tackle Oliver's later. It would be insensitive to strip his bed when he was still on the ward.

As she hauled the laundry bag along the corridor, she saw Samuel seated at his desk. She leant the bag against the wall and stood in the doorway to his office.

'Samuel, you can't stay here like this. There'll be no more food coming over from the manor. Dorothy has suggested you take lodgings in the local pub until you can sort out suitable accommodation.'

'I'll manage here. I'll find someone in the village to come in each day to cook and clean for me. I need to be on site to organise my renovations.'

'Everyone in the village thinks Merewood Farm is cursed. No one will set foot in the place.'

'I'll change their minds. We've just been through a rough patch, that's all. Once the sanatorium is up and running, everyone will see what a wonderful place it is.' He smiled at her. 'And I hope you will too. I understand it wouldn't be seemly for you to stay here in the present circumstances. However, I hope you're still considering my offer.'

Helen shook her head. 'I've got an interview at the Royal Victoria Hospital.'

To her alarm, he rose and came over to her, reaching out to take hold of her hands. 'Helen. I should have made my feelings for you clearer before now. I don't just want you as a nurse, I want you as my wife.'

She stared at him in disbelief. 'Samuel—'

'Think about it, please,' he begged. 'I've never met anyone like you. Your compassion, your dedication. With you by my side, I can make my vision a reality.'

'I can't stay here.' When she tried to pull her hands away, his grip tightened.

'Don't you see? This is a way for you to marry and keep your job.' His eagerness bordered on desperation. 'No hospital will employ a married nurse. But here, as man and wife, we'd be equal. We could achieve great things together.'

'Let go of her.'

Helen jumped at the sound of the low voice behind her. Richard stepped between them, forcing Samuel to relinquish his grasp.

'This is a private conversation,' Samuel spluttered. 'Please leave my office at once.'

'With pleasure.' Richard stood back and gestured for Helen to go first.

She hurried from the room, and he followed.

'Helen. We still have patients... a patient, to attend to,' Samuel called, scurrying after them.

'Oliver's leaving too,' Richard said over his shoulder.

'No, not yet,' Samuel panted.

Helen could hear the pair of them jostling behind her. 'Please don't distress Oliver. He's told me he's happy to leave. Oliver, it's time to—' The words died on her lips as she entered the ward.

Richard and Samuel came to a standstill behind her. Oliver had collapsed across the table, his right hand dangling over the edge. His face lay on his sketch pad, and pencils were scattered on the floor around him.

Richard reached him first, gently lifting his friend's shoulders. Oliver's head slumped forward onto his chest.

'What is it? What's wrong with him? Oliver, wake up.'

Samuel placed his fingers on Oliver's wrist. Then he touched his neck.

'I'm sorry,' he said gruffly. 'He's dead.'

28

'Do you know where Oliver Edwards' drawing box is?' Superintendent Townsend rested his arms on the wings of an ornately carved mahogany chair. Joseph Wintringham had offered him the use of his study, and he had to admit he was enjoying the feeling of power the luxurious surroundings gave him. It certainly made a change from conducting interviews in a room at the station that smelt of disinfectant.

'His what?' Richard replied irritably.

Townsend glanced at Newman. They were struggling to get much out of Locke. 'His drawing box. Apparently he used it all the time. You must have noticed it had gone. It's quite distinctive – antique mahogany with a shell pattern in satinwood.'

'Of course, I didn't notice. I had other things on my mind, such as the death of my friend.'

'Mr Edwards must have had it with him when he died. Both Sister Hopgood and Dr Bingham said he was sketching at the table when they last saw him.'

He saw Richard's expression change and guessed the man was beginning to realise what he was getting at. The drawing box should have been on the table next to Oliver. He knew what its disappearance would signify.

'I didn't notice it.' Richard was loosening his collar and starting to look nauseous.

'Then where's it gone?' The room was hot and smelt of stale cigars, and Townsend guessed Richard was longing to be out in the fresh air. Newman was watching them from a chair at the side of the room. He'd asked his sergeant to try to discern whether the man was as grief-stricken as he appeared to be.

'I don't know where it's gone. Does its disappearance mean he was murdered?'

Townsend rotated his pen with his fingers. 'What do you think?'

'I think you should have been there to protect him,' Richard snapped. 'I thought you were supposed to be keeping an eye on the place.'

'A constable was around all day, either outside the hospital or at the manor. He didn't see anything suspicious.'

To Townsend's frustration, they were interrupted by Frederick Wintringham, who marched in without knocking.

'I've figured out how he did it.' The young man's face was flushed with excitement. He certainly wasn't exhibiting any signs of grief.

'How who did what?' Townsend masked his annoyance, aware he was taking advantage of the Wintringhams' hospitality.

'Bingham.' Frederick waggled a finger at him. 'The crafty beggar. I know how he killed that sparrowhawk. Come with me, and I'll show you.'

'Where is it that you want us to go?' Townsend glanced at Newman, who shrugged.

'The pheasant pens.'

Richard was already out of his seat. Reluctantly, Townsend got up too. He couldn't salvage this interview, so he might as well go

and see what Frederick was talking about. He motioned for
Newman to follow.

'How do the pens work?' Townsend asked Richard as they
trailed after Frederick. 'I'm woefully ignorant on the subject of
rearing pheasants.'

'When they're large enough, the pheasant poults are moved
from the rearing pen to an open-topped pen at the edge of the
woodland. They get used to the habitat – the shrubs and trees – and
start roosting under cover at night. They grow to maturity in time to
be released when the shooting season begins in October. Mere-
wood is famous for its pheasant shoots, though Mr Wintringham
wasn't able to hold them during the war.'

At the pens, Frederick took some grain from his pocket and
easily managed to lure one of the poults out. 'I saw Bingham up
here, feeding them, and wondered what he was doing. Didn't take
much notice at the time. But I've figured it out now. He was
poisoning one of the chicks.'

Richard nodded slowly. 'The sparrowhawk lurks in that tree
over there.' He pointed to a Scots pine. 'If he left the chick at the
base of the tree, she'd devour it.'

'Precisely,' Frederick said in triumph.

'Do sparrowhawks eat carrion? I thought they were hunters,'
Townsend said.

'They'll eat anything when they're hungry enough, which she
was,' Richard replied. 'She had chicks to feed. Morphine would
have knocked out a bird that size pretty quickly. He must have
waited and then scooped her up.'

Townsend considered this. 'You think Dr Bingham fed poison to
a young pheasant, which killed it, and left its corpse for the spar-
rowhawk to find and eat? Would he have the knowledge to do that?'

'I told him that sparrowhawks nest nearby. He's been asking me
a lot of questions about animals and pheasants recently.' Richard

rubbed his bloodshot eyes. 'He said it was because he wanted the farm to form part of his sanatorium.'

'Why would he play such a nasty trick?' Townsend asked.

'To get Merewood Farm, of course.' Frederick was looking at him as if he was an idiot. 'All he cares about is his bloody sanatorium. Baden Knight's withdrawn his offer because it's all over the village the farm's cursed. His workers have said they won't go near the place.'

Richard nodded, muttering, 'Bingham's obsessed with the hospital.'

'It was Bingham's skeleton Sister Hopgood found in her bath. It was his scalpel used to slash my stepmother's portrait. And I'm bloody sure it was his morphine used to poison the sparrowhawk. And what followed each trick?' Frederick jabbed a finger at Townsend's chest. 'The death of one of his patients.'

'We don't yet know how Mr Edwards died,' Townsend replied, although he and Newman were working on the assumption that the pathologist would find morphine in the man's body.

'I know how he died,' Richard growled. 'Bingham killed him.'

29

Richard was desperate to escape into the quiet and shade of Gibbet Wood. It had rained in the night, and everything felt cooler and fresher. He took in a lungful of air in a bid to clear his aching head.

He rubbed his eyes, feeling overwhelmingly tired. He'd only managed a few hours' sleep. By contrast, Frederick seemed to be bouncing with energy. Richard felt a sharp stab of resentment that the young man had pretended to be Oliver's friend yet showed no signs of grief over his death.

As he turned to walk away, he heard Frederick say to Townsend, 'What about Isabel? Bingham must have killed her too.'

He kept walking, not wanting to hear the reply.

While they'd been talking by the pheasant pens, he'd spotted a figure by the lake. When he saw the person was hurrying to catch up with him, he realised it was Helen. She wasn't wearing her nurse's uniform.

He stopped, and as she walked towards him, Richard's eyes followed the contours of her body. She was dressed in a pale green linen frock, and although it reached her ankles, it didn't disguise the power in her legs. What riveted him most was the line of her neck. It was usually covered at the back by her long muslin cap.

'Are you alright?' she panted.

He nodded and took her hand, leading her to their usual spot by the sparrowhawks' nest. It was out of sight of anyone taking the path through the woods to get to the village.

When they reached the nesting tree, they both peered up. There was no sign of activity. He found a patch of grass dry enough to sit on, and they lowered themselves to the ground.

'I couldn't sleep for thinking about Oliver. Picturing him dead at the table in that damned ward. It was a relief to know you were at the manor. Are they looking after you?'

'Dorothy and Joseph have been very kind. I expected to be given a room in the servant's quarters, but they've put me in a guest bedroom. It's the grandest room I've ever stayed in.' She hesitated. 'I couldn't help thinking of Samuel alone at Merewood Farm. I wish he would leave.'

Richard's jaw clenched. 'He'll never leave. That's what this is all about.' He explained Frederick's theory.

Her brow creased. 'Samuel? I can't believe it.'

He wrapped an arm around her shoulder. 'Why was he spending time by the pheasant pens?'

'Because he's been inspecting the farm, making plans for his sanatorium.'

Richard shook his head. 'He did it. He killed them.'

'We don't know how Oliver died. It could have been his heart.'

'Or someone could have poisoned him – like the sparrowhawk. He did it. I know he did.'

Richard waited for her to defend her precious doctor again. She stayed silent, but he knew she wasn't convinced.

'Who else could it have been?' he asked.

'What about Frederick? He was in the ward that morning. He said that Merewood Farm would never be a hospital again.'

Richard considered this. 'I don't know. He's all bluster. I'm not sure he's got the cunning.'

'Georgina was around yesterday morning, too. She's definitely unstable, though she's scared to enter the farmhouse. She believes it's haunted by evil spirits.'

He closed his eyes and leant his head on her shoulder, nestling into her neck. 'I don't know what to think.'

'I'm sorry about Oliver. I wish I could have done more for him.'

'You did more than anyone else. He was difficult, I know that. But he'd suffered.'

She stroked his hair. 'The war left so many scars. Some visible, some not.'

Richard sat up, a sudden movement in the branches of the pine catching his eye. 'Look.' He pointed to the tree. The male sparrowhawk was visiting the nest.

'He hasn't brought any food.' Disappointment laced Helen's voice. 'What do you think has happened to the chicks?'

'They won't have survived without their mother. Too young.' He squeezed her hand. 'He'll go on to find a new mate. He could even breed again this season.'

'Bastard.'

He guessed she wasn't talking about the sparrowhawk. Did she mean Bingham? He found her use of the swear word almost comical. Was he going to see a different side to Helen now she'd discarded her uniform? The thought aroused him, and he had to resist the urge to run his fingers along her neck, across her throat and down to her breasts. Her pale skin reminded him of someone else.

'What about Isabel Taplin?' His voice was unexpectedly hoarse. 'What do you think happened to her?'

'Frederick asked me that question. He wanted to know if she had any boyfriends.'

'And did she?'

Helen shrugged. 'She certainly had admirers. It was difficult to tell if she'd formed an attachment to any of them.'

'I know I said I suspected Victor Protheroe, but let's say it wasn't him. Did Bingham like her?'

She hesitated. 'Samuel always behaved impeccably around the nurses. He can be a little pompous on occasion, but he's always professional.'

'He didn't behave very professionally yesterday.' He saw her blush. 'Anyway, that's not what I asked. Did he like her?'

'She used to flirt with him. I'm not sure if she really liked him, but he was the head doctor and quite a catch. It was a game to her – she liked to show the other nurses how much power she had over men. Of course, Samuel was flattered. He probably imagined the girl was in love with him.'

Richard felt a fool, and not for the first time since Isabel's death. He'd soon come to realise he wasn't the only man she'd played up to. He remembered her laughing about Frederick, calling him a silly boy. She'd thought it was funny when he'd told her that Frederick wanted to marry her. She swore she hadn't encouraged him. He now realised she'd been lying.

'Bingham could have killed her out of jealousy,' he suggested. 'Did you tell the police she flirted with him?'

She shook her head. 'There was nothing to tell. I didn't think there was anything in it. I wasn't in Isabel's confidence, but she never gave me the impression of having a particular preference for anyone.'

'You should mention it to Townsend,' Richard urged. Helen was silent, and he waited, curious to see how she'd respond. Would she do as he asked or stay loyal to Bingham?

Eventually, she nodded. 'Alright. If you think it's important.'

* * *

Samuel crouched low behind the machinery in the north barn. All was quiet apart from the cooing of the doves in the rafters. He found the repetitive sound comforting.

He knew he couldn't stay there much longer. Townsend would come in search of him unless he returned to the farmhouse soon.

That morning, Samuel had woken up in an empty hospital, the ward just a collection of unfilled beds. He looked down and realised he was wearing a white coat. He'd automatically put it on after breakfast, even though he had no rounds to do.

It was time to face the fact he no longer had any patients. And he no longer had Helen.

When he'd seen her earlier, walking by the lake, she hadn't been wearing her uniform. The significance of this had disturbed him and caused him to seek refuge in the barn. It was one thing to wear a dress of an evening, but to walk about in broad daylight without her uniform was quite another. It felt like his world was falling apart, piece by piece.

He was glad that Helen was still close by. As long as she was at the manor, he still had a chance to win her back. Of course, it wasn't appropriate for the pair of them to live under the same roof with the patients gone. But if they were married, it would be another matter.

That oaf, Locke, had designs on her, that much was clear. Samuel had been confident she'd see through his rough charm – but that didn't seem to be happening. He was worried. He had no idea what was going on. Could Locke be involved in the patients' deaths? If he was, Helen might be in danger.

When he heard footsteps, he gave a quick glance to make sure the oil drum was hidden under the tarpaulin. The last thing he needed was for anyone to find his treasures at this stage. Should he tell Helen about them? Perhaps she'd feel more secure if she knew he'd soon have enough money to fund their venture.

Or should he abandon his plans? Take the job they'd offered him at the Royal Victoria? The thought filled him with despair. He knew he couldn't go back to that life any more. Not when he was so close to realising his dream.

But had he gone too far? People had died. His patients had died. Was he to blame? He didn't know what to think.

30

'Do you think Dr Bingham had something to do with Nurse Taplin's death?' Townsend was back in the plush surroundings of Joseph Wintringham's study. As soon as he and Newman had arrived at the manor that morning, Helen had requested an interview with them. He was curious to know why she'd come to them with information about Isabel Taplin now.

'Over the last year, I've considered everyone a suspect. And I'm no clearer to knowing who did it,' Helen replied. 'What about you?'

Townsend saw Newman smile at that and decided to take it on the chin. 'I've never given up on Nurse Taplin. However, I'd be lying if I told you I'm any closer to finding her killer than I was twelve months ago.'

'Just because I'm telling you this, I don't want you to assume that I think Samuel's guilty.'

Townsend nodded. 'Understood. But why are you telling me this now? You say that Nurse Taplin flirted with Dr Bingham, and he was flattered. You evidently believed it was harmless at the time otherwise I think you'd have said something earlier.'

'Because of everything that's happened. This business with the sparrowhawk and—'

'You've been speaking with Mr Locke?'

'It's not just that. I can't understand how Samuel suddenly has enough money to buy a farm. I thought...' she trailed off.

'What did you think?'

'He told me some time ago that he'd been offered a post at the Royal Victoria. The large military hospital in Netley near Southampton. He gave me the impression he wanted me to go with him.'

'In what capacity?'

She flushed. 'At first, I thought he was going to recommend me to the hospital board there. Then...' She hesitated. 'Then it became clear he liked me. He proposed marriage.'

'Did he?' Townsend wasn't surprised by this. He'd suspected that was Bingham's intention. And Locke's, unless he was very much mistaken. Bingham would be the clumsier of the two suitors. 'And how do you feel about Dr Bingham?'

'I admit, I was beginning to develop feelings for him. Those feelings have changed over the last weeks.'

'Why?' He stared at her intently, and she didn't flinch under his gaze. If anyone could give him a clue as to what the hell was going on with Bingham, it was Helen Hopgood. But would she confide in him? And could she be trusted?

'Again, I don't want it to seem as though I think Samuel's a murderer. But he lied to me over David. I believed him when he told me he'd written to St Dunstan's. If I'd known that wasn't true, I'd have written to them myself. I think David was blind and they would have taken him.' Her voice faltered. 'And things would have been different.'

Her distress sounded genuine to Townsend. 'You think he's lying about something else?' he prompted.

She shrugged. 'He was so vague when I asked him how he can

afford to establish a private sanatorium. Yet he keeps trying to persuade me to stay and help him run it.'

Townsend decided to follow his instincts and take a risk. 'Bingham's up to something. Like you, I don't want to jump to the conclusion that it's murder. But unless I know what he's hiding, I can only assume the worst. That's why I need your help.'

'Me? What can I do?'

'You're the one person he's likely to confide in. I think he's desperate for you to stay.' He saw her flush again. 'You play a key role in his plans. I need you to get the truth out of him.'

She shook her head. 'I don't want to mislead Samuel. My feelings have changed over recent weeks, and I wouldn't want him to get the wrong idea.'

Townsend guessed she was talking about her relationship with Richard Locke. He glanced at Newman, who nodded his encouragement. It was time to start forcing things out into the open. 'We're treating Captain Jennings, Mr Cowper and Mr Edwards' deaths as murder.'

'Oliver was murdered?' She sounded more resigned than shocked.

'The pathologist is running more tests, but his initial findings confirm what I suspected.' He paused. 'And I'm sure you suspected it too. Oliver Edwards died from an overdose of morphine. His body is being examined for any signs of an injection.'

'Poor Oliver.' Helen blinked back tears. 'And poor Richard.'

'I need your help to find out what's going on here. It may or may not be Bingham, but someone's behind the deaths of those men. We have to find out who that is.'

'How?'

Townsend ran his fingers over the ornate carvings on Joseph Wintringham's antique mahogany chair. 'Just keep saying no. Until he's forced to confide in you.'

31

Helen gazed around the empty ward. Like Merewood Farm, the room was now neither one thing nor another. It no longer bore any resemblance to a hospital ward. Nor did it look like the drawing room it had once been. It was an empty space that held no trace of the hundreds of men that had slept within its walls.

She thought of Morgan calling to her, wanting her to pay him some attention; Albert asking her to read a passage from one of Emma's letters; Nathan sitting quietly by his bed reading; David winding up his clock and staring out of the window; and Oliver bent over one of his sketches.

Helen decided this would be the last time she entered the ward. She never wanted to set foot in Merewood Farm again. From now on, she'd organise the return of the medical supplies from the south barn.

Despite Samuel's protests, she'd insisted that Richard be allowed to move the remaining furniture from the ward. Once that was done, she'd go upstairs and pack her trunk. Dorothy had offered to store it for her and have it sent on once Helen was settled in a new position. All the belongings she needed for the present were in her room at the manor.

Without turning, she could tell that Samuel had entered the ward. She didn't have to see his face to know he was wearing a pained expression.

Helen went over to the window and watched Richard and Nathan carry the last of the beds down to the south barn. Samuel came to stand beside her.

'Have you seen Superintendent Townsend?' he asked. 'I want to talk to him. When we were saying goodbye to Albert, I saw Locke take a cup of tea into the ward. It was on the table when I was talking to Oliver.'

She recollected Richard had left the kitchen carrying a cup of tea and a slice of cake. She vaguely remembered washing up the cup and plate. Could Oliver have ingested the morphine? It seemed unlikely to her. He would have noticed the bitter taste.

'Superintendent Townsend and Sergeant Newman were at the manor earlier. I believe they've left for the day but plan to return in the morning,' she replied. 'I don't think they intend to come back to the hospital now it's empty.'

'I'll speak to them up at the manor tomorrow. I'm glad they're not coming back here. Their presence is highly disruptive.'

'Samuel, there's nothing left to disrupt.' The fact that he was still wearing his white coat felt like some kind of cruel joke.

He contemplated the bare ward, shaking his head. 'I don't understand how things went so wrong. I let the patients down.'

'We let them down. Morgan, David and Oliver were in our care.' She swallowed hard, fighting the tears that were welling.

'No,' he said softly. 'It was my fault. I never understood the danger they were in. I was too preoccupied with my plans for the sanatorium. You were right to get Albert and Nathan away from here. I should have listened to you.'

'Will you leave here now, Samuel? I don't believe in curses, but there's been too much death – the place feels tainted by it.'

'No.' He shook his head vehemently. 'I still believe in Merewood Farm. It has so much to offer. Just give me time, and I'll prove it to you.'

'How?' She gestured to the empty ward. 'Can you really afford to turn this into a sanatorium? It isn't even a hospital any more.'

'Helen, please.' He reached out for her hand and then seemed to think better of it. 'You must trust me. I realise I should have told you of my intentions earlier. I don't just mean about my plans to buy the farm. My marriage proposal still stands. I always wanted you to be a part of my life here and not only as a nurse. I truly believe we can transform this into so much more than a hospital – it would be a place that heals minds as well as bodies.'

'Too much needs to be done before we can think of housing patients here again.'

By his slight smile, she knew he was encouraged by her use of the word *we*.

'It's all in hand. I just need you to believe in me.'

These vague statements, along with his self-satisfied expression, persuaded her she had to go along with Townsend's plan. Something about Samuel's confidence told her that if she prevaricated long enough, she'd find out what he was hiding.

'I'm sorry, I just don't think it can be done.' She walked through the patio doors. 'I wish you luck. I hope you can make it a success.'

'I'm not sure I can without you by my side.'

She turned and gave a sad smile. 'There are many competent nurses who'll be more than willing to take employment at a private clinic.'

'I'm not asking you to marry me because you're a competent nurse.' Samuel held out his hands in a pathetic gesture. 'I know I haven't been the most romantic suitor. I never have the right words.

But I meant it when I said I've never met anyone like you. Your compassion makes you a good nurse.' He paused, then added softly, 'It also makes you a desirable woman.'

Inwardly, she cursed Townsend, even though she knew she wasn't goading Samuel because the superintendent had asked her to. For Morgan, David and Oliver's sakes, she had to find out the truth.

Helen gave a helpless shrug. 'I'm sorry, your plans are too vague. I admire your dedication to your patients, and I'm sure you could achieve great things. But is skill enough? I fear you'll require more money than you have at your disposal for such an ambitious venture to work.'

'I wish you'd trust me.' He looked as desperate as he sounded. 'Is there nothing I can do to persuade you to stay?'

Feeling she was getting close, she turned and walked away, calling over her shoulder. 'I'm going to finish my inventories in the south barn. I don't intend to return to the hospital.'

'Helen,' he called.

She kept walking. But not at her usual brisk pace.

'Helen.' Samuel caught up with her. 'Come with me. I have something to show you.'

'Samuel, I...' She made a show of resisting.

'Please,' he begged. 'Just give me a few minutes.'

She let him take her arm, and to her surprise, he led her away from the farmhouse. They seemed to be heading in the direction of the manor, then he veered right, and they walked along the dirt track that linked the two barns.

'Where are we going?'

He didn't answer but kept glancing around as though checking to see if anyone was watching them. When he stopped at the north barn, she wondered if he was playing some sort of trick. Her skin began to prickle.

The tall doors groaned as he opened them and she reluctantly followed him inside. It was full of old farming machinery and smelt of metal and rust.

'What are we doing here?' For the first time, Helen felt a shiver of fear. Despite what Richard had said, she hadn't believed Samuel capable of murder. But why had he brought her to the north barn?

Samuel didn't reply. He had his back to her and was pulling on a sheet of tarpaulin. She edged closer and saw that underneath was an old oil drum. It was tucked in a corner behind a stack of hay bales.

He bent over and reached inside the oil drum for something. Could he have a weapon hidden in there? She took a few steps away from him, ready to run for the door if he swung around with a knife or cosh.

When he hefted something out of the drum, it seemed to be more awkward than heavy. The object was square and wrapped in coarse white linen. Samuel propped it up against the wall and gently pulled back the fabric to reveal a painting. She moved nearer and saw that it wasn't just one; two others were stacked behind it. He arranged them so all three were lined up against the barn wall.

Each picture was a scene from the Merewood estate. One was of the lake with Gibbet Wood in the background. Another was of Merewood Manor as you looked up at it from the lake, and the third was of Merewood Farm. The one of the farmhouse must have been painted in June, as the jasmine was in flower.

Helen shook her head to indicate she didn't understand.

'Victor Protheroe painted them.' There was something almost reverential in the way Samuel said it.

She stared at the three oil paintings. And then realised their significance. These pictures would be valuable. Since Protheroe's death, his work had become highly collectable, and his paintings were selling for quite considerable sums.

'There were two more. I sold them. They raised enough for me to buy Merewood Farm,' Samuel explained. 'After I sell these, I'll have the money to pay for the renovations.'

Helen was silent while she digested this. Then she asked, 'Do they belong to you?'

Samuel nodded. 'Victor and I became close friends. He left them in the art studio. I'm sure he intended for me to have them.'

She wasn't sure that was true. 'What are they doing here?' She motioned to their rustic surroundings.

'Everything stored in here will form part of the sale. When I buy Merewood Farm, they'll be legally mine. Not that they aren't anyway,' he added hastily.

'But...' She was at a loss. She had no idea if he would be considered the legal owner of the paintings or not.

'No one knows of their existence. When I sent the other two to a private auction, I told them they were a present from Victor. That he'd been grateful to the physician who'd saved his injured hand and enabled him to continue to paint.'

Helen knew this wasn't true.

'When did you find them?' she asked.

'A few months ago. It was like they were given to me by God. I went to the art studio searching for inspiration. Looking for a way to keep our beloved hospital going. And I found these.'

Her pulse began to race. 'Mr Wintringham had a buyer for Merewood Farm.'

To her astonishment, he went down on his knees. For an awful moment, she thought he was going to ask her to marry him again.

'Helen. I need you to forgive me. I've done some bad things, but when you hear why, I think you'll understand.'

'What bad things?' Her mouth was dry and her voice thick.

'I put Yorick in your bath. And I'm ashamed to say I took a scalpel to Mrs Wintringham's portrait. On occasion, I even stopped the clock in your office and broke the mantles of the wall lamps.'

She slowly released the breath she'd been holding. 'And the sparrowhawk?'

'That was rather clever. I fed the poison to one of the pheasant chicks...' He must have seen the horror on her face because he stopped abruptly. 'I'm sorry. I had no idea the bird meant so much to you. Dear Helen, please forgive me.'

'Why did you do it?' It came out as a whisper.

'I didn't know how else to get rid of Baden Knight. He was my only competition for the farm. You remember he used to come to the wards to preach? I sometimes see him when I'm out walking, and we've talked about the hospital. He thinks the place is cursed. He's always urging me to leave, telling me the spectres of the murdered nurse and the artist who'd killed himself haunt the farm. I told him Protheroe died in London, but he said it didn't matter. His superstitious nonsense gave me the idea.'

'You wanted people to believe Merewood Farm was cursed?' She felt a mixture of anger and disbelief.

'With Knight out of the way, I knew Wintringham would have no choice but to accept my offer. No one else would want the farm.'

'Did you need more ghosts?' Her voice was stronger now. 'Morgan, David and Oliver?'

'No. No. You can't think that.' He scrambled to his feet and lurched towards her.

Helen screamed, throwing out her arms to stop him from coming any closer. Behind her, she heard the groan of the barn doors opening.

Richard flew to her side. Before Sergeant Newman could stop him, he'd pushed Samuel to the ground with one swipe of his hand. Superintendent Townsend grabbed Richard's arm and pulled him back.

Breathing heavily, Helen looked down to where Samuel lay. He made no attempt to get up, he simply stared in fright at Townsend.

'I-I thought you'd gone,' he stuttered.

Then he turned to Helen, and she saw the hurt in his eyes as it dawned on him she must have tricked him.

32

'You know what I'm going to ask, don't you?'

Samuel shrank down into his chair. His office door was open, and Sergeant Newman stood outside. He had no idea what Superintendent Townsend was going to ask. All he knew was that he was terrified. Things were unravelling at such speed. One minute, he'd been in the north barn with Helen; the next, he was back in his office with Townsend.

What hurt him most was Helen's betrayal. She must have known Townsend was lurking outside the barn. In fact, he suspected she'd been acting on his instructions. How could she be so cruel?

'I want to look in your medicine cabinet again.'

Before Samuel could rouse himself from his thoughts of Helen, Townsend was at his side, pulling open the desk drawer.

'Still here, I see?' The superintendent held the key between his thumb and finger. 'Not in its secret hiding place?'

'I've been extremely busy,' Samuel mumbled.

Townsend wasn't listening. He'd already opened the cabinet and was pushing aside the bottles and vials.

'One, two, three, four, five.' He swung around to face Samuel. 'You said you had six vials of morphine. I can only see five.'

'But... but there were six. You saw for yourself.' Samuel felt his chest contract.

'Then what has happened to the sixth vial?'

He wiped the sweat from his brow, wondering if he was having a heart attack. 'I have no idea.'

'Don't you? Because I have a very good idea of what happened to it. It was administered in a fatal dose to Oliver Edwards.'

'No,' Samuel gasped.

'Oh yes. According to our pathologist, he died of morphine poisoning.'

'Richard Locke. He took Oliver a cup of tea,' he wheezed.

'That was when Albert Gates was leaving. How many hours before morphine takes effect?'

Samuel recalled talking to Oliver after Locke had driven Albert and his father to the station. Had the cup been empty? He couldn't remember.

'Oliver may have only got around to drinking the tea later in the day. Or...' He glanced at the medicine cabinet. 'It's possible he found the key in my drawer and took an overdose. He wasn't a happy man.'

'He took the same drug *you* used to kill the sparrowhawk. The sparrowhawk that *you* left on the kitchen table for the maid to find. Or did the bird kill itself too?'

'I don't know anything about—'

'I heard everything you said to Sister Hopgood. And Frederick Wintringham saw you loitering by the pheasant pens. He guessed how you did it. You poisoned one of the chicks and waited for the sparrowhawk to eat it. You've been taking quite an interest in farming recently.'

'That's because I intend to retain some aspects of the farm. Tending to animals will form part of my patients' therapy.'

'You still intend to open your sanatorium?'

'Yes, of course. Why shouldn't I?'

'Three patients have died in your care. I question whether you should still be practising as a doctor. I'm not sure I'd want a relative of mine to come and stay in your sanatorium.'

Samuel wanted to say that he'd refuse admittance to anyone associated with Townsend. Instead, he took a deep breath and summoned as much dignity as he could.

'All three of those patients were suffering from complicated conditions due to their wartime experiences. Suicide is a possibility, although I certainly haven't ruled out foul play. That's a matter for a coroner to decide. But I can hardly be held responsible for what happened. And I should remind you that this is not my private clinic. It's an auxiliary hospital that has been sadly neglected by the Red Cross.'

'Yet you still intend to buy it? It seems you led Mr Wintringham to believe you were funding the purchase with some money you inherited from your parents?'

'Ah, well, I didn't exactly say that.' Samuel sunk low in his chair, wishing Townsend would sit down too, instead of towering over him.

'Both your parents are alive and well, I believe?'

'I never said—'

'We know exactly where you got the money from. By your own admission, you've acquired a collection of paintings by the late artist Victor Protheroe.'

'That's correct. He gave them to me as a gift.'

'Did he? That's not something he can corroborate, is it?' Townsend drummed his fingers on top of the medicine cabinet. 'Can you tell me why you hid the paintings in the north barn?'

'I moved them for safekeeping. All the items in the south barn are being returned to the Red Cross. I didn't want to risk them getting lost amongst all the medical equipment.'

'Why not bring them here to your office? Surely, this would be a safer place than inside an old oil drum?'

Samuel stayed silent. He realised that with every utterance, he was incriminating himself further.

'I suspect you hid them in the north barn because you didn't want anyone to know of their existence. And because you knew the contents of the north barn had been included in the deeds of sale. Thus, in your mind, becoming legally yours when you purchased Merewood Farm.'

That was exactly what Samuel had thought, although he'd never admit it to Townsend.

'Do you have any correspondence between yourself and Mr Protheroe mentioning the paintings? You must have written to thank him for such a valuable gift.'

Samuel wondered if he should demand to see a solicitor, or would that condemn him even more in the superintendent's eyes? It might appear as though he were admitting guilt.

Townsend hadn't finished. 'Or did you find the paintings when you were clearing out the art studio and realise what you'd stumbled across? How do you intend to pay for the running of your sanatorium?'

'I've told you. My patients, or their families, will pay for their care. There are many ex-servicemen who came back from the war suffering from mental ailments. Their families will be willing to pay good money to have them treated in a private clinic, away from prying eyes. I'll return these men to their loved ones in good health.'

Samuel was pleased with this answer. Only when it was too late did he realise the implications of what he'd said.

'Morgan Jennings, David Cowper and Oliver Edwards wouldn't have been able to afford your fees, would they? Is that why you got rid of them?'

'I planned to take non-fee-paying patients too. I would never have deserted those men. I wanted them to stay here with me. And Albert Gates and Nathan Smith. I could have given them better treatments and studied their responses to them. What I learned from them would enable me to help others. My wealthier clients would have effectively paid for their care.'

Townsend ignored him. 'I'm going to summarise what we know about recent events. Your skeleton' – he gestured to Yorick, who was still propped up on his stand in the corner – 'was placed in Sister Hopgood's bath. The following night, Morgan Jennings left the ward, and the next morning, his body was discovered floating in Merewood Lake. Chloral hydrate taken from *your* medicine cabinet and wine from the case Mr Wintringham gave *you* was found in his body. Next, the portrait of Mrs Wintringham was slashed with a scalpel and the eyes gouged out. The damage was done with one of *your* scalpels, as were the cuts to David Cowper's wrists.'

'Those weren't my scalpels. They're just scalpels that were used here at the hospital.'

'By doctors?'

'Yes, of course by doctors.'

'And as you're the only remaining doctor, I would suggest that they're your scalpels. Then we come to the sparrowhawk and Oliver Edwards.' Again, Townsend rapped his fingers on the medicine cabinet. 'Both poisoned with vials of *your* morphine.'

'It's not my morphine, and nor were they my scalpels. They're medical supplies issued to the hospital. I didn't want those patients to die. Quite the opposite. I wanted to save them. Treat them so they could go on to lead fuller lives than they had been able to since the war.'

'It seems to me your tricks are a precursor to your murders. You follow the same pattern.'

Terror was beginning to paralyse Samuel. 'You must believe me. I never hurt those men. I'm a doctor, I save lives. I don't take them. I admit, I played those harmless tricks, but never on my patients.' He could smell the sweat that was soaking his shirt. 'I think I'd like to speak to a solicitor.'

'I think that would be a good idea. I'm glad you appreciate the seriousness of these accusations. And I'm sure you know what the penalty for murder is. Why don't you ask your solicitor to go straight to the police station in Winchester? We can meet him there.'

'I have no intention of going anywhere. I have patients to...'

Samuel's words petered out. He was unbearably hot and realised he was still wearing a white coat. He didn't even remember putting it on that morning.

As the full meaning of Superintendent Townsend's words sank in, he started to shake uncontrollably. The penalty for murder? Did he mean...

A vision of a length of rope tied into a hangman's noose swam into his mind. Then darkness descended. He had the sensation he was sliding off his chair – but felt nothing when he hit the ground.

33

Richard had walked down to the lake to stare at Merewood Farm. He had no idea why. Perhaps it was a form of punishment. Every time he looked at the farmhouse, he was reminded of his failure to protect Oliver.

He was interrupted by Dexter jumping into the water and Frederick demanding if he'd seen Townsend.

Richard shook his head. 'Not this morning.'

Since they'd carted Bingham off to hospital in a Black Maria the previous day, there had been no sign of any police officers.

Frederick began to stroll towards the farm. 'Then I'll start without him.'

'Start what?' he called after Frederick. 'The police haven't finished there yet.'

'Searching for clues. They haven't charged him with her murder. I'll prove to them he did it,' Frederick yelled over his shoulder.

Richard guessed he was talking about Isabel. He knew he should stop the man from pulling the hospital apart. But he didn't have the energy.

Instead, he made his way into Gibbet Wood and waited for Helen at their usual spot by the sparrowhawk tree.

When she arrived, he could see she was upset.

She lowered herself to the ground beside him. 'Before I left, Joseph took a telephone call from Superintendent Townsend. Samuel's been released from hospital. He says he's still sick, but the doctors decided he was well enough to be taken into police custody. They've charged him with the murders.'

He heard the tremor in her voice as she said these last words and put an arm around her shoulder.

'I'm sorry. About Oliver. About all of them. But I can't believe it of Samuel.' Helen took a handkerchief from the pocket of her cardigan and dabbed her eyes.

Her use of Bingham's first name still irritated him. 'I believe it. And I hate the bastard for it. He's as good as admitted it.'

'He admitted he was responsible for those horrible tricks. But why would he kill the patients?'

'All that mattered to him was his bloody sanatorium. And they weren't the sort of patients he needed.'

She frowned. 'No. He wanted them to stay with him. I'm certain he did.'

'Did he? Are you sure they weren't beginning to offend his pride? The man's got a huge ego. Albert and Nathan were safe enough, they were making progress. Didn't you say he'd even started to write a case study on Albert? But what about David and Oliver?'

'They were more complex,' she admitted.

'He wasn't healing them, that's for sure.'

'Why would he kill Morgan?'

'Because he didn't like him. Or the way he flirted with you.' He saw her flinch and added, 'It wasn't your fault.'

'Morgan used to vex Samuel, nothing more.'

Richard didn't argue. In his opinion, Morgan Jennings had been the sort of chap who charmed the ladies but got under the skin of other men. His arrogance and blatant disregard for rules would have infuriated someone like Bingham.

'It's over now. Time to move on.' He squeezed her shoulder. 'You're no longer Sister Hopgood of Merewood Hospital. And very soon, I'll no longer be the estate manager of Merewood Manor. We're free to do whatever we want.'

'He's back.'

For a heart-stopping moment, Richard thought she was referring to Bingham. Then he realised she was looking up at the Scots pine.

'Over there.' She pointed. 'On the left-hand side.'

He peered up at the tree and saw movement on one of the branches. Then the male sparrowhawk came into view. And he wasn't alone. Further along the branch, a female sparrowhawk was eyeing him warily.

Richard smiled. 'I do believe he's found a new mate.'

He couldn't help thinking this was a good omen. They sat watching the pair's awkward courtship until the birds suddenly took flight and disappeared from view.

'Have you heard from the Royal Victoria?' he asked.

'I've been invited to attend an interview at the hospital. It would be nice to live by the sea. I'd always assumed I'd return to the city. But I've seen so much during the war, I don't think I can go back to my old life in London. I want to escape from all the memories and begin again.'

'Escape?' He regarded her curiously. 'Have you been a prisoner?'

She nodded. 'The war took over my life. In some ways, I relished it. After my mother died, being a nurse gave me a sense of purpose. I was happy to do my duty.' She brushed her dark hair from her brow. 'But part of me got lost along the way.'

Richard understood what she meant. 'I was thinking of moving to the south of the county. My mother lives in Fareham. She'd be happier if I were nearby.'

'What about your father?'

'He died some years ago.' He hesitated. 'I've promised my mother a day out. I usually drive down to Fareham to pick her up, and then we go into Southampton. Why don't I drive you to your interview? If you don't mind my mother accompanying us, I could drop you off and pick you up afterwards.'

'Would she mind?'

'She'd like to meet you. Also, there are a couple of livery stables I want to take a look at on the outskirts of Southampton. You'd be doing me a favour if you'd have tea with her while I went to see them.'

'In that case, I accept your kind offer. I thought you liked the stables you saw in Andover?'

'They'd remind me of the plans I made with Oliver. Like you, I need to get away from here. Too many bad memories.' And not just of Oliver, he reflected sadly. 'I'm seeing Oliver's widow tomorrow to arrange his funeral.'

'Have they released his body?'

Richard nodded. 'It was morphine that killed him.'

'Yes, but weren't they checking for injection marks? Did they find any?'

'I don't know. How else could you administer morphine?'

'You can take it orally. It's possible someone put it in Oliver's tea.' She paused. 'Did he have a cup at Albert's send-off?'

Richard thought back to the scene in the kitchen with Joseph and Dorothy, Albert and his father, and Nathan and Kate. 'Everyone in the kitchen was standing around, holding cups and saucers, and eating cake. Oliver didn't want to be the only one sitting at the table.

He couldn't manage to eat and drink standing up, so he refused to have anything. You know what he was like.'

She smiled. 'He hated anyone to help him.'

He frowned. 'I took a cup of tea and slice of cake into the ward for him and left them on the table. I don't remember seeing them when... when we found him.'

'I took the empty cup and plate away and washed them up.'

'Didn't you say you heard Bingham talking to Oliver while I was running Albert and his father to the station? How quickly would morphine take effect?'

She wrinkled her nose. 'Difficult to say. It depends on how much was in the tea and how fast he drank it. I think it would have made the tea taste very bitter.'

Richard stood up. 'I don't care how he did it. Bingham killed Oliver and now he's on his way to the gallows.' He saw Helen shiver and held out his hand to help her up. 'I'm sorry, that wasn't a nice thing to say.'

In silence, they strolled out of the woods and down the slope to Merewood Lake.

Helen contemplated the empty hospital. 'I wonder what will happen to it now?'

'Joseph's still trying to persuade Baden Knight to reconsider. But I doubt he'll succeed.'

'Perhaps the place is cursed. I never want to go back there.'

Richard felt her tense. 'What is it?'

She was squinting at the farmhouse. 'Someone's in there. Is it Townsend?'

He followed her gaze and saw a tall figure in one of the upstairs windows. 'It's Frederick.'

'He's in my room.' Helen corrected herself. 'My old room. What's he doing there?'

'Looking for clues.'

Her brow creased. 'Clues? Clues to what?'

'When he heard they were going to charge Bingham with killing the patients, he was angry they hadn't included Isabel Taplin's murder.'

'He thinks Samuel killed Isabel?' Her expression told him she wasn't convinced.

'It's possible. Frederick's hoping to find some evidence.'

'In my room?'

'It was once her room, though, wasn't it?' Richard regretted the words as soon as they left his mouth.

34

Helen stood by the window. For years, she'd looked up at Merewood Manor from the hospital below. Now she was staying there as a guest of the Wintringhams, she was relieved her room was at the back of the house. She had no desire to gaze down on Merewood Farm.

Dorothy had given her a comfortable guest bedroom on the eastern side of the manor, overlooking the walled kitchen garden. Georgina was in the room next door, and Frederick's bedroom was on the opposite side of the corridor. His windows must face the lake and Merewood Farm. Dorothy and Joseph's private quarters were on the western side of the house with a view of the woodland.

Beyond the wall of the kitchen garden was Richard's cottage. She saw him get into the old Vauxhall and drive off. He must be going to see Oliver's widow.

His offer to take her to the Royal Victoria Hospital had surprised her. Now she had more than just the interview to feel nervous about. It wasn't the prospect of meeting Richard's mother that made her anxious. More what that meeting represented.

Perhaps she was being presumptuous, but she suspected marriage was on Richard's mind.

It was certainly a tempting proposition. She and Richard were well-suited. She'd once thought that she and Samuel were compatible, then realised it was simply that they worked well together. Aside from their profession, they had little in common.

With Richard, it was different. He seemed to enjoy her company. Since she'd moved into the manor, they'd taken daily walks together, strolling hand in hand, confiding secrets and sharing wartime experiences.

Dorothy was certainly encouraging the relationship. She'd lent Helen a smart suit that she assured her would impress the hospital board and Richard's mother.

Today, she was back in uniform. She straightened her white cap, tied an apron around her waist and went downstairs to where Dorothy and Nathan were waiting.

'Morning, Sister Hopgood.'

She smiled at Nathan. 'I'm not sure I am Sister Hopgood any more.'

He grinned. 'You are to me. And to Albert. I got a letter from him this morning, and he asked me to tell you they've set a date for the wedding.'

Dorothy clapped her hands together. 'How wonderful. Perhaps you'll be next,' she teased.

'I don't know about that,' Nathan mumbled.

'The vans will be here soon.' Helen bustled them out of the front door to spare Nathan's blushes.

She'd seen him out walking with Kate on more than one occasion. What's more, she'd heard them talking together. Nathan had been chatting animatedly with no trace of a stutter, his expression eager, his eyes shining. She'd detected no sign of the twitching that was once so incessant. Watching him, she'd longed to tell Samuel of his progress.

At the south barn, a Red Cross van was waiting, and a couple of orderlies jumped out. More vans arrived throughout the morning until the barn was finally empty. The doors produced a satisfying hollow echo when Helen pulled them closed.

After days of being idle, the manual work was invigorating. She wasn't accustomed to having no one to look after and didn't know what to do with her time. She wiped her hands on her apron and decided to go in search of Chester. Georgina had said she wanted a cat at the manor, preferring him to Frederick's dog.

Helen strolled down to the farmhouse that had been her home for nearly three years. She admired the ornate red brick façade. The exterior was as pretty as ever. She had no intention of going inside.

Dorothy appeared, brushing dirt from her pinafore. 'What are you thinking about?'

'Merewood Farm. It seems to take a hold of people. Samuel was obsessed with the place.'

'I think he was obsessed with you too.' Dorothy took her arm. 'I'm glad you escaped his clutches.'

'Thank you, Dorothy, for everything you've done. For giving me a room at the manor. You've all been so kind.' To Helen's surprise, even Georgina and Frederick were being civil to her. But then, everything had changed since Samuel's arrest. Accusations were no longer flying, and it seemed the only people who still believed in the curse were Baden Knight and Georgina.

'It's a pleasure having you, my dear. I think your presence is good for Georgina.'

It was true, the girl had calmed down. Helen suspected it had nothing to do with her and more to do with the adoration of Clifford Knight. She said as much to Dorothy.

'He does seem extremely taken with her. I don't believe she's in love with him. Not like she was with Morgan. But she enjoys the attention.' Dorothy winked. 'Even she can see that he has much to offer.'

Apart from money, Helen didn't think Clifford did have much to offer. He was a plain-looking man of about thirty-five, whom she found extremely dull. However, he was certainly a more advantageous match than Morgan had been.

A sudden howl caused them to jump. Chester came tearing across the yard, Dexter in pursuit.

'Leave it, Dexter, you stupid dog.' Frederick appeared at the kitchen door of the farmhouse and frowned at them. 'What are you doing here?'

'We've cleared out the south barn,' Dorothy replied. 'All the hospital equipment has been returned to the Red Cross.'

'About bloody time. We can start getting this place back on its feet.' Frederick mopped his brow with a handkerchief.

Dorothy touched his arm. 'Why don't you walk with us to the manor. Lunch will be waiting.'

'What? Is it lunchtime?' He seemed distracted. 'I'll check on the pheasants, then see you back at the manor.'

'Alright, my dear.'

He strode off, yelling for Dexter so loudly that Helen had to cover her ears.

Dorothy shook her head in exasperation. 'What you said about the farm is true. It does seem to take hold of people. Frederick's obsessed with the place. But, of course, it's where Isabel Taplin lived.'

It was ironic, Helen mused, that Frederick Wintringham was the sort of person Samuel had planned to treat in his sanatorium. A troubled young man in need of psychological help to deal with his problems. And from a wealthy family who'd be prepared to foot the bill. She didn't say this to Dorothy.

She called to Chester, and the cat appeared, though he wouldn't come close enough for her to pick him up. As they strolled to the manor, Helen coaxed him into following.

'Tell me, my dear. Do you believe Dr Bingham killed Isabel Taplin?'

Helen shook her head. 'I always thought it was Victor Protheroe. His mood could be volatile, and he used too much cocaine.'

Dorothy nodded. 'I heard the rumours. He left so suddenly – and we now know he left five of his paintings behind. Then to kill himself. He must have been guilty. I heard he'd wanted to paint the girl, and she refused.'

'I think Isabel would have liked to have sat for the painting, but Matron wouldn't let her.'

'It's a shame. I'm sure it would have made a beautiful portrait.'

'What's happened to the paintings? The ones Samuel hid in the oil drum. Who do they belong to?'

'No one's contested Joseph's claim to them. They're currently hanging in his study. I'm trying to persuade him to move them into the drawing room. They're lovely pieces, and I don't want them tarnished by his cigar smoke.'

'You're keeping them?'

'Joseph is putting them up for auction. I might ask him to let me keep the one of the manor.' She gazed at Frederick, who was now on the outskirts of Gibbet Wood, Dexter at his heels. 'Part of me hoped Victor Protheroe's estate would lay claim to them.'

'Why?' Helen asked in surprise.

'Because if Joseph can raise enough money from selling the paintings, he doesn't need to sell Merewood Farm.'

Helen saw the problem. 'You think he'll give it to Frederick?'

'That's what I'm afraid of.' Dorothy smiled sadly. 'My husband and I rarely quarrel. When we do, it's usually about our children.

Joseph believes that if he gives Frederick what he wants, the boy might become less... well, you know, less fixated on what happened to Isabel. I fear it will have the reverse effect. As you said, Merewood Farm does seem to exert a hold over people.'

Helen privately agreed with Dorothy. Nothing good was likely to come from indulging Frederick in his obsession.

When they reached the manor, she went upstairs to change out of her uniform before lunch. As she passed the door of Georgina's bedroom, she could hear retching from within. She hesitated. She didn't want to get involved, but the nurse in her couldn't ignore the situation.

'Georgina, it's Helen. Can I help?'

The door opened, and Georgina peeked out. She checked the hall to see if anyone was around before pulling Helen into her room.

'I'm feeling rather nauseous. It's my nerves.' She suddenly dashed over to the washstand and vomited into the basin.

One look at the girl's clammy face and queasy expression told Helen that nerves weren't the problem.

'Have your monthlies stopped?'

'I've never been very regular.' Georgina wiped her mouth with a handkerchief and sank down onto the bed. Resting on the embroidered bedcover was a Victorian rosewood box inlaid with flowers. She snatched up some of the items lying beside it, threw them into the box, and snapped the lid closed.

A photograph fell to the floor. Helen picked it up and sat beside Georgina. She'd seen the snapshot before. It was of Morgan just after he was promoted to captain. He looked every inch the hero with his broad shoulders and square jaw. She smiled at the familiar insolent grin and thick blond hair.

She handed the photograph to Georgina. 'Is the baby Morgan's?'

'It's why he asked me to marry him.' She gave a faint smile. 'He would have gone through with it, too. Even if Joseph had refused to help us.'

Helen thought this was true. Morgan probably would have done the right thing by the girl, though God knows how they would have managed for money. She supposed Dorothy would have persuaded Joseph to come to their rescue.

She noticed Georgina was playing with a ring on her left finger.

'Did Clifford give you that?' It was a large sapphire on a gold band. Helen was no expert, but the gem looked real enough to her, which meant it hadn't come from Morgan.

'It's Patrick's ring.'

Her confusion must have shown.

'Patrick Wintringham. I met him at Mummy's wedding. He's some sort of distant cousin of Joseph's. We started courting. He gave it to me before he joined up.'

'You never married?' Helen remembered the gossip she'd heard in the village. The rich banker who was awarded medals for his bravery on the battlefields of France. When he'd returned to England, he'd called off his engagement to Georgina and married a colonel's daughter.

'By the time the war was over, he'd been ensnared by some other woman.' Georgina sniffed. 'Everyone I love gets taken away from me.'

'I'm sorry.'

'I kept his ring. When I found out I was pregnant, I thought I might as well make use of it. I told Morgan I was going to wear it and say he'd given it to me. He couldn't have afforded one. Mother wouldn't have approved, but Morgan saw the funny side of it.' Georgina pulled the ring from her finger. 'The irony is, Patrick married and became a father seven months after the wedding. They hushed it up, of course. Said the baby was premature.'

Helen noticed the way she placed a protective hand on her stomach when she said this.

'How are you feeling? Have you had any problems?'

Georgina shook her head. 'Apart from the sickness, I feel fine.'

'That's normal. Come to me if you experience any other symptoms.'

'You won't tell anyone?'

'Of course not.'

'Not even my mother?'

'No. My only concern is for you and the baby. You won't do anything silly to try and get rid of it, will you?' Helen had seen enough botched abortions to know the risks.

'I want this baby.' Tears welled in Georgina's eyes. 'I've wanted one for a long time.'

'What do you plan to do?'

'I need to marry Clifford quickly, so he'll think it's his.' Georgina opened the rosewood box and placed the ring and photograph inside. She snapped the lid closed and turned a small silver key in its lock. 'I'm putting all this behind me. You mustn't tell anyone what I've told you. All that matters now is getting married and giving my baby a good home.'

Helen nodded, feeling queasy as she stood up. The smell of vomit and the girl's cloying floral perfume were making her feel sick. As was the thought of poor Morgan lying dead on the shores of the lake. She wondered if the baby was a boy. Morgan would have liked a son, she was sure of that.

She left the room feeling sorry for Georgina. And even sorrier for Clifford Knight.

35

Richard stood by the window of Joseph Wintringham's study and watched Helen chatting with Nathan in the garden.

Joseph came to stand by his side. 'Dorothy tells me you're taking Helen to meet your mother today. That can only mean one thing.'

Richard smiled. 'I'm thinking about it.'

'Do it. Always marry a sensible woman over a simpering one. Talking of which, I hope to get Georgina off my hands soon. Knight's son seems keen to marry her. I hope he does it before he discovers what she's really like. I won't be sorry to get shot of her.'

'Any chance of Knight coming back with an offer for the farm? He can't still believe there's a curse.'

'Man's an idiot. Kept wittering on about bad things happening to anyone who owns the place. He's going to buy the land but says he doesn't want the farmhouse.'

'What will you do with it?'

Joseph rubbed his chin. 'Frederick plans to live there.'

'Is that a good idea?' Richard was reluctant to say too much, but he could see Joseph understood his meaning. He could also see the confusion and sadness in the older man's eyes.

'He's going through a rough patch at present. The war and all. It might help him to feel more settled if he stays there.'

'He's young. I'm sure with time he'll get over his... er, problems.' Richard wasn't sure of this at all, and his voice lacked conviction.

He stared down at Merewood Farm, its red walls almost glowing in the bright sunshine. The place had always been an oddity. What would it be like when farming activity resumed, and it stood in the midst like a forgotten tomb? With Frederick inside.

He remembered Helen talking about the scars of war – some visible, some not. Frederick had been a scared boy, sent into hell. He'd escaped at the expense of being branded a coward. Then he'd fallen in love with a woman he worshipped as an angel, and someone had snatched her from him. Would he recover?

Richard wouldn't be around to find out. He'd be glad if he never set eyes on Merewood Farm again.

He left the manor and was almost at the gate when Georgina came skipping toward him. She looked pretty and childlike in a sleeveless blue summer dress, her golden hair pinned beneath a pink straw hat.

'Mummy says you're taking Helen to meet your mother.'

Richard reflected on how insular their world had become. At one time, his life had been private. His taking someone to visit his mother certainly wouldn't have been a cause for comment by the Wintringhams. But the war had thrown them together more closely and now everyone seemed to know everyone else's business.

'You introduced me to her once.' Georgina had her hand on his arm.

Richard had regretted that as soon as he'd seen the expression on his mother's face after spending five minutes with Georgina.

'Helen has an interview at the Royal Victoria Hospital at Netley, and I'm taking my mother to Southampton for the day. It's nothing more than that.'

She smiled, clearly not believing him. 'You're planning to ask her to marry you, aren't you?'

'No,' Richard lied. He'd be far away from Merewood Manor and Georgina when he did propose to Helen.

'Clifford's asked me to marry him,' she said without enthusiasm.

'Do you want to marry him?'

'He's keen to start a family. And so am I. I can't afford to wait any longer.' She played with a tendril of hair. 'I wanted your baby, but you didn't ask me to marry you.'

'Oh.' Richard didn't know what to say in response.

'Morgan would have made a good father,' she said wistfully.

Frankly, Richard doubted this. He couldn't imagine Morgan staying at home with a crying baby. Though he supposed fatherhood could change a person. He was hoping to find out one day. Thankfully not with Georgina.

'At least Clifford has money, so we can escape from here.' She cast a glance in the direction of Merewood Farm. 'I hate that place. It will destroy Freddie.'

Richard nodded. Sadly, he thought she was right.

As Georgina skipped away, he reflected on how fickle she was. She seemed genuinely to have cared for Morgan. Yet before the poor man was even in his grave, she'd turned her hungry violet eyes on him – pawing him and practically begging him to take her back to his cottage. And now she'd switched her attention to Clifford Knight, poor bugger. He had no idea what he was letting himself in for.

* * *

Helen gazed out over Southampton Waters. She thought the interview had gone well, though it was difficult to tell. She knew that if they offered her a post, she'd accept it.

And what of her relationship with Richard? If he found stables nearby, they could meet on her days off. Away from the unreal environment of Merewood, they'd be able to decide on their true feelings for one another. Helen envisioned long walks along the beach, hand in hand, watching the gulls swoop overhead.

But she tried not to feel too happy. It was an emotion she didn't trust. A high was always followed by a low – and the higher you went, the steeper the drop. She preferred to keep things balanced.

'Do you like it here?' Richard asked.

She nodded, and he took her hand.

Mrs Locke smiled at them and turned to look at the hospital. She was a tiny woman with grey hair pinned neatly into a bun. When they'd arrived at her cottage, she'd been waiting. Instead of inviting them in, she'd jumped into the back of the car and said, 'Let's have an adventure.'

Richard had made hasty introductions and started the engine again.

'Call me Mary. Richard's told me what's been going on in his letters. Nasty business. I'm sure you don't want to dwell on that. So let's enjoy the sea and sunshine, and you can both forget about Merewood for the time being.'

And they had. They'd driven through the prettiest countryside Helen had ever seen and then along the coast before parking in Southampton. Richard had treated them to lunch in Mary's favourite restaurant, then driven to Netley in time for her interview.

Richard and his mother had originally planned to motor along the coast and return for her later. But when they'd seen the Royal Victoria Hospital, they'd decided to stay and explore the grounds of the building. It was an amazing structure that stretched for a quarter of a mile along the shores of Southampton Water.

When Richard dropped them off at a beachfront cafeteria,

buying them tea and cakes, before he went to view stables nearby, Helen prepared herself for the second interview of the day. She had no doubt Mary would take this opportunity to interrogate her.

But she soon discovered that Mary Locke was far too shrewd for interrogations. Instead, she asked gentle questions and showed a genuine interest in the answers. Helen found herself telling Richard's mother about her childhood, her training as a nurse, and her time in the field hospitals in northern France. Conversation then turned to Merewood.

'You can imagine my relief when Richard was discharged from the army. It terrible what happened to him and Oliver.' Mary sipped her tea. 'I was glad they were able to stay together and grateful to the Wintringhams for helping them.'

'You've been to Merewood?'

'Yes, a few times. I liked Mrs Wintringham very much. She took me to visit Oliver in the hospital. It was comforting to see how well he was being cared for.' She looked apologetically at Helen. 'I'm afraid I don't remember you. The ward was full of patients, nurses, doctors. I do remember meeting the matron, though. A most impressive woman.'

Helen smiled. 'She was. I miss her. She's retired from nursing now. Everything changed after she left.'

'The burden of being head nurse fell to you?'

She nodded, realising how tired she was. 'The hospital should have closed sooner. I wish it had.'

'I could sense from Richard's letters that all wasn't right at Merewood. It began with the death of that young nurse, didn't it?' Mary held up her hand. 'I'm sorry. I promised you we wouldn't talk about that.'

'I don't mind. Being away from it all helps me to put things in perspective. The hospital was a good place once. I was proud of the work we did there and the lives we saved.' Helen shrugged. 'That time is over, and we need to move forward and put the war behind us.'

'You're so right.' Mary patted her hand. 'I'm glad my son's found a sensible woman. I once feared he'd make an offer for that Vane girl. He introduced me to her when I visited the manor. I could tell he was smitten. Fortunately, nothing came of it.'

Helen wasn't surprised by Mary's comment. She'd seen how Georgina was around Richard and had long suspected a dalliance. However, she wished he'd told her about it himself. Perhaps when they knew each other better, he'd feel able to confide in her about his previous girlfriends. She was sure there must have been more than just Georgina.

When she saw the Vauxhall pulling into the motorcar enclosure, Helen was sorry her conversation with Mary was at an end. It had felt liberating to talk freely with someone far away from the confines of Merewood.

They stood up and went out to meet Richard by the car.

'I shouldn't have liked to have seen Georgina Vane wearing my ring. Or my brooch. But...' Mary slipped her arm through Helen's. 'I'd be very happy for you to have them.'

'Richard and I are still getting to know each other.' She forced a smile, a familiar feeling of apprehension creeping over her. She was right not to trust happiness. Disappointment usually followed the emotion. Like the excitement she'd felt when her father had told them they were going on holiday. 'Your brooch?' she enquired.

'When my husband asked me to marry him, he gave me an engagement ring and a sweet little brooch as a present. I wanted Richard to have them after his father's death to keep for when he married – as sort of good luck charms. My husband and I had a long and happy marriage, and I want the same for Richard.'

'How lovely,' Helen murmured.

'It's not a showy ring. A simple solitaire diamond on a gold band. And the brooch is a beautiful grey pearl in a twisted silver setting.'

36

When Helen saw Superintendent Townsend and Sergeant Newman standing on the patio outside the ward, she decided it was a sign.

She'd spent a sleepless night going over what Mary Locke had said. The brooch she'd described sounded identical to the one Isabel Taplin had been wearing on the day she was killed. Had Richard given it to her? And even worse, taken it back when he'd murdered her? Perhaps he'd asked her to marry him, and something, or more likely someone, had caused him to regret his rash proposal. Had he found out about her other romances?

'Sister Hopgood.' Townsend raised his hat, and Newman nodded at her.

'I found out something yesterday that I think you should know.' Her words came out in a rush.

Townsend gestured to the ward. 'Do you want to go inside? Perhaps you'd feel more comfortable in your old office.'

She glanced around to make sure no one was in earshot and then shook her head. 'No, thank you. I'd prefer to stay out here.' Quickly, she told them about Mary's brooch.

Newman let out a low whistle.

Townsend's eyes narrowed. 'Were you aware of a relationship between Mr Locke and Nurse Taplin?'

Helen shook her head.

The superintendent was silent for a while. Then he said slowly, 'Is it possible Mr Locke could have harmed the patients?'

She'd be lying if she said the thought had never crossed her mind. But it seemed unlikely to Helen that he could be involved in any deaths other than Isabel Taplin's.

'No. I don't believe so.' She realised the implication of the question. 'Does that mean you think Samuel's innocent?'

Did Townsend share her doubts about his guilt? She remembered the look on Samuel's face when he discovered a bottle of his wine was missing. She'd seen and heard only sadness when he said he hoped Morgan had enjoyed it. Not guilt or remorse.

Townsend held up his hands. 'I didn't say that.'

'We're considering every possibility,' Sergeant Newman said diplomatically. 'Take Captain Jennings, for instance. Did he and Mr Locke get along? Perhaps there was some jealousy over Miss Vane? You say Mrs Locke mentioned meeting her once?'

'Richard no longer appears to care for Georgina.' Helen realised she might sound like a possessive girlfriend and added, 'I can't think of any reason why he would want to kill Morgan or David.'

'And Oliver Edwards?'

'They were close friends. Oliver once saved Richard's life.'

Newman appeared unimpressed. 'Perhaps the debt of gratitude was beginning to weigh on Mr Locke? From all accounts, Oliver Edwards wasn't an easy man to get along with.'

'Oliver's temper was mainly due to frustration at the loss of his arm. Richard knew it sometimes caused him to lash out at those around him.'

'Particularly if he'd been drinking whisky?' Newman suggested.

Helen felt a sense of apprehension wash over her again. 'Whisky?'

'Mr Edwards had drunk some before his death,' Townsend explained. 'Not a huge amount, but enough to contain a lethal dose of morphine. There was no sign the drug had been administered intravenously. And whisky would have disguised the bitter taste more effectively than tea.'

'Was there whisky at Albert Gates' leaving party?' Newman asked.

She shook her head. 'There was not. We never consumed alcohol in front of the patients. Apart from the wine, there was none in the hospital.'

'We'll be making a thorough search of every room to check,' Townsend said. 'Did you ever smell whisky on Mr Edwards' breath?'

Helen closed her eyes. She remembered helping Oliver to remove his shoes when he returned from his day out with Richard. 'Just once.'

37

Helen wondered if she'd been wrong to go to Townsend. What would Richard think when he found out? His mother could have been describing a completely different brooch.

But then there was the whisky. She'd smelt it on Oliver's breath when he'd returned from his outing to the stables. Richard knew the patients weren't allowed to drink.

And had he been too eager to believe in Samuel's guilt? He'd insisted she told Townsend about Isabel's flirtation with Samuel, even after she'd said she didn't think there was anything in it. Was Richard simply toying with her?

Yet he seemed such a kind man. When she'd asked for his help with Albert and Nathan, he'd willingly given it. And she'd never detected alcohol on his breath. Or seen any bottles of spirits in his cottage, though she'd only been into the parlour. Surely, he wouldn't have taken her to meet his mother if his feelings weren't genuine?

When she reached the manor, Frederick was standing by the gates, staring down at the farmhouse.

'Was that Townsend I saw you talking to? What's he up to?'

'He didn't really say. I suppose they're still looking for evidence to convict Dr Bingham.' She shivered at the thought of the gallows.

Frederick shifted from foot to foot. 'I'm having my doubts.'

This took her by surprise. 'What about?'

He scratched his head. 'Bingham. Do you think he killed Isabel?'

She could hear the desperation in his voice and see it in his eyes. 'I can't see why he would.'

He appeared almost tearful. 'No. Nor can I,' he groaned.

She wondered if she could trust him. He'd known Richard for some years and been friends with Oliver. And, of course, he'd had feelings for Isabel. But she'd have to tread carefully, given his obsession with the nurse.

'There are some things I don't understand—' she began.

'Lunch,' Dorothy called from the garden. 'Come along, you two.'

'I might have discovered something,' he said in an urgent whisper. 'Come and find me by the pheasant pens later.'

During lunch, Dorothy quizzed her about her day out with Richard. Helen gave polite responses, aware that Georgina was listening intently. It was safer to describe her visit to the Royal Victoria Hospital than to reveal her conversation with Mary.

She noticed that Frederick picked at his food, his gaze constantly straying to the window. He stood up abruptly before dessert had been served and said he had to check on the pheasants.

'Richard will go later,' Dorothy protested, but Frederick had bolted from the room.

'Leave him to it. He's upset because Townsend's poking around the farmhouse again.' Joseph picked up his spoon and started shovelling apple crumble into his mouth.

'Why?' Georgina squealed. 'Why does he keep coming back here?'

Joseph rolled his eyes, clearly wishing he hadn't mentioned it.

'He's probably just examining Dr Bingham's office and bedroom.' Dorothy placed a hand on her daughter's arm. 'Eat some dessert, it will do you good.'

Georgina accepted a serving of crumble, looking at it pensively rather than eating it.

Helen managed a few mouthfuls and chatted to Dorothy until the plates were cleared away. As soon as she could politely leave, she stood, saying she was going for a walk. Fortunately, no one suggested accompanying her, and she darted up to her room to change into her walking shoes and put on a straw hat.

Outside, the sun was high, and she felt it burning her arms as she crossed the grass and went over to the pheasant pens. There was no sign of Frederick. She assumed he'd gone into the woodland in search of shade.

The smell from the birds was strong, and Helen made her way into a dense stretch of trees where the air was cooler and sweeter. She walked deeper into the woodland, reflecting that it was the only part of the Merewood estate she would miss.

There was no sign of Frederick, and she supposed he must have gone down into the meadows with his shotgun. She was about to turn back when she heard a rustling nearby. It sounded like an animal rooting around in the bracken.

Helen followed the noise until she reached a grove of oak trees. She spotted Dexter scampering through the undergrowth. Then she saw Frederick.

It took her moment to realise what he was doing. He'd slung a length of rope over a low branch of one of the trees.

Helen began to run towards him when she saw he was tying it into a hangman's noose.

'No!' she screamed. 'Frederick, that's not the answer.'

38

'Well?' Dorothy called to Richard as he made his way across the lawn of the manor.

'My wife is asking how your day out went,' Joseph explained. 'Helen didn't say much at lunch. Did your mother take to her?'

He and Dorothy were sitting on deckchairs covered by a large red parasol. It was rare to see them relaxing together. They reminded Richard of the holidaymakers they'd seen sunbathing on the beach at Netley, except the Wintringhams wore far more expensive clothes.

He smiled. 'By the end of the day, you'd think they'd known each other for years.'

Dorothy clapped her hands. 'I predict wedding bells before the year's out.'

Richard made a non-committal reply. The end of the year might be a bit soon. He needed time to get himself established once he left Merewood. The livery stables he'd seen would fit the bill nicely. It was a secure business; the owner was retiring, and it was close to where Helen would be. But he wanted to modernise the place before proposing. He had a feeling that to entice Helen away from nursing, he'd have to make her fall in love with more than just himself. She'd need to love his way of life and be an active part of it.

Joseph grunted. 'He's got to set himself up first. What were the stables like?'

'I've put in an offer. If it's accepted, I'd like to leave after the pheasant shoot.'

'Fair enough. Frederick will take over when you go.'

Richard saw Dorothy was about to comment on this and decided to make his escape. 'I'm just going to check the pens now.'

'Frederick's gone to do it. Didn't even finish his lunch.' Joseph shifted the parasol to give them more shade. 'I've got another job for you. Get down to the hospital and see what Townsend's up to.'

'He's at the farm?' Richard thought they'd seen the last of the superintendent.

'Him and that sergeant. God knows what they're looking for. See if you can find out.'

Richard nodded, groaning inwardly. He had no wish to be interrogated by Townsend again. He'd wanted to catch up with Helen to talk about the previous day. He'd seen her heading to the woods, and his visit to the pheasant pens was just an excuse to spend an hour or two with her in their favourite spot.

Instead, he strode down to Merewood Farm, wondering what reason he could give Townsend for being there. He decided just to be honest and tell him that Joseph had sent him to see what was going on.

The patio doors were open, but when he went inside, the ward was empty. Richard walked along the corridor, peering into each room. It felt strange not to hear the chatter of the patients or the pompous voice of Bingham.

'Hello,' he called.

'Up here,' came the reply from above.

Richard climbed the stairs and stood on the landing, guessing which room they were in. It was one he had no desire to enter again.

'In here, Mr Locke,' Townsend called.

Reluctantly, he entered the room that had once been Isabel's. His eyes were immediately drawn to the window. How often had he looked up at it, pretending to be engaged in some task or other by the lake or in the garden? Eventually, she'd appear and hold up her fingers to indicate what time she could meet him. He'd nod and scurry away, hoping no one had seen their exchange.

He realised Townsend and Newman were standing by Helen's open trunk. Anger flared.

'Is it really necessary to go through Helen's things?'

'We wondered why her trunk was still here. Do you know when she packed it?'

'It was after you arrested Bingham. She said she never wanted to set foot in this place again.' He'd been conscious of Isabel's accusing presence as he'd helped Helen gather her belongings. 'She's taken what she needs to the manor, and this will be stored until she moves to a new hospital.'

Richard had been surprised by how few possessions Helen had. She explained how itinerant she'd been since her mother's death. First living in nursing quarters in the Nightingale School and then travelling between field hospitals in northern France before ending up at Merewood Farm.

The only thing she'd had plenty of was toiletries. Bottles of lotions, jars of cream and cakes of soap. He'd been touched when she'd confided in him about her bathing ritual.

The house that came with the stables had a large upstairs bathroom. He planned to make it fit for a queen. Once they were married, he'd fill it with cosmetics and all the fragrant bath oils she seemed to love. He'd promise to run her a warm bath every day. And he'd buy her some clothes. Dresses that would make him proud to call her his wife.

Richard wondered if he'd be able to persuade her to get rid of that damned uniform. He'd seen the pride she'd taken in neatly folding her collection of blue tunics, starched aprons and muslin caps.

'Have you seen that before?' Townsend was pointing to something in the trunk.

Richard saw that the clothes had been pushed aside to expose a metal box. He took a step closer and smiled when he saw what it was – a Red Cross first aid tin. Perhaps he should resign himself to the fact that even if she became Mrs Locke, part of her would always be Sister Hopgood. Knowing Helen, she probably still had a stock of emergency field dressings and a bottle of tannic acid to treat burns.

'I've seen many of those before,' he replied with a grin. 'In every field hospital I was unfortunate enough to land up in.'

'Take a look inside,' the superintendent ordered.

Richard grew uneasy. He glanced from Townsend to Newman, but their expressions gave nothing away.

Trying to hide his dread, he knelt down and lifted the lid of the tin. He wanted it to contain dozens of bottles of pills and potions lying on a bed of bandages. But he knew they wouldn't be asking him to open it if that was what was inside.

What he saw made him fall backwards onto his heels. A cold sweat spread over his body, and his breathing became shallow. He closed his eyes, hoping that when he opened them, the image would be gone. But it was still there. Oliver's mahogany drawing box with its decorative shell inlay.

With shaking hands, he lifted the drawing box out of the first aid tin. Worse was to come.

At the bottom of the tin was David Cowper's little gold clock in its leather pouch. Beside it was Morgan Jennings' silver cigarette case with his regimental emblem engraved on the front.

39

'Frederick, I know you're unhappy. But things will get better, I promise.' Helen held out her hands to him. 'Come with me to the manor. We can talk there.'

He ignored her, tugging at the rope to make sure it was secure. She wanted to run to the cottage to fetch Richard, but she couldn't leave him. When they got back, it might be too late.

She looked again at the noose. 'Frederick. This isn't the answer. Isabel wouldn't have wanted this. She would have wanted you to find someone new. Give it time, and things won't seem so bad.'

'Always so caring, Sister Hopgood.' A mocking smile hovered on his lips. 'Don't worry. It's not me who'll be hanging from that noose.'

It took her a moment to register his meaning. When she did react, it was too late. As she turned to run, his hand shot out and gripped her arm. She winced at the pressure.

He grinned. 'You're the one who decides that suicide is the only way out.'

Helen gasped, trying to understand what was happening. 'Why would I do that?'

'Guilt. Over what you did to those poor patients.'

'I-it wasn't me,' she stammered. 'Nobody could think that.'

He laughed. 'Townsend will when he looks in your trunk. I've left him a few clues to find.'

His words chilled her. At the same time, she felt a flutter of hope. Townsend was nearby. Screaming wouldn't help – no one would hear unless they were already in the woods. But she might manage to escape to the farmhouse. Hope faded when she noticed Frederick's shotgun lying on the ground. He would shoot at her if she tried to run.

'What clues will he find?' Her words came out in short rasps.

'Morgan's cigarette case, David's clock and Oliver's drawing box. I left the lid of your trunk open, practically inviting him to search it. I'm sure he won't be able to resist. And when he does, he'll find wicked Sister Hopgood was in it with Bingham all along.'

His hand tightened around her arm, and she winced in pain. Would Townsend think she was responsible for the patients' deaths? He was beginning to have his doubts about Samuel, she was certain of that. Surely, he'd realise someone had put those things in her trunk. Or had she got it all wrong? Perhaps Townsend did suspect her? Either way, he'd come in search of her. But would he be too late?

Frederick was attempting to drag her towards the noose, and her straw hat fell to the ground. Panic was starting to suffocate her.

She felt Dexter's nose rubbing against her leg. The dog whined, sensing something was wrong.

'Why?' she whispered. 'Why did you do it?'

'I wanted the hospital. Bingham wanted the same thing, and he showed me how I could get it.'

Helen's mouth gaped. Could Samuel and Frederick have been in it together? Then she remembered Samuel's face when Richard had knocked him to the floor of the barn. His confusion had been genuine.

'I don't believe you.' Her voice was stronger. 'Samuel wouldn't have helped you.'

'If it wasn't for him, I'd never have done any of it. I'd seen him sneaking around and decided to find out what he was up to. I was in the kitchen, watching the corridor, when he came out of his office with that skeleton. I heard all the fuss afterwards and couldn't figure it out. He didn't seem the type to play silly jokes. Then I saw him chatting with Baden Knight and knew.'

'Knew what?' She stopped struggling and tried to relax her body. It worked, and the intensity of his grip lessened.

'He was trying to scare Knight off so he could keep the hospital going. At first, I assumed he was doing it to stop my father from selling the farm. It was a clever idea. But not clever enough. I didn't think one silly prank would do it. That's when it came to me.'

'You killed Morgan?'

'Bloody right I did.' He sounded proud of his achievement. 'Bingham did me a favour. I'd never have thought of it otherwise. Couldn't have Georgie marrying that chancer. Silly bitch. She really knows how to pick them. First Richard and then Morgan. It was great fun. I stole the wine and chloral hydrate from Bingham's office. Idiot always keeps the key to the medicine cabinet in the same drawer. I knew Morgan was meeting Georgie. Slut used to have sex with him. After she'd gone, I stumbled to the lake, pretending to be drunk. I offered him the drugged wine. He drank it, then when he got drowsy, I questioned him about Isabel.' Frederick frowned. 'He didn't seem to know anything, so when he passed out, I dragged him into the lake.'

Helen shuddered, picturing Morgan's sodden body lying on the shore. At least he hadn't suffered. Unlike David.

As if reading her mind, Frederick said, 'David was all Bingham's fault. I didn't like doing that to the man.'

'Then why did you?'

'Because Bingham went to see my father and made an offer for the farm. I listened at the door. Bloody cheek of the man. That's when I realised what he was really up to. Pulling that stunt with Dorothy's portrait. I saw David sitting alone on the patio and decided to give Bingham more than he bargained for.'

'David had done nothing wrong. He was a good man.' Her fear was dampened by anger.

'Didn't have much of a life, though, did he?' Frederick waved his free hand in a dismissive gesture, causing the rope to swing. 'I didn't enjoy cutting his wrists. But I had to make it look as if whoever slashed the portrait committed the murder. Turns out the man was blind after all.'

Helen closed her eyes, feeling sick. Despite her revulsion, she had to ask, 'How do you know?'

'I held the scalpel in front of his eyes. He didn't see the danger he was in. Even when I lifted his hand, he didn't say a word, he just seemed surprised by my touch. When I sliced through his wrist, he flailed out, but he couldn't see me.'

Helen's legs began to tremble, and she knew she wouldn't be able to stand for much longer, let alone run. She tried to steady her breathing. 'What about Oliver? I thought you liked him.'

'I've told you.' Frederick's voice rose. 'It was Bingham's fault. After what happened to David, I expected him to stop. Then I saw him by the pheasant pens. Bastard kept walking around the estate as if he owned it. Scheming to get his hands on the farm. My farm. I didn't like what he did to that sparrowhawk.'

'You didn't have to kill Oliver.'

'He was the only one left. And do you know what? When I

offered him the whisky, I think he suspected. He gave me a strange look, then knocked it back. I think he wanted out.'

'No. I don't believe that.' Helen was wracked with guilt. She'd left Oliver alone in the ward when she'd gone to speak to Samuel. 'He was making plans for the future.'

Frederick ignored her. 'The hospital was finally empty, and I knew Townsend was onto Bingham. All I had to do was sit and wait. I took a little memento from each of the patients. If you hadn't goaded him into confessing he'd played the tricks, I'd have used them to point Townsend in the right direction. Wish I'd known about those paintings of Protheroe's. That was sneaky of Bingham.'

'You've got what you wanted. Why kill me?'

'I told you. You're going to kill yourself. Isabel never liked you. She said you were stuck up and looked down on her.' Frederick suddenly twisted her arm, causing her to cry out. 'Did you kill her?'

'No,' Helen whimpered. 'I did not.'

'Then who did?' he yelled. 'Tell me.'

'I don't know.' The pain was intense and she wanted to make it stop. But if she told him who she suspected, the consequences would be devastating.

He lowered his head so that his face was almost touching hers. 'You're lying. I can see that you do know.'

She jerked her head back, feeling spittle on her skin. 'I don't.'

'You must do. You have to tell me.' Like a rag doll, he lifted her up and pushed her head through the noose. 'You were always there amongst it. In that cursed hospital.'

Dexter let out a howl and pawed at his master, sensing his distress.

'The hospital was never cursed,' Helen screamed as he pressed the rope against her neck. 'It was always the manor.'

40

Townsend watched Richard's reaction. Either the man was an accomplished actor, or he really hadn't known what was in the first aid tin.

Richard was breathing heavily. 'Bingham must have put them there.'

'You said yourself, Dr Bingham had already been taken into custody when Sister Hopgood packed her trunk.'

'Helen didn't kill those men. I know it.' Richard gestured to the tin. 'Someone put those things in there. The trunk has been sitting here for days.'

'You seem very sure. Is that because it was you who put them there?' Townsend suggested.

'Don't be ridiculous.' Richard's fingers gripped the side of the trunk.

Townsend decided to increase the pressure. 'Tell me about the brooch.'

'What brooch?'

'The one your mother described to Sister Hopgood. The one you gave to Isabel Taplin.'

Newman had reached out a hand to help the man to his feet, But at these words, Richard fell back onto his heels.

There was a long silence before he spoke. 'It was stupid of me. I should have told you before.'

Townsend rolled his eyes at Newman before asking, 'Why didn't you?'

'Because I found her body. You were bound to think I'd killed her if you'd known she'd been with me that afternoon.'

'Tell me what happened,' he prompted.

Richard's shoulders drooped. 'She had a few hours off. I'd seen her in the morning, and she said she could come to my cottage at two o'clock. So I made sure I was there.'

'And what did you do?'

Richard gave him a scathing look. 'We talked. And kissed.'

Georgina Vane had said the same thing about the last night she'd spent with Morgan Jennings. An awful lot of talking and kissing seemed to go on at Merewood, Townsend mused. 'Had she visited your cottage before?' he asked.

Richard nodded. 'We'd been seeing each other for a while.'

'And you gave her the pearl brooch?'

'I was in love with her. I thought she felt the same way about me.'

Townsend tensed. Were they getting close to a confession? 'And you discovered that she didn't? That must have hurt.'

'I don't know how she felt,' Richard snapped. 'I never got the chance to find out.'

Townsend frowned and indicated to Newman to take over the questioning.

'What time did she leave your cottage that afternoon?' the sergeant asked.

'Around four o'clock. She would walk along the track behind the walled garden of the manor and go into the woods on the eastern side. Then she'd come out to the south so it would appear as though she was coming back from the village.'

'So when Sister Hopgood told you she was missing, you knew where to look?'

Richard nodded. 'I followed the route she would have taken.'

Newman tutted. 'Why didn't you tell us this when you found her?'

'I've told you. I knew what you'd think.'

'You'd be right,' Townsend growled. 'It's what I'm thinking now. You were in love with her. You discovered she'd been seeing someone else, perhaps Frederick Wintringham, and were jealous. You killed her and took your brooch back.'

Richard seemed close to tears. 'No. I didn't. Whoever killed her must have stolen it because she was wearing it when she left my cottage.'

Townsend glanced at Newman, who shrugged. They stood in silence, watching the figure hunched on the floor.

Townsend decided to take a different approach.

'Did you and Oliver Edwards often drink whisky together?'

Richard wiped his eyes and peered up in confusion. 'Whisky? No. I don't drink alcohol.'

Townsend was surprised by this. He could see Newman looked equally perplexed. The man clearly didn't comprehend the significance of the question. Something wasn't right.

'The pathologist found whisky in Mr Edwards' body as well as a lethal quantity of morphine. Was it a drink he favoured? We can't find any bottles of whisky in the hospital. Where would he have got it?'

Richard clasped his hand to his mouth. 'Oh my God,' he whispered.

'What is it?' Townsend asked urgently. 'Tell me what you know.'

Richard stared into the trunk at the cigarette case, the clock and the drawing box.

Suddenly, he was on his feet. 'Helen,' he yelled, running for the door.

Newman reached out to grab him, but Richard was too quick. Townsend had to hold onto his sergeant to stop him from falling over.

They raced down the stairs, calling for Richard to stop, despite the fact it was obvious he had no intention of obeying. By the time they reached the ward, he was tearing across the patio.

Townsend and Newman started to run even though they knew they couldn't match the man's speed. They only managed to catch up with him when he paused on the outskirts of Gibbet Wood.

Newman pulled out his handcuffs, but Townsend gestured for him to hold back. His instinct told him that Richard wasn't trying to run away.

'Where are you going, Mr Locke?'

'Helen. When I was walking down to the farm, I saw her by the pheasant pens.'

Townsend looked over to the pens. 'She's not there now. What—'

Richard held up a hand. 'Hush.'

The three men stood still, listening.

A sudden cry came from somewhere in the woodland, followed by the howl of a dog. Townsend couldn't make out where the noises were coming from and felt a wave of panic. He wasn't sure what was happening. All he knew was that they had to stop it.

Suddenly, Richard was sprinting through the trees. Townsend couldn't achieve the same speed but managed to keep the man in his sights. His chest felt like it was about to explode. He could hear Newman's laboured breathing and knew the older man wasn't far behind. The sound of a woman screaming and a dog barking made him keep going.

Richard disappeared into a grove of oak trees, then he heard him roar, 'Let her go.'

He and Newman staggered after him, emerging into a clearing. Gasping for breath, they saw Frederick Wintringham forcing Helen's head through a hangman's noose. A shotgun was at his feet.

Richard charged at Helen. When he reached her, he clasped his hands tightly around her waist and held her aloft.

Townsend kept running, manoeuvring his body at the last moment to come in low, shoulder forward. With an almighty lurch, he managed to barrel into Frederick and bring him to the ground. He fell on top of him and stayed there until Newman had kicked the shotgun out of reach and snapped a pair of handcuffs around Frederick's wrists. Dexter circled them, barking furiously.

Townsend saw Richard remove the rope from around Helen's neck. To his relief, her breath came in deep, strong gasps.

'Good tackle, sir,' Newman panted, wiping the sweat from his brow.

41

Frederick struggled; his wrists handcuffed in front of him. Newman dragged him out of the woods and shoved him in the direction of the manor. When the young man stumbled, Richard couldn't resist giving him a hefty clout around the head.

'Sergeant Newman and I will take care of the prisoner,' Townsend said drily, pushing him out of the way. 'Walk with Sister Hopgood and stay in our sight. We still have matters to discuss.'

Richard took hold of Helen's hand. 'I'm not going anywhere.'

Townsend and Newman marched ahead, hauling an unwilling Frederick between them. Dexter trailed after them, whimpering.

To Richard's dismay, Helen pulled her hand away from his. 'I'm fine,' she muttered.

'I had nothing to do with Isabel's death, I swear,' he whispered. 'It's true I gave her my mother's brooch. She was wearing it when she left my cottage that afternoon. When I found her body, it was gone. I promise you I never hurt her.'

She didn't reply, and he found himself on the receiving end of one of her cool stares.

Townsend rapped on the door of the manor and barged in when it opened. 'Where's Mr Wintringham?'

'The family are having tea in the drawing room.' The butler stood back, wide-eyed, as Sergeant Newman tugged a handcuffed Frederick into the hallway.

'Take this dog into the kitchen and give it some water,' Townsend ordered. 'I need to use the telephone in Mr Wintringham's study. Newman, make sure everyone stays in the drawing room.'

The butler patted Dexter and tried to coax the dog into following him.

Richard helped Newman drag a rebellious Frederick across the hall. In the drawing room, Dorothy and Georgina were seated on the sofa, and Joseph was standing by the mantelpiece. They gave a collective gasp as the group stumbled through the door.

'What the hell's going on?' The cigar between Joseph's lips dropped to the carpet, and he quickly stamped on it.

Newman thrust Frederick into a delicate occasional chair by the door. For a moment, Richard thought the seat would break.

'Father. Tell them to let me go.' Frederick flexed his wrists against the metal restraints. 'I found Helen in the woods. She was trying to hang herself, and I dragged her down. These idiots got the wrong idea.'

'Take those cuffs off immediately.' Joseph was bearing down on Newman, and Richard placed himself between them.

'He killed the patients. Morgan, David and Oliver.' Thinking of the three men made Richard want to weep. 'Your son is a murderer.'

'Don't be so bloody ridiculous. They've arrested Bingham.' Joseph looked like he was about to strike him.

Although he was reluctant to hit the older man, Richard clenched his fists, preparing to defend himself against the blow.

Dorothy was on her feet, tugging at her husband's arm. 'Calm down, Joseph.'

Georgina was silent for once. She sat motionless on the sofa, her mouth gaping.

'Bingham did it, not me.' Frederick tried to stand, raising his handcuffed wrists in a futile gesture. 'And Helen helped him. That's why she was planning to hang herself. Townsend knows it.'

When Richard shoved Frederick forcefully back into the chair, Newman made no protest.

'Where is Townsend?' Joseph roared, his face crimson.

'He's making a telephone call, sir.' Newman appeared unperturbed by Frederick's writhing and Joseph's fury. 'He'll join us shortly.'

'Where's Helen?' Dorothy asked. 'Is she hurt?'

Only then did Richard realise Helen hadn't followed them into the room. He moved towards the door and felt Newman grip his arm.

'Stay here, Mr Locke. Superintendent Townsend told you not to go anywhere.'

'Why? What's he done?' Joseph demanded.

Richard thought better of ignoring Newman's command. The Wintringhams were now all regarding him with suspicion. He couldn't afford to make any more trouble for himself. As long as he had Frederick in his sights, Helen was safe.

'Well?' Joseph was towering over Newman.

'It's Isabel, isn't it?' Frederick's eyes were narrow and his voice low. 'What did you do to her?'

'I didn't do anything.' Richard was fervently grateful for the handcuffs around the man's wrists.

Newman obviously sensed the danger and kept one hand on Frederick's shoulder. 'If I could ask you all to sit quietly, Superintendent Townsend will answer any questions you have.'

'Where is the bloody man? How long does it take him to make a telephone call?' Joseph strode to the door. He was about to open it when Townsend entered, forcing him backwards.

Helen followed the superintendent into the room and hovered by the door. Richard tried to catch her eye, but she wouldn't look at him.

Dorothy went over to her. 'Helen, my dear, what's going on? Are you hurt? What happened?'

Helen's hand went to her neck. 'Frederick tried to kill me.'

'She's lying,' Frederick yelled, leaning forward. 'She tried to kill herself. She was in on it with Bingham.'

Richard was about to push him back, but Newman got there first.

'Where the hell have you been?' Joseph jabbed Townsend's chest. 'Tell your sergeant to let my son go.'

'I used the telephone in your study to arrange for my officers to collect your son and take him into custody. I need to question him at the station,' Townsend replied calmly, brushing Joseph aside. 'I've also been upstairs to the family bedrooms. Sister Hopgood showed me where each one was.'

'Without my permission,' Joseph snarled. 'You're going to regret this.'

Townsend ignored him and turned to Richard. He held out his hand. 'Mr Locke, is this the brooch you gave to Isabel Taplin?'

Richard heard Georgina gasp. He glanced from her to the object lying in Townsend's palm. It was his mother's grey pearl brooch.

He nodded. 'I don't understand—'

'You?' Frederick spluttered. 'You and Isabel?'

'No! Now I know this is all lies.' Joseph waved a finger at Townsend. 'Frederick wasn't even here when that girl died. He loved her. He would never have killed her. You didn't find that in his room.'

'You're quite right. We found the brooch in a rosewood box in Miss Vane's bedroom. I'm afraid I had to pick the lock,' Townsend said apologetically to Georgina. 'I presume you have the key on your person?'

For a few moments, the room was silent. Then Georgina started to sob.

Richard stared at her in disbelief.

'How dare you go into my daughter's room.' Dorothy flew to Georgina's side and clasped her hand. 'Get out of this house immediately. I won't stand for any further accusations.'

'We'll be leaving shortly. And we will be taking Miss Georgina Vane and Mr Frederick Wintringham with us.'

'Mummy... I...' Georgina was whimpering.

'Did you murder that girl?' Joseph grabbed Georgina by the shoulders and shook her violently.

'For God's sake, let her go.' Dorothy jostled her husband away. 'Of course she didn't.'

'Then how did she get that brooch?' Joseph demanded.

'I found it,' Georgina whispered.

Joseph relaxed his hold on her and turned to Townsend. 'Why would Georgina kill that nurse?'

To Richard's surprise, it wasn't Townsend who answered but Helen. And she directed her words at him.

'She was jealous because you'd been in a relationship with her and then discarded her in favour of Isabel Taplin.'

All eyes were upon him, and Richard felt hot with shame. He nodded slowly, unable to look at Helen.

'Did Georgina know about the brooch?' Helen asked.

'I once showed it to her,' Richard said hoarsely.

'I thought you were going to give it to me,' Georgina screeched.

'You can see Mr Locke's cottage from your bedroom window, can't you, Miss Vane?' Townsend said in a soft voice. 'When you saw

Isabel Taplin leaving his home that day, you must have guessed why Mr Locke was no longer interested in you. It must have been very upsetting for you.'

'Don't say anything, Georgina,' her mother warned. 'We were all in the garden that afternoon. Don't you remember, Joseph?'

Her husband ran his hand over his cropped grey hair. 'Georgina was in her room for some of the time.'

'Did you follow Isabel Taplin?' Townsend continued. 'You must have been angry when you realised what was going on. Perhaps you hoped to win Mr Locke back?'

'How could you be so cruel?' Georgina shrieked at Richard. 'When I said I'd tell everyone at the hospital what she was getting up to, she laughed at me. She said it wouldn't be a secret for much longer as you'd asked her to marry you. How could you do that to me?'

'You?' Richard grasped the back of a chair to steady himself. 'You stole the brooch and pulled the scarf around her neck?'

'It wasn't fair,' Georgina sobbed.

Helen regarded her sadly. 'You said everyone you loved got taken away from you. First Patrick and then Richard.'

'And Morgan,' Georgina whimpered. She turned her desperate violet eyes on Helen, clearly hoping for sympathy.

Frederick, who'd been listening in silence, suddenly leapt from the chair causing Newman to stumble.

'I loved her,' he bellowed, flinging himself at Georgina.

Before he could reach his stepsister, Townsend attempted another rugby tackle, forcing Frederick onto the carpet. With a sigh, Newman crouched down, muttering something about his knees, and sat on top of the young man.

'You murdered the father of my baby,' Georgina screamed back at him, then began to make a strange wailing noise.

Dorothy wrapped her arms around her daughter, begging her to calm down. Joseph loomed over Townsend and Newman, yelling at them to get off his son. A scratching could be heard at the door, and Dexter gave a low mournful howl.

Richard stood motionless, watching the chaos surrounding him. He stared at Helen, trying to force her to look at him. When her cool green eyes finally met his, he saw his vision of their future together disintegrate.

Frederick stopped fighting and lay face down on the carpet. He twisted his head so he could peer up at Helen.

He smiled at her, though there were tears in his eyes. 'You were right. It wasn't the hospital that was cursed – it was the manor.'

42

'Sister Hopgood.'

Helen smiled at the incongruous sight of Superintendent Townsend dodging out of the way of nurses pushing patients in wheelchairs and porters wheeling trolleys from ward to ward.

'This is a far cry from Merewood Hospital,' he said.

'There are one hundred and forty wards here and over a thousand beds. And miles of corridors.'

'The scale of it is incredible.' He stood back to allow a group of nurses to pass. 'Is there somewhere private we can talk?'

She nodded.

In her office, Townsend walked across to the arched sea-facing windows to admire the view of Southampton Water.

Helen sat behind her desk, curious to know what had brought him to the Royal Victoria Hospital. Presumably he wasn't here to take the sea air. She didn't rush him. Every day, she did what he was doing and stood by the windows to gaze out over the estuary. The never-ending view reinforced her belief that she'd made the right decision in coming to Netley.

Townsend turned and pulled up a chair. 'Frederick Wintringham was found hanging in his cell this morning.'

Helen felt a mixture of pity and relief. 'I'm sorry for the Wintringhams, though I'm glad there won't be a trial. For everyone's sake.'

'It wouldn't have been a pleasant ordeal, and the outcome would have been the same. I've no doubt a judge would have sentenced Frederick to the gallows.'

Helen's hand went to her neck as she remembered the scene in Gibbet Wood.

'And Georgina?'

'A judge is likely to be lenient when sentencing, given her condition. However, she will have her baby in prison. Her mother wants to take care of it once it's born.'

'At Merewood?'

Townsend shook his head. 'I heard Mr and Mrs Wintringham have separated.' As he stretched his legs and adjusted his trousers, Helen noticed the creases were as precise as ever. 'Do you think Mrs Wintringham knew what her daughter had done?'

Helen nodded. 'I'm sure she suspected, though perhaps she wasn't certain.'

'You're probably right. There's something else. Samuel Bingham has been released from custody. He's paid for his misdemeanours. I believe it's his intention to seek an interview with the hospital board here.'

She gave a faint smile. 'I don't think I have anything to fear from Dr Bingham.'

'Maybe not. I'll leave it up to the hospital board to decide if he's fit to practice. From a criminal perspective, I don't suppose he presents a threat. However, if he does cause you any problems, let me know, and I'll use my influence to see that he's removed.'

'Thank you. I doubt that will be necessary. I'm just surprised he's given up on his plans to buy Merewood Farm.'

She saw Townsend's look of surprise.

'You haven't heard? The farm was destroyed.'

Helen blinked. 'How?'

'It burned to the ground.'

'Was anyone hurt?'

'Joseph Wintringham has a few scalds but nothing serious. He poured petrol inside the ward before throwing a lit rag into the building. He burned his hands in the process.'

Images of Merewood Hospital filled Helen's mind. Of the busy times, with ambulances pulling up each day, bringing fresh casualties. Of Matron, Isabel, Samuel and all the patients until finally, there had just been Albert, Nathan, Morgan, David and Oliver. 'So Merewood Farm is no more?'

'A pile of ashes. I thought Mr Locke might have told you? He's purchased a livery stables not far from here.'

'We haven't kept in touch.'

She watched his expression change and wondered what was coming next. He seemed to be weighing up his words.

'You may feel let down by Mr Locke's behaviour.' It was a statement rather than a question. 'However, I want you to know that I don't think he ever believed you were guilty. Even when we found those items in your trunk.'

'Unlike my suspicions of him?' She felt a twinge of remorse.

Townsend held up a hand. 'That's not what I meant. You were under considerable strain after everything that had happened. All I'm trying to say is that when Mr Locke ran into those woods, his only thought was to save you – at any cost to himself.' He cleared his throat. 'Other factors may have caused you to reconsider your relationship. All I can say is that I have no doubt of the depth of his feelings for you.'

Helen was touched that Townsend had been moved to tell her this.

'Believe me, those feelings were reciprocated. Although Richard behaved foolishly, he's not a bad man. Ending our relationship was one of the most difficult decisions I've ever had to make. But being a nurse is my vocation. I can't marry and continue with my work.' From Helen's point of view, there was nothing more to be said. She'd dreamt of marrying Richard and having children. But that's all it had been. A dream. She knew her calling.

Townsend stood up. 'I'm sure many patients will be grateful for the choice you've made.'

'Thank you, Superintendent Townsend.'

'Goodbye, Sister Hopgood.'

'Matron.'

'Sorry?' Townsend looked confused.

'The hospital board told me they'd received a letter from Dr Bingham. He wrote at length about my skills, and they decided to offer me a senior position. I'm no longer Sister Hopgood. I'm Matron Hopgood.'

AUTHOR'S NOTE

Merewood Manor and Merewood Farm are based on Minley Manor and Home Farm in Minley, Hampshire.

Minley Manor is a Grade II listed country manor house built in the French Gothic style between 1858 and 1860 for Raikes Currie, a Member of Parliament and partner of the bank Curries & Co.

His grandson, Laurence Currie, introduced a water tower, kitchen garden, and walled gardens to the estate and extended the woodland. In 1896, he had Home Farm built. The model farm had a decorative tudoresque façade and included a dairy, pigsties, bull boxes, and calf and cow sheds.

During the First World War, it wasn't Home Farm that became a hospital, but Minley Lodge, a grand house on the Minley Manor estate. The Commandant was Mrs Laurence Currie, and the Curries met all the hospital's expenses.

In 1935, the Ministry of Defence purchased the manor and its estates. Home Farm was an active dairy farm until the mid-20th century and was still used by the MoD until the 1990s.

In recent years, Minley Manor has found new owners and is now an events venue. However, the MoD still owns Home Farm and thousands of acres of surrounding land. Despite other buildings within the estate being listed, Home Farm remains unlisted. It's now derelict and in need of restoration.

In 2020, the MoD submitted plans to demolish the farm. The Victorian Society sent a letter to the Secretary of State for Defence, urging them to rethink, highlighting the farm's architectural and historical significance. SAVE Britain's Heritage took legal action to block the demolition under permitted development rights, and with the support of the Victorian Society, they've applied for Home Farm to become a listed building. So far, that hasn't happened, and the future of Home Farm remains uncertain.

ACKNOWLEDGEMENTS

I'd like to thank the following people for their support and encouragement: my parents, Ken and Barbara Salter, with special thanks for their help with research; Jeanette Quay for her patience and for changing the B word I used to describe this book; and Barbara Daniel for reading early drafts more than once and providing valuable advice.

I'm always grateful to my editor, Emily Yau, but never more so than for her detailed feedback on this book. Thanks to all the other brilliant members of the Boldwood Books team.

As ever, I'm indebted to the numerous people, books, libraries, museums and archives that contributed to my knowledge of this period.

ABOUT THE AUTHOR

Michelle Salter writes historical cosy crime set in Hampshire, where she lives, and inspired by real-life events in 1920s Britain. Her Iris Woodmore series draws on an interest in the aftermath of the Great War and the suffragette movement.

Sign up to Michelle Salter's mailing list for news, competitions and updates on future books.

Visit Michelle's Website: https://www.michellesalter.com

Follow Michelle on social media:

X x.com/MichelleASalter

facebook.com/MichelleSalterWriter

instagram.com/michellesalter_writer

BB bookbub.com/authors/michelle-salter

ALSO BY MICHELLE SALTER

The Iris Woodmore Mysteries

Death at Crookham Hall

Murder at Waldenmere Lake

The Body at Carnival Bridge

A Killing at Smugglers Cove

Standalone

Murder at Merewood Hospital

Boldwood

Boldwood Books is an award-winning fiction publishing company seeking out the best stories from around the world.

Find out more at www.boldwoodbooks.com

Join our reader community for brilliant books, competitions and offers!

Follow us
@BoldwoodBooks
@TheBoldBookClub

Sign up to our weekly deals newsletter

https://bit.ly/BoldwoodBNewsletter

Printed in the USA
CPSIA information can be obtained
at www.ICGtesting.com
LVHW051620180124
769269LV00051BA/2536

9 781837 510788